UNENDING MAGIC 1

Unending Magic

Bargains with Beasts 3

STACIA STARK

one
Kyla

Getting to Tikal was no joke.

It involved a portal to the middleground, another portal to Antigua, a small colonial town in Guatemala, a chicken bus to Guatemala City, and a flight—on a plane that was little more than a lawnmower with wings—to Flores.

By the time I landed, my wolf was pissed. She hadn't enjoyed any part of the trip, and I couldn't exactly blame her.

After all, neither had I.

As soon as I landed in Flores, I focused on filtering every scent I came across. I had no doubt this place was filled with mages, keeping an eye out for any other paranormals who might be looking into their activities.

My wolf wanted to run to Tikal. I wanted to do the same. But we didn't have the time. Instead, I booked a private transfer. The driver's name was Juan, and he spoke much better English than my bad Spanish. The drive went faster than I'd anticipated, thanks to his history lesson about the Mayans, who'd inhabited the area from the sixth century BC to around the tenth century AD. Apparently, a good chunk of the archaeological remains were still underground.

While I'd assumed the demigod would've been buried

beneath one of the huge temples, I was actually headed *away* from the temples. Juan dropped me on the outskirts of the site, clearly concerned about leaving me.

"I'll wait for you," he told me.

"No, thank you. I'm meeting some friends." A lie, but relief crossed his face, and he nodded.

"Enjoy your time here."

And then I was alone. Glancing at the map I'd lifted from Lennox Rees's little information room, I got my bearings, shoved Angelica's ring into my mouth, rendering me invisible, and took off at a steady jog.

The mages had stationed guards in nondescript clothing all over the area. Several of them were wearing giant cameras around their necks, while a few more wore fanny packs and baseball caps. A sad attempt to fit in with the tourists, but I could see—and smell—their magic a mile away.

Their presence reinforced that I was in the right place.

The demigod was located outside the national park, deep in the forest. He'd originally gone to sleep far beneath the earth but was now in the cave that had been created when the McCormick coven had raised him from his coma-like sleep.

It took me an hour to hike to the cave, keeping my footsteps light. Finally, I heard voices.

I caught sight of twenty or thirty mages, all armed with guns. I had no doubt they were also armed with that stolen power. I crouched, watching the area for a few hours, while I stored away everything I noticed about the guards, their shifts, and just how much attention they were paying to their surroundings.

I couldn't just check out the security. I had to know what we were working with.

My wolf liked that idea, and I padded toward the cave. I'd expected it to be warded, but that likely would've stopped them from being able to access their stolen power.

I crept into the mouth of the cave, and my eyes adjusted to the dim light.

I'd once seen photos of the Reclining Buddha in Thailand. The demigod was large enough that he reminded me of those pictures. Only, he wasn't gold, and he wasn't reclining with his eyes open.

Even with him lying down, his shoulder ended far above my head. His feet were as long as my body and crossed at the ankles, while his wrists were encircled with what seemed like miles of Naud chains. My wolf snarled at the sight.

I couldn't even attempt to soothe her. I wanted to rip out these mages' throats in the worst way.

The guy had tried to take a nap for a few thousand years and woke up in chains, surrounded by humans who were feasting on him. I was betting he was *pissed*.

Unfortunately, as much as I wanted to do a little slaughtering, this was supposed to be a reconnaissance mission. Even if I hadn't promised Evie that I'd just come to spy, I was massively outnumbered by these fuckheads.

Soon, I soothed my wolf.

We'd once been trapped, just like this. A soundless growl left my throat.

And that was when the ground began shaking.

Little wolf, why are you here? A voice sounded in my

head.

I went still. I was invisible. But this guy was a demigod. The mages were running for cover, but from what I could see, the earthquake wasn't unexpected. Obviously, it was one of the few ways the demigod could show his displeasure.

"I'm here to figure out how to free you," I whispered, hoping he'd hear me. I wasn't sure if the whole talking to him in my head thing would work.

I wish to sleep.

"I know. I'm sorry they woke you up."

Come closer.

I padded toward him, and even though his eyes were closed, I had a pretty good feeling he could see me.

Other side, he instructed. Pushy bastard.

A low laugh sounded in my head, and I froze. Could he—

Read your mind? Of course. Why do you think I spoke to you? You're the only one here who isn't attempting to suck my power dry.

"Yeah, sorry about that." I crossed around those massive feet, aware that his toenails were the size of my face.

This side of his body was closest to the cave wall. I took a good look and went still.

Ah, you see it.

Yes, I fucking saw it.

Strapped to the demigod's side, looking absurdly small, given how big he was…

Was an empty sword sheath.

Return my sword and remove these chains so I can sleep. Please.

The last word sounded foreign. He likely hadn't ever used the word before.

I stared at the demigod and forgot how to breathe. My suspicions were correct.

Selina had been clear. Steal the sword from Finvarra and return it to its owner. Or the worlds burn. Well, I'd found the owner. But if I returned the sword and sent him back to sleep…

The portals to our world would close.

Forever.

two
Kyla

"There you are!"

Evie leaped, flinging her arms around me. Her blond curls seemed to be exploding from her ponytail today, and I couldn't help but laugh. The short period of time when we hadn't been speaking—right after she learned I'd known Nathaniel was her mate—had felt as if someone were pulling out my fingernails one by one. It was good to be back in sync.

"Yep. I'm back."

"What did I tell you about disappearing to Guatemala without a word?"

I peeled her off me and leaned against my desk. "Actually, we've never had that conversation."

Evie attempted to give me a hard stare, but she just looked cute. My mouth trembled, and her eyes narrowed.

"What did you find out?"

I sighed. I wasn't ready for that subject just yet. "Did you guys get anything else out of Rees?" Lennox Rees was the son of Alistair Rees, the man behind Humans for Equality. The man was half paranormal himself, although we weren't sure exactly what he was. When his father had died, he'd taken over, and thanks to Evie's planning, we'd managed to take him down, along with every single HFE lab.

Now he was chilling in one of Nathaniel's reinforced cells.

Evie gave me a long look. But she allowed the change of subject. "No. Rees is still swearing he has no idea how the mages are harnessing the demigod's power."

"And Gabriel?" My voice was a low growl. The mage council leader was usually a hermit—when he wasn't being a grade-A psychopath. When he'd realized we knew he was working with HFE, he'd set a trap—a trap that had nearly killed Xander.

"Nothing." Evie turned to pace. "We may have Rees, but he's not talking. Gabriel has disappeared, and Taraghlan hasn't been seen either."

I snorted. The seelie king was probably lying low. The wolves wanted to rip out his throat, anyone still alive from HFE would be livid that his *activities* had led us back to them, and Finvarra currently owned the only sword that could kill him.

Our prey was running out of allies, and my wolf was pleased.

"And Selina?" I asked.

Evie frowned. "I'm still looking for her. Unfortunately, she left no clues. Aubrey is a mess." She turned to face me, her mouth flattening. "Tell me what happened in Guatemala."

I sighed. "It's not good."

Selina's prophecy had been clear. And I'd spent a little time exploring the demigod's cave before I left, searching for as much information as I could find. The etchings in the cave were faint, but I'd taken pictures.

Selina had never told me exactly when the realms would burn. But those etchings had made it relatively obvious.

If I was right, we had just over a month.

Evie was still studying my face. "Lay it out for me."

I didn't want to. Because this was the kind of information she couldn't unknow once she knew it. With just a few words, I was going to rip all my friends' lives apart.

"It's bad, then." Evie's voice was soft.

"Yeah." I took a deep breath. "I know where the sword needs to go."

Her eyes lit up. I just shook my head.

"I found the demigod in Guatemala. The one the McCormick witches woke. The reason the portals are open."

And once I gave him what he wanted and sent him back to sleep…

"We have until the winter solstice."

And already, the leaves were beginning to change color. We had *weeks*.

"Okay. So, you give him back the sword, and then what?"

"We remove the Naud chains, and he goes back to sleep."

I watched Evie. And I saw the moment she understood. Grief hit her all at once, and I wished I could take the words back as she slid to her knees. I crouched in front of her, with no way to soften the blow.

"The portals only opened because he woke up. If he goes back to sleep…" She choked on the words, her eyes already bleak. "Danica…"

A dead weight pressed on my chest at the thought of Evie being separated from her sister forever. "We'll figure out another way. We won't just accept this, Evie."

The door swung open. Nathaniel slid a glance at me. One that said we'd be talking later. But he was already picking Evie up, cradling her in his arms. "What is it, darling?"

I backed out of the office, giving them some space. My wolf ached for a run. How many more lives would I have to ruin with this news?

And where the fuck was Selina?

She'd told us that if she saw anything else related to the sword, she'd let us know. And then she'd disappeared.

Selina had proven she was on our side. I considered her to be almost like a funny, wise aunt—although she was still young and hot. The fact that no one knew where she was… That was the cherry on top of my shit sundae.

I'd gone too many days without sleep and, more importantly, without enough food. I knew better. My wolf got *mean* when she was hungry. I turned to get into my car, and Nathaniel stepped out of the office.

"Guatemala."

Nathaniel was like that. He didn't need to say any more. My wolf hung her head. *I* lifted mine higher.

"You didn't say I couldn't go."

His eyes burrowed into mine. It wasn't often he gave me his Alpha stare, and I dropped my own gaze. Even after all this time, resentment slid through me.

Nathaniel was a good Alpha. More like a brother than the brother I'd had. And yet…

"You haven't played that game since you first joined my pack."

Despite the situation, a faint smile curved my mouth.

When Nathaniel first found me, I wasn't exactly pleased with my new life. I was dominant, but nowhere near as dominant as Nathaniel. Our pack still talked about the power struggle we'd been engaged in.

Well, *I'd* been engaged in the struggle. Nathaniel had likely just been amused.

Any order he gave me, I searched for a way out. When he told me I wasn't allowed to run as a wolf, I shifted and made sure I kept to a walk. When he told me I was to stay within his territory, he found me on the very edge of that territory, several states away. And when he'd told me I wasn't allowed to hunt humans, I'd hunted his wolves, fighting for dominance and working my way up the pack.

"I didn't consider going to Guatemala a game," I said. "You never would have allowed me to go, and now we have key information that we need."

"Did you ever consider that maybe I would have allowed you to go with backup?"

I blinked. Since he'd turned off the Alpha stare, I lifted my head. "No."

He sighed, pinching the bridge of his nose.

"You are not to work on the portals, the demigod, or the sword without asking me first. Is that clear?"

My wolf understood dominance and orders. It was the human side of me that wanted to gut Nathaniel where he stood.

"Understood," I ground out.

"Kyla…" I knew that tone. Nathaniel was done being Alpha, and now he wanted to be my friend.

I turned and walked away.

#

Kyla

When I'd originally been making plans to steal the sword from Finvarra, my strategy had been simple—get him to invite me into his castle, where I would shamelessly rob him and disappear into the night.

I scowled, pacing back and forth in Evie's office. She was still in pack territory, so it was the perfect place to think about what would come next… without her realizing exactly what I was planning.

Unfortunately, we didn't have the time to convince Finvarra to be my buddy. I had plenty of charm at my disposal when I needed it, but it would take *years* of using that considerable charm on Finvarra before he would trust me enough to hang out in his home. And while I'd hoped to find something to bribe or blackmail him with so he would deign to see me, I had no time for that now.

No. Now, if I was going to return the sword to its rightful owner, I was going to have to steal it first.

Unfortunately, that meant figuring out a way into Finvarra's castle. I'd start by sneaking into the castle and memorizing the layout. It would likely take a few days before I figured out where he had the sword hidden, so I'd find an inn located in one of the unseelie towns close by. Maybe one of the locals would unwittingly give me some kind of clue about Finvarra and his habits.

With Nathaniel's order lingering in my mind, I put my first plan together. It was difficult to even think about that plan, thanks to the way Nathaniel had phrased his order. But my Alpha had forgotten the way I could twist his words.

Guilt coiled in my stomach. I didn't *want* to be the pain in the ass who made everything more difficult for Nathaniel. But just because he was Alpha didn't make him right.

So I rolled my shoulders and turned, opening the cupboard next to Evie's desk.

Wow, would you look at that? We were almost out of pain charms. That wasn't a good way for any business to operate.

Shutting out every other thought, I stared at the space where those pain charms would usually sit. I definitely needed to go to Gary's and stock up on some things for the office. Along with charms, there were probably a few other spells we needed to stock up on.

I repeated that thought over and over until it solidified in my head.

Go to Gary's. Get the pain charms.

Go to Gary's. Get the pain charms.

I replayed the thought again and again as I got into my car. My hand froze as I attempted to turn the key.

Blowing out a breath, I pictured the empty spot in that cupboard where the pain charms would usually sit. Then I pictured the pain charm Evie had recently used after she'd fought the roc.

It needed to be replaced. There were *lots* of things in our office that needed to be replaced at Gary's.

I focused on that pain charm the entire drive to Gary's, picturing myself walking inside, finding the pain charm, and walking back out again.

That's what I would do.

I managed to snag a parking spot on Main Street, right outside Gary's store. Reaching for my phone, I called Nathaniel.

He answered immediately. "Kyla. Tobias was wondering if you were coming for dinner."

I ignored that. "Is it okay if I do some work on the portal stuff?"

I ended the call before he could say no and turned off my phone. And then I moved.

He'd ordered me to ask him. And I had.

The heavy chains of the Alpha's order in my mind disappeared. I reveled in the temporary freedom.

Nathaniel knew exactly how I operated, which meant every pack member in Durham was getting a message right about now—all of them alerted to be on the lookout for me.

It was a good thing I wouldn't be in this realm for too much longer.

Selina had made it clear that this was *my* fight. If Nathaniel took me out of the game, people I loved would die.

And realistically, the chances of my living long enough to deal with the consequences from my Alpha were low.

I slid out of the car and grabbed my purse, hightailing it into Gary's. His store had recently been refurbished, but it smelled the same as always—the scent of magic and herbs and gnome winding toward me.

Gary was standing on his stool behind the counter, gaze on a copy of *Durham Denizens*. He looked up and gave me a nod.

"Long time, no see."

"Busy, busy," I said, reaching for the pain amulets. "I need some help."

"I had a feeling you would. Selina said you'd come looking for something magical. And she left this for you." He held up what looked like a ball of red thread.

I sucked in a breath and strolled toward him. Selina may have disappeared, but she'd done whatever she could to help us before she left.

"What is it?"

Gary placed it on the counter. "It's based on something called Ariadne's Thread. Also known as a clew. I don't know where you're going, but Selina said to tell you that your problem won't be getting in. It'll be getting out. Use this, and you'll be able to find your way out."

"Thank you." I hesitated. "Uh, you don't have any family in the other realms, do you?"

Gary slowly lifted his gray head, his eyes meeting mine. "Why?"

We had to be careful who we told. But Gary was on our side. He'd keep his mouth shut. And more importantly, he was a good man who deserved to have his family and friends close.

"Anyone you know who is between realms needs to make sure they're where they want to be by the winter solstice."

His skin had lightened. "Where they want to be forever?"

I nodded. He studied me for a long moment. "This is the kind of information that could cause a panic."

"Yes."

"And you told me anyway."

"You've more than earned it."

"I appreciate that. Don't you worry about us. We'll make sure we're well hidden in this realm."

"Okay. Good." My skin prickled. A pack member was guaranteed to see my car outside Gary's store soon. "I need to go."

He handed over the ball of thread, along with the pain charms. I reached into my purse, my fingers brushing the stone that allowed me to call the unseelie king. Despite the situation, I smirked. I pulled out my wallet, and Gary shook his head.

"Get gone."

"Appreciate it."

Ten minutes later, I was driving toward the portal to the unseelie realm. Unfortunately, Ryker and Hunter were on my ass. Hunter flashed his lights at me, his black Jeep practically kissing my bumper.

I ground my teeth and reached for the earbuds in my center console.

Hunter and Ryker were dominants—basically Nathaniel's mouthpieces. If they gave me an order, I'd have to follow it. Unless I wanted to challenge them.

My wolf was half the size of Ryker's. Even I had to admit he'd wipe the floor with me.

I shoved the earbuds in, connected them to my phone, and turned up my music as loud as my sensitive ears could stand. Popping Angelica's ring into my mouth, I grabbed the small backpack I'd kept packed after my trip to Guatemala and pulled up as close to the portal as I could get.

I was out of the car before they stopped. I'd even left my car running, but they'd take care of that.

Thanks to the ring, I was invisible. They wouldn't be able to see me, but they'd scent me. *I* could get through the portal. But if Ryker and Hunter attempted to get into Finvarra's realm without an invitation, they'd have to fight his guards.

And they'd never alert those guards that I was in the unseelie king's realm uninvited, no matter how pissed they were at me.

My chest clenched.

Family. They were my family. Nathaniel was my family too.

But if I didn't find this sword and return it to the demigod, our realms burned. This was the only way to protect that family.

And I was just the wolf for the job.

#

Finvarra

I knew the moment the wolf entered my realm.

I had, of course, been expecting her.

She wouldn't have expected *me* to be alerted to her presence. In truth, *I* didn't understand what she'd done to deserve the betrayal.

If I had any room left in me for softer emotions, I would

likely pity the little wolf. I knew what it was to be double-crossed by someone I'd foolishly trusted.

Kyla was after the sword. And the thought of her in *my* territory, attempting to steal something that was crucial for my revenge—something that could fall into my enemy's hands?

"Your Majesty?"

Lutrin's breath fogged in the air. I'd lowered the temperature significantly with my displeasure.

"My apologies," I ground out.

"Is something wrong?"

"Wrong? No. But there's something I need to handle." I glanced at the table of advisers who were currently trading insults. "We will resume this at another time."

That was enough to make them fall silent and stare at me. Mouths dropped open, eyes widened, but I was already gone.

My power allowed me to remain invisible and watch the wolf as she attempted to breach my castle. Unlike Taraghlan, I didn't have a tunnel she could sneak into. And I'd ordered my guards to pretend they couldn't see her.

It was best to study your allies—and your enemies—before you engaged them.

#

Kyla

I wanted to switch to my wolf form. It was better for sneaking. But I needed to keep the ring in my mouth, and there was a chance it would fall out with my shift. Decisions,

decisions.

For now, I let my wolf come to the forefront of my mind, my senses on alert. And I paced twenty feet from Finvarra's guards, my footsteps silent, even to their strange, pointed ears.

There would be no encircling of Finvarra's castle and searching for a weak point. Because some forward-thinking ancestor of his had built the castle into the *side* of a mountain.

Looking at the size of that castle, at the wards making the air appear incandescent in places, and at the hundreds of guards dressed in slate uniforms...

I suddenly felt very, very small.

I shook that away. Enough of that. Small was a good thing. No, small was a *great* thing. Small meant I could get into that castle undetected. I just had to—

Had that guard just looked right *at* me?

Angelica's ring was nestled safely beneath my tongue. My heart tripped, and I eyed the guard, my wolf on the hunt.

He was staring straight ahead once more. Just like all the other guards.

I prowled toward him, careful to stay silent. His pulse was a slow, steady thump in his neck. He didn't smell like fear, but there *was* a thread of anxiety buried beneath his calm. Was it the usual anxiety one would feel if they had to work for a tyrant like Finvarra?

Or was it more?

I waved my hand in front of his face. He didn't blink.

Hmm. Maybe I'd imagined it.

I stuck out my tongue.

Nada.

Turning to go, I swung back around with no warning and lifted my T-shirt, flashing the guard.

His gaze dropped. His cheeks turned red.

Son of a—

Dropping my shirt, I turned to run. I'd come up with a new plan.

For now, I was busted.

I was three steps from the portal back to my realm when a hand clamped down around the back of my neck.

I spat out the ring and slipped it into my pocket. It wasn't doing me any good anyway.

I didn't have to look. I could scent the unseelie king easily. He smelled like amber and pine.

"Finny boy. Fancy seeing you here."

"What are you doing sniffing around my castle, wolf?"

How had he known I was here? Had I messed up somehow? I'd used the ring, just as I'd used it in Guatemala.

Something in my chest wilted. I'd already messed this up. If I was in charge of making sure my friends survived the apocalypse, we were all dead.

Maybe I could talk my way out of this.

I glanced up at Finvarra's face. "Um, did you happen to see…"

He lifted one dark brow, and his gold eyes glittered at me. That huge hand tightened around the back of my neck.

"Did I happen to see you display your breasts to one of my guards? I certainly did."

"I'm wearing a bra," I muttered. Of *course* he'd seen that. "Look, there's been a misunderstanding. I was coming to see you. To talk. I think we could work together…"

One of Finvarra's guards stepped forward, blocking my way. I poised to leap, but the unseelie king slid into motion, already perp-marching me toward the castle.

Oh, hell no.

I turned wolf, ducking out of his hold and displaying my teeth.

My fangs were very large and very white. I was proud of them.

Finvarra didn't look impressed. No, the bastard *clicked his fingers* as if I were a golden retriever, expected to follow him home.

My snarl ripped through the air.

The unseelie king just looked bored. "You're in my realm, wolf. And you came here of your own free will, carrying this."

Leaning down to my torn clothes, he picked up the ball of thread Gary had given me. Satisfaction gleamed in his eyes as he pulled that thread apart and removed something else.

I craned my head, and he was obliging enough to lean down, unwrapping a piece of paper from a sparkling gem. He held up the paper for me to read.

I'm sorry.

Selina's handwriting.

Her words rang through my head loud and clear.

You will trust someone who will betray their word.

That gem was likely some kind of tracking spell, or perhaps even the reason Angelica's ring had been useless. Selina had betrayed me. She'd disappeared, but she'd still managed to betray me.

It was a good thing I was in wolf form. Because if I were in my human form, I likely would have burst into tears. And I wasn't a crier.

Finvarra jerked his head at the guard, who swiped the ring from the ruins of my jeans.

"You have two choices," Finvarra said, while I attempted to come to terms with Selina's duplicity. "Follow me into the castle for a conversation, or be carried."

I growled. He just lifted a hand, and I rose a few inches off the ground, his magic holding me in place.

My yelp made me sound like a startled puppy.

He lowered me back on the grass, his gold eyes burning into mine. "This is *my* realm."

I caught the subtext. Not only was it Finvarra's realm, but he was god here.

Sticking my nose in the air, I trotted past him and toward the castle.

three
Kyla

Unsurprisingly, as soon as we reached the castle, Finvarra gestured for me to follow him into the library.

I could count on one hand the number of times I'd seen him in this castle, and they'd mostly been in that library.

The library where I'd made the deal with him to steal his enemy's sword in the first place.

You'd think I would hate the place. But…I couldn't.

Huge, towering bookshelves lined the long walls, while the mezzanine held more books. When I peered up, I caught sight of a few comfortable chairs, arranged together and overlooking the library.

The thought of Finvarra sitting up there with *friends* was laughable. The unseelie was the definition of a cold, arrogant bastard.

A fire burned, taking some of the chill from the air. But I liked the chill in this realm. As a wolf, I was always hot. Summer in Durham was my nightmare.

Finvarra lifted a throw from a chair by that fire and dropped it in front of me.

"Shift."

I let out a low, threatening growl at his tone. Finvarra

ignored that, turning away dismissively to stare into the flames.

I shifted, wishing desperately for my clothes. I wasn't shy by nature, but there was something about being naked in front of Finvarra that made me feel almost vulnerable.

Wrapping the throw around me—and it was soft enough that I *would* be stealing it when I left—I leaned against the back of the closest chair.

"What were you doing here?" Finvarra turned, and his expression was blank once more, those eyes ice-cold.

"I told you, I wanted to talk to you."

"I'll rephrase. What were you doing here with Angelica's ring in your mouth?"

How could you screw me like this, Selina?

I wanted to believe she had reasons for doing everything she did, but I could see no logical way for this little meeting to be a good thing.

"I was just checking out the lay of the land. You've got a secure place here."

"Why do you want the sword?"

"I don't know what you're talking about."

I'd almost told him. Almost spilled the entire story. Almost believed that Finvarra would take my word and allow me to save the realms.

But that look on his face…

It was a feral kind of rage—there and gone in an instant. No, telling him what I wanted and why was a bad idea. I didn't know much about the unseelie king, but he seemed to pride himself on his self-control.

The sword was his blind spot. His beef with the seelie

king was the one thing that made him seem almost…human.

"Fine," he said, waving a hand. "You'll stay here until you choose to be truthful with me."

"Nathaniel's not going to like that."

His eyes darkened, and he turned until he faced me fully. Those strange ears of his were blade-sharp, and I counted at least three knives on him—that were visible, at least.

I went perfectly still, my mind creating and discarding escape plans. If it were just me and Finvarra and those knives, I'd bet on myself any day. I was a scrappy bitch, and my wolf was *fast*.

But I could sense his power, hidden beneath the surface. Could sense the well of it, so deep I didn't know where it ended.

There was a lethal predator in this room, and it wasn't me.

"If you're not operating alone, then your Alpha ordered his wolf to sneak into my realm and attempt to steal my most valuable possession. Is that the case, little wolf? Will my people go to war with yours?"

Fuck.

"No. Nathaniel didn't know what I was doing," I admitted, my mouth dry. "But he won't just allow you to keep me here. He's Alpha for a reason."

"You came into my realm with that ring. That means your little wolf friends don't know for sure if you even went through the portal or if you were attempting to throw them off the hunt."

"They'll be able to scent me."

"Perhaps." He gave an indolent shrug that made me

want to rake my claws down his face. "But I'm guessing your Alpha knows exactly what kind of troublemaker you are. Do you really think he'll put all his people at risk for a wolf who refuses to fall in line? One who is so selfish she would risk starting a war?"

The backs of my eyes burned. God, I hated this man. I refused to speak—wasn't even sure if I could—and he just studied my face.

"Stubbornly silent. Unsurprising, if unoriginal." He glanced toward the door, and I scented another fae who appeared within moments.

"Since I'm a *merciful* ruler, you can show the little wolf to her room. Something tells me it won't take long before she craves her freedom enough to admit exactly why she was attempting to steal from me."

#

Finvarra

If I'd expected Kyla to be cowed by our conversation, I would have been disappointed. Sure, I'd practically tasted her grief when I'd implied her Alpha would no longer want a hellion such as herself—a button I would push and push until she told me what I needed to know.

In reality, I knew the Alpha just enough to dislike what I'd seen of him, and to know that he considered the little wolf his sister.

He would move mountains for her. So would the other dominants.

And yet Kyla chose to believe my words.

It was interesting. Anyone who had spent more than five minutes with the wolf would consider her to be completely invulnerable to things like *feelings*.

It was always good to know your enemies' weaknesses.

Although I hadn't expected *her* weaknesses to be so obvious.

My mind raced as I attempted to consider just why she would need that sword. The obvious answer? She was working for Taraghlan. My greatest enemy. While she'd stolen the sword from him originally, she'd only done so because of the deal we'd made.

The deal that had preserved the alliance between Samael's people and my own.

It had been fascinating, striking that deal. The wolf had jumped in with both paws, more than willing to deal with me if I left Danica out of it.

I'd begun learning exactly who she was in that moment, and her movements had been helplessly predictable ever since.

She was more than willing to sacrifice herself for her friends, her pack...anyone she was loyal to. And yet the moment they attempted to shield her, she refused to cooperate.

Because, deep down, she didn't believe she deserved such loyalty.

Again—*fascinating*.

And I could wield such a weakness against her without even blinking.

That obsessive need to protect those she loved—even at the expense of herself—meant she was likely a puppet who'd been sent here to steal my sword, thanks to another deal she'd heedlessly agreed to.

The question? Who exactly was pulling her strings? And why?

Though Taraghlan was the obvious answer, I found it difficult to believe she would allow herself to be trapped by a deal with him. He'd endangered the people she loved, and the little wolf would never tolerate working with someone who'd done such a thing.

But he had allies. And the sooner I knew exactly who Kyla was working for, the sooner I could retaliate.

#

Kyla

The bedroom Finvarra gave me was surprisingly comfortable, considering he'd decided I was his prisoner.

Although, from what I'd seen of his castle so far, it was unlikely there were any small, dim, cold rooms to choose from. Except for the dungeons, which were undoubtedly located beneath his castle. I shuddered at the thought and dragged my attention back to the room.

It was shaped like a semicircle, the obscenely large bed placed against the main wall. That wall was a light blue, with delicate silver flowers climbing along what looked like hand-painted vines up toward the ceiling.

Nightstands flanked the bed, each of them holding crystal vases filled with wild flowers, their scent delicate, even to my sensitive nose.

But it was the ceiling that made me catch my breath.

Finvarra had put me in one of the towers. And the stone had been cut away—a huge skylight in its place. The sun had set while I'd been talking to Finvarra, and outside, the stars gleamed down at me, so close I felt as if I could touch them.

There was also a curtained contraption that would allow me to block out the light if I didn't want to wake with the sun. I studied it and shrugged, strolling back toward the bed.

I wasn't here to sleep in. I was here to get the lay of the land and steal Finvarra's sword.

And I'd already fucked that up so badly, tales would be told of this for centuries.

"But I'm guessing your Alpha knows exactly what kind of troublemaker you are. Do you really think he'll put all his people at risk for a wolf who refuses to fall in line? One who would cause a war?"

I sat on the edge of the bed. Finvarra was attempting to get under my skin. I *knew* that.

But that didn't mean he wasn't also right.

I *was* a pain in the ass.

I followed orders because I had to—and because along the way, I'd decided Nathaniel was the kind of leader I could respect. But a part of me had always chafed under those orders.

The pack had a hierarchy. I was near the top, but both Ryker and Hunter could take me in a fight.

For now.

I pushed that thought away. I had no desire to be one of the Alpha's dominants. It was my instinctive urge to *win* that had caused so many problems in my life.

I never could have anticipated that Selina would turn on me. Some tiny part of me hoped it was part of her larger plan. Perhaps I needed to be staying within the castle, so I'd have the best chance of stealing that stupid sword.

I'd carefully memorized everything she'd ever said to me about my future. There was a distinct possibility that I was marked for death. And that I had to accept that death to avoid a much worse fate.

I took a deep breath and shoved that thought down where I could ignore it some more. For now, I'd use this time to gather as much information as I could before I made my move.

Finvarra thought he had me at a disadvantage. Thought he could lock me up in here and I would be begging him to let me go.

A flash of cage bars slid through my mind, and I shuddered.

I'd been in much, much worse situations.

So, I would enjoy Finvarra's hospitality, all while figuring out a way to steal the sword.

He might be ancient, but his arrogance would cost him this time. And I couldn't wait to make it happen.

four
Kyla

Finvarra summoned me for dinner. And it *was* a summoning. One of his people had brought me a pair of sweatpants and a t-shirt, and I'd been pacing, considering everything I'd learned about his castle so far, when a knock on the door made me turn slowly.

The messenger dropped his gaze as soon as my eyes met his.

The poor boy looked like he was a teenager. Of course, he could be hundreds of years old, for all I knew. Still, I felt like a bully.

"His Majesty requires your presence at dinner."

"Fine," I sighed. If I didn't eat, I'd get weak, bitchy, and, eventually…feral. And after my imprisonment in the underworld, I was much more likely to turn feral than the average wolf.

I pushed away that little memory and followed the messenger down the stairs, through the wooden door—previously locked—and along the corridor.

Memorizing my route was easy, even with the strange unseelie magic messing with everyone's scents. Beneath all of them was one scent that put me on edge and made me want to bare my teeth.

The scent of snow and magic, pine and amber. Finvarra.

The messenger scurried in front of me, clearly not enjoying the experience of a werewolf prowling behind him. The scent of his fear didn't help me keep my control, so I focused on my plans.

The portal I'd come through wasn't my only option. While it was the most convenient, it was also the most well-guarded, and Finvarra would have increased his guards.

But there was another portal close by. I'd used it once with Danica, and it would take me to another part of Finvarra's realm—the swamp of Ilis. I just needed to get to a pub called the Harpy's Hell, where I'd take that portal to the swamp, pop through another portal, and be back in my realm within a couple of hours.

I had options.

The thought calmed my wolf. The messenger opened a door and gestured for me to walk in front of him. I tamped down the urge to show him my teeth—my wolf enjoyed when her prey was afraid.

Be nice. Save that shit for Finvarra.

If Finvarra hadn't been waiting for me, I would have sucked in a startled breath. This obviously wasn't a formal dining room, despite the luxury that dripped from every inch of it.

The unseelie king had a fondness for fires, and one burned low to my left. To my right, it was as if someone had sliced off a chunk of the stone, leaving the room open to the elements. Finvarra's realm was cold to most—exceptionally comfortable to my wolf, although I'd never admit *that*—and it had begun to snow lightly. Some kind of ward kept the snow from falling into the room, allowing the cool breeze to play along my skin.

Behind me, Finvarra practically radiated amusement. I'd stalked to the edge of the room, gazing out at the winter wonderland of his realm.

He knew I loved it, the bastard.

Slowly turning, I raised one eyebrow at him. "Your ancestor certainly had great taste."

A slow smile spread over that irritatingly perfect face. "*I* made the updates."

"Awesome. Maybe you should turn your attention toward interior design and away from kidnapping."

That smile widened, more a display of teeth than anything. I stifled a growl. "*Is* it kidnapping when someone enters your home?" Finvarra mused.

Since I wasn't entirely sure—all I knew was that he was most definitely the bad guy here—I stalked toward the table. It would have seated six but had been set with two place settings. Clearly, this wasn't where Finvarra conducted his formal dinners.

The polished wood gleamed beneath the glow of what seemed like hundreds of candles. Food was already waiting, and the scents curled toward me until my mouth was watering. From the satisfaction on Finvarra's face, I was pretty sure he knew.

He waved his hand, and the silver domes disappeared from the dishes in front of us. My stomach growled, loud enough that the unseelie king's lips twitched. But I forced myself not to eat just yet.

He studied me. "What's the problem?"

"I know what happens to people who eat in the fae realms."

"Do you truly want to starve to death, wolf? It turned you feral last time."

That hadn't *just* been the lack of food. I'd also been unable to shift. Still...

Finvarra rolled his eyes. "The seelie realm works differently from mine. Eat."

Fae-speak. I snorted. "Swear to me that I can eat your food with no consequences."

He angled his head. "I swear you can eat my food with no consequences. You are, after all, already my prisoner."

I sat back in my seat and watched him. His mouth curved. "I swear you may eat in my realm without being tied to it in any way."

Another wave of that hand, and a little of everything appeared on my plate. He was hoping to unsettle me with his blatant displays of magic. I just gave him a toothy grin.

"Thanks."

A nod, and he did the same to his own plate. I studied the food.

I'd gotten spoiled in the pack. I couldn't cook, but Tobias, Nathaniel's butler slash cook slash assistant, insisted on feeding me whenever he could. The submissive took personal affront whenever he scented drive-thru burgers on me.

"Kyla," he would say, "why must you insult me this way? Do you not enjoy my food?"

Tobias was better at the guilt trip than most mothers. Not that I would know anything about that.

"Wolf?"

Finvarra was studying me. I took a deep breath and struggled to hold back a moan. I didn't even know what it was—something savory and meaty, with pastry, vegetables…

I came up for air after my fifth serving. Finvarra looked vaguely appalled.

"I'm a werewolf, bro. If I'm eating your food, I'm not eating your people."

He ignored that not-so-veiled threat. "Are you ready to tell me why you attempted to steal from me?"

I opened my mouth, unsure exactly what I'd say.

Thankfully, the door to our left opened, and I clamped my mouth shut. Finvarra's expression tightened, and he turned.

"Forgive the interruption, Your Majesty. We have… news."

The unseelie was dark-haired, as most of them tended to be. But he was small, almost slight. While his face was attractive, he sneered at me, and the expression made him look like an angry weasel.

"Thank you, Lutrin," Finvarra ground out. "I'll be right there."

"Don't let me keep you." I got to my feet and placed my napkin on the table. "I'm done."

Lutrin narrowed his eyes at me when I approached. He held my gaze longer than most, instantly raising it once more after it had dropped. But I gave him a wide, we-both-know-my-dick-is-bigger-than-yours smile.

His hands lit with a blue glow.

My wolf pushed me aside with no warning and snarled at the threat.

Then Finvarra was there, his hand clamped around the back of my neck as he steered me from the room.

"Must you antagonize everyone you meet?" he ground out.

Shaken from the way my wolf was *still* occasionally half feral, I pasted a smirk on my face.

"Oh, but I must," I simpered. Finvarra let me go, and I swept past him, ignoring the messenger who appeared once more.

"I know the way," I snapped.

The messenger paled and glanced over my shoulder.

Finvarra must have nodded, because the messenger melted away. I didn't look back, just stalked back to my room. The moment I reached it, the door swung shut behind me automatically, locking instantly.

I snorted. I could rip through that door if I wanted to. In fact, my wolf could burrow beneath the stone I was standing on. And oh, how she wanted to.

But this wasn't the kind of situation I could get out of with strength alone.

No, I needed to be smart. Smart and sneaky.

Finvarra had let me into his castle. And before I was done here, I'd make sure he regretted it.

#

Finvarra

Lutrin swallowed as I watched him. His interruption

couldn't have come at a worse time. After the wolf had eaten almost everything on the table, she'd seemed to be less…savage.

And more likely to think logically.

I'd seen it in her eyes. It was the closest she'd come to telling me what she was up to.

"Your Majesty?"

"What. Is. It?"

"Your cousin is here."

I could understand the interruption. Taeso hadn't visited for years, always convincing me to meet him in his own lands. If he was here, it was likely important.

"Where is he?"

"The library."

I nodded and turned to go. "Ah, Your Majesty, if I may?"

Glancing over my shoulder, I raised one brow.

Lutrin swallowed. "It's just… I wonder if having the wolf here is a distraction we don't need."

"Of course it is. The fact remains that she's here—either with or without the blessing of her Alpha—and attempting to steal the sword she stole for me. I need to know why."

I rarely explained myself to anyone, even my most loyal advisers. I turned to go, and Lutrin cleared his throat once more.

"What is it that you want, Lutrin?"

"She's an enemy. One who snuck in here to take something that belongs to you. She should be dead."

I studied him. Oh, he hadn't appreciated that the little wolf had presented herself as a threat to him. He might have magic, but the wolf was smart and sneaky. She would rip out his throat if she got the chance. And instead of dealing with that threat himself, he expected that I should kill her.

"Do you or do you not remember the day I signed a treaty with Samael—who is now the underking? His mate, the underqueen, is the little wolf's best friend. And the wolves? We still have an alliance. Make no mistake," I said, my voice soft, "if I have to kill the wolf, I will. But to do so would mean declaring war. That is not the kind of decision one makes lightly."

And that was more explanation than I gave anyone regarding my actions. Perhaps it was actually more for me—a good reminder of the consequences of any decisions I made regarding the wolf. Especially since she unerringly knew exactly how to infuriate me.

Lutrin was studying the floor. I turned and stalked out, making my way to the library. Unsurprisingly, my cousin waited with a glass of my best whiskey in his hand as he lounged in *my* seat.

He glanced up at me with a challenging grin, and I shook my head. I should never let him meet the wolf. They would likely become fast friends.

"Tae."

"Fin."

I poured a whiskey of my own and leaned on the wall. "It has been some time since you visited."

His expression sobered. "It's not a happy visit, I'm afraid. My father refuses to see reason. He will be dead within the month."

I closed my eyes. I enjoyed my uncle's company, although we'd never been particularly close. His mate had died while I was still young, and so I'd never known the Drusin my family spoke of. The one who loved life and laughed often. I'd only ever known the Drusin who stayed alive for Tae but longed to join his mate.

And *this* was why my advisers were so determined for me to marry. Drusin was currently the heir to my throne. After he died, Tae would be the sole unseelie in line. If something were to take out both of us... And with war on our doorstep, that was not *un*likely.

Should the both of us fall, civil war would rip our realm apart as those closest to my bloodline fought for the throne.

Tae was still watching me. "I don't want it."

I angled my head. "The fact that you don't want power is one of the most compelling reasons to give it to you. The best rulers understand the weight of that power."

"Don't analyze me. You need to find a mate."

"I won't be pushed into a loveless bonding."

"Your parents…"

I stalked to the window, gazing sightlessly out at the snow. For some reason, my thoughts returned to the little wolf. I'd seen the way her eyes had lit in appreciation at the view. Perhaps the only thing we had in common.

Tae had gone silent behind me. My parents hadn't started out loveless. No, they'd once been famed as a love *match*—something that was extremely uncommon among royalty.

Except my mother hadn't been royalty. No, she'd been the youngest daughter of a minor nobleman who, with four other girls, hadn't had the time or the inclination to rein in his wild child.

My father had already been king when they met—by chance—when he was touring the kingdom.

"Fin…"

"I've ruled for long enough now that my power has only grown. You may not want the throne, and since I would have to be dead for you to take it, I'm quite happy to keep it myself. But I know you would be an excellent king."

He heaved a sigh, but I didn't take the sound as a concession. He wasn't going to let this go. The ghost of a smile teased my lips. I would expect nothing less from my hardheaded cousin. We were, after all, family.

"Well then," he said after a long silence. "Why don't you tell me about the female werewolf everyone is talking about—and why exactly you've got her locked away?"

five
Kyla

The next morning, Finvarra sent a messenger who insisted I join the king for breakfast. Maybe the king had taken my little joke about eating his people seriously.

I'd woken early, poking around the room and riffling through the closet. At some point, likely while I was at dinner, Finvarra had ordered someone to fill it with clothes in my size. Most of them were the kinds of clothes I usually wore—activewear, jeans, joggers. But there were also several dresses, a formal gown, and something that looked a lot like…armor.

Shaking my head, I grabbed the closest pair of jeans and a T-shirt. My wolf approved of the quality of the clothes, which further irritated me, but I pasted on a smile when the messenger led me down to Finvarra's dining room.

That smile widened when I caught sight of the man waiting at the table.

"Well, well, well," I purred. "And just where has Finny boy been keeping *you*?"

The fae glanced up and grinned back at me. "I was about to ask the same thing."

Like most of the unseelie I'd met so far, he was attractive. The dimple that flashed in one cheek also made him much more approachable than Finvarra. His eyes were green, but I could see a hint of family resemblance in those high cheekbones.

"Brother?" I asked.

"Cousin."

"Ah." I sat at the table and began loading my plate with eggs, French toast, bacon, sausage, and fruit.

His eyes widened, and I almost chuckled. "Werewolf."

"That's right. A *female* werewolf."

"That isn't close to the most interesting thing about me."

His eyes lit, and he leaned across the table. "Is that so? Well—"

"No flirting with the werewolf, Tae." Finvarra prowled across the room and sat down.

I glowered at the unseelie king. "What's your problem?"

He pointed at Tae. "Younger. That means he can tolerate more alcohol."

Tae grinned. "You can *tolerate* it. It's the morning after that begins to present a problem when you're ancient."

I smirked. I liked this guy.

Finvarra slid me a look, and I shoved another forkful of eggs into my mouth.

"Tae, meet Kyla," Finvarra rumbled, pouring himself some coffee.

"What about you?" Tae asked me. "Can werewolves get drunk?"

"Oh yeah. But we have to drink a lot very quickly. We also metabolize it quickly. That means our hangovers hit hard. But if you time it right and pass out at the perfect point, you'll sleep through that hangover."

Tae raised an eyebrow. "Fascinating."

I hadn't seen him yesterday, but so far, this guy was the best person in this castle. "Do you live here?"

His face darkened slightly. "No. My father is dying, and I came to deliver the news in person."

"I'm sorry."

"Thank you." He played with his spoon. I took another helping of everything.

"Do you always eat this much?"

Finvarra smirked. "Last night, she had five servings."

Tae's mouth dropped open. I couldn't tell if he looked impressed or appalled, so I was going to assume he was impressed.

"Werewolves metabolize everything rapidly. They quite literally need to feed the beast inside them," Finvarra said. "Without enough food, they risk turning feral before they waste away. Isn't that right, little wolf?"

Of course he would bring that up.

"How do you even know so much about werewolves?" I muttered sullenly.

"I know a lot about everything."

I sneered at him. Tae looked like he was trying to suppress a laugh.

"So, Kyla," Tae said. "What exactly are you doing here?"

"I caught her stealing from me," Finvarra said mildly, pouring himself more coffee.

"I wasn't stealing," I snapped.

"Only because you didn't get that far."

I *hated* this man. Tae sent me a sympathetic look, and I shoved more food into my mouth and sent him one back. It could be worse. I could be *related* to the unseelie king.

"We're traveling today," Finvarra announced, sparing me a glance. "You'll need to change to formal dress. One of the servants will find you a cloak."

"Wolf, remember?"

His lips curved. "Ah. And my realm must be the ideal temperature."

"I certainly didn't say that." Only because I didn't need to. The bastard knew.

Tae cleared his throat. "Well, I'll just be—"

"You're coming too." Finvarra gulped the rest of his coffee and got to his feet. "We leave in half an hour. Don't be late."

He strode out, and I glanced at Tae. "Where do you think we're going?"

He sighed. "I don't know."

"Why do you have to go with him?"

"I probably shouldn't tell you this—Fin would likely kill me—but I'm his heir." His expression turned haunted. "At least, I will be when my father dies. The unseelie king has no wife or children, something his advisers have been hounding him about for at least a century. Since I'm the backup plan, Fin likes to make sure the people see me. He also wants me to learn the ropes, as you'd likely say in your realm."

"You don't want to rule."

His eyebrows shot up. "What makes you say that?"

I chose not to point out that no sane person would want

UNENDING MAGIC 47

the unseelie throne and the headache that likely came with it. Especially since it probably meant turning into someone like Finvarra. "Your voice changes when you talk about it."

"You're very perceptive."

I shrugged. He studied me for a moment longer and then sighed. "No. I don't want the throne. I don't want the responsibility, the endless meetings, the war councils, the politics. I've seen what it's done to Fin."

"You mean he wasn't always a—"

"Careful," Tae said, but a smile tugged at his lips. "That's my cousin you're talking about. But no. He wasn't always like this. And that drives a wedge between us."

I could imagine it would. When Tae said he didn't want the throne, and Finvarra knew it was because he didn't want to end up like him? Ouch.

"I need to go get dressed." Tae smirked at me. "You may want to do the same."

I gestured at my leggings and T-shirt. "Why? What's wrong with this?"

He just sighed, got to his feet, and strolled out.

I finished my breakfast and wandered back up to my room, where I found a dress lying on my bed.

At least Finvarra's people hadn't chosen anything close to the monstrosities Danica and I had been forced to wear to meet the seelie king. The dress was long, a blue so dark it was almost black, and speckled with tiny jewels across the boobs.

This was not ideal. If we were leaving the castle, it meant I would be even farther from the sword.

Hopefully, it wouldn't be for long. I could use this time

to study Finvarra…and to attempt to figure out exactly where he would hide the sword that had the ability to end his life.

Someone knocked on my door, and I turned as a woman entered.

"My name is Shemia." She smiled. "His Majesty asked me to help you get ready."

"Thanks. But I know how to put on a dress."

Her expression stayed perfectly placid. "Of course. However, you might want some help with your face and hair."

I eyed her. "Why?"

She blinked. "Why?"

"Yeah. Why does my face need to be done? Where are we going?"

"Ah. His Majesty is taking you to a part of his kingdom called Greleris. He does this occasionally—surprises the nobles with a visit to ensure everything is functioning as it should."

Because he was a giant control freak. Made sense.

Based on the warning look he'd given me at breakfast, there was no way I was getting out of this. Nathaniel might even be interested in any information I learned for the long-term—especially if their alliance ended up broken.

"Kyla?"

I jolted myself out of my thoughts. "Yeah. Okay, let's do this."

She smiled and waved her hand. A vanity appeared in the middle of the room, and I stared at her.

"I just lifted it from somewhere else," she murmured.

"A simple magic."

Simple, my butt. But I nodded and sat down.

"I'll do my own hair." It was currently relaxed—I went through stages, sometimes preferring my natural hair, sometimes changing things up. But I knew how I liked it styled. Shemia simply nodded.

"Makeup?"

"Don't go overboard, please."

"No. I'll keep it natural."

I'd bet Shemia could likely achieve the "natural" look in half the time it took me. Why did natural makeup take almost as long as full glam, anyway? I pondered that after I'd swept my hair into a loose bun, leaving a few pieces to fall around my face.

When I was done, I kept my eyes closed as Shemia's brushes tickled my face. At one point, I opened my eyes to find five different brushes all working on my face while she watched carefully.

Talk about multitasking. Yes, she could definitely do this much faster than I could.

Just a few minutes later, she pronounced me ready. I glanced in the mirror. My lashes looked longer and fuller, and she'd darkened my lids just enough to add some depth without being overdone for the middle of the day. The color she'd applied to my cheeks made me look naturally flushed, and my lipstick was a nude on the browner side of the spectrum.

She'd gotten it right. And she hadn't attempted to make me look like a doll. She got points for that.

"Thanks, Shemia."

"Let me help you into your dress."

A few minutes later, I was standing in front of the full-length mirror she'd had transported into my room. She'd found matching shoes with a low heel.

If I didn't know I could shift the moment I felt threatened, I likely would have felt like prey in a dress and shoes I'd struggle to run in. But my wolf could be free in the blink of an eye.

"You look beautiful."

"Thank you."

"Here's a purse to match." She handed it to me. "I think you need to meet His Majesty downstairs now."

I didn't have anything to put in the purse. My phone certainly didn't work here. But I opened the drawer next to my bed, unzipped my own purse, and plucked out the stone Finvarra had given me to call him to deal with Fenrir months ago.

I didn't want to risk a curious servant finding it and telling Finvarra I still had it.

She escorted me to the main stairs, and I picked up the hem of my dress, ensuring I didn't trip on it.

If there was one thing turning into a werewolf had given me, it was natural grace. Even in heels, my wolf balanced perfectly. Before I'd been turned, I'd felt a little like Bambi every time I'd worn heels.

Tae and Finvarra were both waiting, dressed in what I was guessing was courtly attire.

Finvarra's gaze trailed down my body and back up again. When his eyes met mine, they heated.

Well. I barely held back a flush. We stared at each other

in silence, until Tae stepped forward, giving me a low bow.

"The stars pale in comparison to your beauty," he intoned.

"Give me a break," I muttered, and he grinned up at me. I couldn't help but glance back at Finvarra, who was now talking to one of his servants.

His Majesty was wearing head-to-toe black—not uncommon for him. But it was the black crown he wore that caught my attention.

He should have looked ridiculous. For most people, the crown would have worn them. Not Finvarra. The jewels glinted in the light, slightly crooked on his head, as if he'd shoved it on as an afterthought. My hands itched with the need to straighten it, and he glanced at me, raising his eyebrow.

"Problem?"

"Nothing," I muttered.

"Hmm." He studied me some more, and I just waited him out. But my eyes slid up to that crown before I could stop them.

I flicked my glance back down, but he just smirked at me. "Cataloguing the jewels for your next embarrassing theft attempt? I'm almost inclined to leave it lying around to tempt you."

God, I hated this man.

Tae wiped a hand over his mouth, clearly hiding a smirk. I narrowed my eyes at him, and he shrugged. "You have to admit, that's kind of funny."

Finvarra just turned. "Follow me."

Tae strolled after Finvarra without hesitation. I trailed

behind them, after a glance toward the main entrance of the castle—and all the guards.

How exactly were we traveling?

Since Finvarra wasn't the type to explain, I allowed my wolf to take the lead. She noted each scent, but within moments, my gaze was stuck to the tantalizing slice of bare skin right beneath Finvarra's pointed ears. His dark hair fell behind his shoulders, and his pulse beat in the side of his throat.

It would be so, so rewarding to rip into that throat.

The unseelie king stiffened, paused, and slowly turned his head.

"Keep walking, Tae," he ordered, his voice just louder than a whisper. Tae took one look at me and winced. But he complied, strolling away.

"Do you imagine me your *prey,* little wolf?" Finvarra purred, stalking toward me.

My wolf refused to back down. And neither did I.

I just stared at him silently until he angled his head in that strange, inhuman way he did.

His hand struck out, reaching for my chin. But my wolf was close enough to the surface that I was just a hair faster. I batted his hand away, my claws slicing out as I snarled.

"And there she is."

"Excuse me?"

"Why is your wolf so close to the surface? Are you close to going feral?"

Again.

He didn't say the word, but we both heard it. I showed him my teeth, and he just raised one eyebrow in that endlessly amused way he did.

"It's close to the full moon," I muttered. I could feel it, just days away. Finvarra studied me.

"And instead of frolicking, you've been caged. Poor little wolf."

It was a taunt, but I refused to respond to it. He just smiled, but there was no humor in it.

"But you allow your wolf enough freedom that you have to overcome the urge to tear out my throat."

"To be fair, that urge has always been there. Your trachea would look perfect on my desk. I'd use it as a pencil holder."

He took a step closer. I planted my feet. *Now* the dress annoyed me. If I shifted, I'd have to change clothes again. And yet Finvarra was too large and too close.

To my surprise, that was actual *humor* curving his mouth now. My threat had genuinely amused him. Goody.

"The region we're visiting is densely forested. You can run there. Now, if you're finished with your murderous impulses—the impulses you'll never achieve—we need to leave."

The bastard's hand moved once more. But this time, I miscalculated. He wasn't going for my chin.

The unseelie king *booped* me on my nose.

Then he turned and sauntered away.

#

Finvarra

We stepped into the portal room, and Kyla gasped

behind me. Tae slid her a grin, and I held back a sigh.

"You have a portal. In your castle."

"An internal portal," Tae said. "Fin can take it to any portal within this realm."

I slid him a look. That wasn't a lie. But it wasn't the whole truth either. This particular portal was one of the biggest mysteries in my realm—and yet it was a mystery I would never solve.

Kyla glanced over her shoulder. "You don't travel with an…entourage?"

"They'll travel behind us and will meet us tomorrow," Tae said.

Kyla raised one eyebrow, clearly storing that information away. Her gaze flicked to the portal, and I saw the moment she realized it was hidden from all but my most trusted people.

"Hand," I demanded.

The little wolf hesitated, and I waited her out.

"Finvarra has to keep the destination in his mind," Tae murmured. "Since you don't know where you're going…"

She sent him a grin that, for reasons I didn't understand, made me want to set him on fire.

"So if I went through by myself, I'd end up who knows where?"

"Correct," I ground out. "Move."

She strolled over to me, every muscle moving in a graceful roll that drew attention to the way her dress cupped her breasts. The way it fell over her hips and the curve of her ass.

With a poisonous look up at me, she took my hand,

immediately looking away. That hand was ridiculously small and delicate in my own. I slid a glance at Tae as he reached for Kyla's other hand.

He sent me a shit-eating grin and circled around, grabbing hold of my shoulder instead. "Now *that* reaction was interesting," he murmured to me.

"If you weren't my heir…"

"This is cozy." Kyla gestured to all of us, standing in front of the portal. "But can we move this little journey along?"

"Things to do?" Tae asked her.

I just sighed, fixed our destination in my mind, and stepped into the portal, taking them both with me.

The portal released us, and Kyla immediately pulled her hand free of mine.

The forest clearing was located close enough to the summer palace that we wouldn't need further transportation, yet far enough away that no one could arrive through the portal without the guards being alerted.

"State your… Your Majesty!" one of the guards choked out.

I just waited, and he turned his attention to the castle, obviously alerting Marnin to my presence.

Kyla strolled a few feet away, taking in the forest. Her nostrils flared, and I couldn't help but wonder what information that incredible nose was giving her.

"Your Majesty," a deep voice said. "What a welcome surprise."

Kyla snorted, and for a moment, my lips wanted to curve. The insincerity in that voice was obvious to anyone who had ears.

I turned. "Marnin."

The fae was older than I was. He'd been close to my father once. But now he was wearing long blue robes, and on his head…

Behind us, Tae sucked in a breath. I kept my expression blank. "Well now. That looks almost like a…crown."

Marnin flushed. "Merely a reminder of whom we all serve, Your Majesty."

I let my gaze stay on his face for a long moment. I could practically scent the sweat gathering on his brow beneath the sapphire crown he wore.

"That crown looks like a reminder of the seelie king," Tae mused. His expression had turned carefully neutral. This was why I insisted on bringing him with me on occasions such as these. Because one day, he would likely be the one to rule every single one of my people. Including those who wished to rule themselves. Such as Marnin.

Marnin's eyes went wide. "The sapphire is the jewel of my house," he ground out.

I just waited.

Marnin was allowed to rule these lands—and enjoy residence in the summer palace—simply because I didn't have the time or inclination. And because thinking of this place made me think of my mother.

But somewhere along the way, he'd decided to take my inattention as an opportunity to crown himself king of this territory.

The question? Just how loyal were the nobles who lived here? And more importantly, how much of the greater population had he swayed to his cause?

Marnin removed the crown. Tae smiled. I just angled my head. "Ensure the royal chambers are clean."

Marnin glanced at Kyla, clearly wondering who she was.

"Is there a problem?" Tae asked softly.

"No." But resentment glimmered in Marnin's eyes. The kind of resentment that had festered. I had gone too long without visiting the outer regions of my kingdom.

Because you turned all your attention to Taraghlan.

Marnin turned, summoning a servant with a wave of his hand. I glanced at Kyla.

Her blue eyes had narrowed, her gaze sweeping our surroundings for threats. For some unknown reason, that made me grit my teeth.

"Relax, wolf. No one will attack you here."

She ignored me. "I'll be the judge of that."

Tae slid me a sympathetic look.

Marnin had finished speaking with his servant, who took a long second to gawk at us before scampering away.

"Was there any reason in particular for this visit?" Marnin asked.

"Do I need a reason to visit my lands? To stay in the palace my mother adored?"

"No, of course not." Marnin glanced away, his gaze finding Kyla once more.

"Ah, and is this your new pet werewolf, Your Majesty?"

So word had already reached this part of my kingdom. Just as I'd expected it to.

The little wolf stiffened. And she didn't look at me.

Her body language told me everything I needed to know.

She expected me to mock her publicly. To allow others to do the same.

I kept my gaze on the wolf. "Kyla Hill is my guest," I said softly.

That meant she was *mine* to torment—and mine alone.

I caught Kyla's surprise in the way she angled her head.

"Of course. Of course," Marnin said. "May I escort you to your chambers, Your Majesty?"

I studied him. My father had been friends with him only because he believed in keeping his enemies close. Something I'd clearly learned from him, if my insistence on bringing Kyla here was any indication. And even though I'd been too busy to visit these lands, I'd still ensured my spies reported back to me.

I knew all about his late-night meetings in the clearing he thought hidden. The plans he thought secret.

Marnin was a threat that would need to be removed. Soon.

"You may."

six
Kyla

It was easy to see why this place was known as the summer palace. There was still a mild chill in the air and several inches of snow on the ground. And yet, flowers bloomed throughout the forest as we walked away from the portal.

I would need to run tonight *and* tomorrow. My wolf would demand it. I'd prefer even more snow since some genetic flaw had made my wolf completely white.

We stepped out of the forest, and Marnin smiled his smug little smile and gestured for us to follow him—as if he owned the place. Already, I could tell he was going to be a thorn in Finvarra's side.

I should have celebrated. I was, after all, a thorn in his side myself. But I just plain didn't like Marnin.

My breath caught in my throat, and I forced my expression to turn neutral as I felt Finvarra's attention. I could almost sense his amusement, the bastard. But…this place…

"It's beautiful, huh?" Tae murmured, so low my wolf just heard it. "Easy to see why Fin's mother loved the place."

Ah. Another reason for Finvarra to be pissed. That little weasel Marnin was setting himself up as king of the castle his mom had adored.

And I could see why she'd adored it.

Unlike Finvarra's castle, which was more of a fortress, the summer palace was open to the elements, with few walls in place that I could see. The unseelie must run almost as hot as I did, because if Evie or Danica were here, they'd be curled up in front of a fire.

My heart ached for my friends.

But we were already stepping into the palace. I knew the guards were there—I could scent them just a few feet away in places. But unlike in Finvarra's castle, they lingered out of sight, giving the pretense there *were* no guards.

The first room was clearly for visitors to wait to see if they were admitted into the next level. Comfortable-looking furniture was grouped throughout, while my gaze caught on flashes of white—servants dressed in robes, who were carrying food and drink.

That was one thing Finvarra had going for him. I could accuse him of many things, but so far, I'd never seen him summon a servant for a drink. No, he used his magic whenever possible—shifting things the way Shemia had shifted the vanity into my room.

The sand-colored tiles beneath my feet were flecked with some kind of glittering stone. The same stone had been inlaid in the walls, only the pieces were much larger, allowing some incredibly talented artist to create intricate designs.

We passed a water feature that splashed into a tiny pond, and I caught sight of a plump blue-green fish.

Another servant trotted up to Marnin, murmuring to him. He smiled, glancing back at us. "Your chambers are ready. We also have people available to see to…all your needs." His gaze swept over to us, and I barely prevented my mouth from dropping open.

Had he just offered to set us up with some sex workers?

I wondered what Finvarra would say if I took Marnin up on that offer. A slow grin spread across my face, and Tae elbowed me in the ribs. "Don't even think about it."

Finvarra was eyeing Marnin the way I looked at my prey.

Maybe this trip wouldn't be so bad after all. Finvarra had been cold as ice with Marnin, and it was evident that the fae was terrified of his king and completely unprepared for Finvarra's visit. Maybe, if I was really lucky, I'd get to see Finvarra smite him.

My wolf perked up at the thought of violence, and if I didn't know better, I'd think Finvarra had *felt* her. He slowly turned his head, until he was looking me in the eye.

I will be responsible for any throats that are ripped out here. Are we clear?

My mouth dropped open, and I froze. Tae grabbed my arm, hauling me with him. "You okay?"

"No," I hissed. "His Majesty just clawed his way into my head."

Tae choked on his laugh. "You mean he used his power to talk to you?"

"It's invasive as hell, and I won't tolerate it."

He sighed. "Let's discuss that when we're in our chambers."

Damn right, we would discuss it. I gave Finvarra my dirtiest look, and amusement crossed his face for the first time since we'd stepped through the portal.

Great.

#

Finvarra

Kyla paced back and forth, sending me occasional dirty looks. I sat on the sofa, stretching out my legs as I sighed, pinching the bridge of my nose. "You're overreacting."

I knew enough about women to know those two words were like pouring gas and throwing a lit match.

Her eyes widened, narrowed, and turned feral. That look punched into me in a way I didn't want to think about.

The royal chambers were made up of four suites connected to a main sitting room, which had plenty of space to take meals and relax. Kyla had fallen silent as she'd taken in the tasteful art, comfortable seating, and the view over the garden into the forest in the distance. The magic of the summer castle ensured all rooms had a balcony and view, regardless of where they were actually situated.

"A simple conversation," I muttered.

She folded her arms. "It's not a conversation if you're just shoving words into my head."

"Would it help if I taught you how to speak back to me?"

Interest flickered in her eyes, followed immediately by suspicion.

This woman exhausted and annoyed me in equal measure.

"Toddlers can speak this way," I snarled. "You may

choose to stay ignorant, but I'll speak to you however I want."

Unsurprisingly, the little wolf's eyes fired at that. Tae gave me a look.

"Stay out of my head," Kyla snapped, stalking into her room. The door slammed, and Tae sighed.

"Must you antagonize her?"

"Yes," I muttered darkly.

"I don't see why Lutrin had to come with us." Tae stretched out his legs. My adviser would be here within hours, and Tae hadn't been pleased to learn that information.

"You know why."

"Now? While this court is a mess?"

"He's useful to me."

Tae rolled his eyes, getting to his feet. "I don't need to tell you that you're playing a dangerous game," he said. "If Lutrin realizes…"

"My guards have been alerted." My tone told him the conversation was over, and Tae shook his head.

"What are you going to do about Marnin's little meetings?"

"I haven't decided yet." If I arrested him, it would seem as if it were based on rumor and speculation. Yet those meetings were becoming dangerous, and Marnin grew more arrogant with each noble he turned to his side.

"I could—" my cousin began.

"He'd sense your power."

"Arresting a traitor who is conspiring to take your throne doesn't make you like your father, Fin."

I fisted my hands, immediately besieged by images of

what my father had done to his enemies over the centuries. I wasn't a good man. Would never be. But I'd decided long ago that there were some things I wouldn't do for power.

As usual, the thought of my father darkened my mood. Getting to my feet, I stalked to the small bar in the corner and poured myself a drink.

"Whiskey?"

"No," Tae sighed. "I'm going to go do what I do best."

I smirked at that. "Convince beautiful women that you're a soft, kind male beneath your tough exterior?"

He grinned back at me, and for a moment, it was as if we were children again. "No." His grin faded. "I'm going to pretend to be the naïve, fumbling heir who has no real idea about court politics and can be easily manipulated by those who know the right buttons to press."

I raised my glass in a toast. "Good hunting, cousin."

#

Kyla

I'd been warned not to say anything to the servants that I didn't want everyone in this palace to know. Thankfully, Shemia was the one who arrived to help me dress for dinner. Finvarra wouldn't have ordered her to come if he hadn't trusted her, but I was currently craving solitude more than I ever had before.

"Which gown would you like to wear?" Shemia asked.

Somehow, Finvarra had arranged for more gowns in my size to be waiting in the closet, along with a couple of pairs of jeans, T-shirts, and sweats.

"Do I really need to change?" I waved one hand at the gorgeous blue dress I was still wearing.

Shemia gave me a sympathetic smile. "Yes. The dress you're wearing is beautiful, but suitable only for the day."

I sighed as I took in the gown she laid on my bed. It was a red so dark it was almost black, with a longer train and even more embellishment. I was torn between refusing to wear it and doing whatever I could to fit in so I could study Finvarra for weaknesses—and perhaps even find an ally or two who'd help me with my sword plans.

"What's with all the formality here?"

She sighed, helping me out of the blue dress. "His Majesty allows those whom he has put in charge of each territory to rule that territory as they see fit. While they all answer to him, many of them prefer the old ways. This part of the kingdom is called Greleris, and it's difficult to travel to—thankfully His Majesty directed us to the right portals so we could take a shortcut—and that difficulty has meant that the people here have kept the old traditions longer than most."

Now that was interesting. I filed that information away as Shemia helped me dress for dinner, and within half an hour, I was ready, my only rebellion leaving my hair down.

Finvarra and Tae were waiting in the sitting room, and Tae grinned at me. "Tired of the formality yet?"

"You have no idea."

Finvarra merely nodded and turned away, clearly deep in thought. The door opened, and I automatically sneered as Lutrin appeared.

Great.

The last thing I wanted to have to do was ask that motherfucker to pass the peas.

He narrowed his eyes at me and turned to address Finvarra. "Dinner is being served, Your Majesty. Marnin has gathered his highest-ranking court members."

"*Court* members?" Finvarra kept his voice silky, but Lutrin gave him an apologetic nod. "It appears your suspicions were correct. His greater plan appears to be underway."

Finvarra's expression had turned inscrutable. I wished I knew what he was thinking.

"Let's go," he said.

We all trailed after him. Lutrin seemed to know I was in far too dangerous of a mood for him to breathe down my neck, because he followed Tae, who gave me more than enough space.

The formal dining room lay at the back of the palace, as far from the entrance as you could get and still be within the main building. Like the entrance, there were no walls, allowing the jasmine-scented breeze to ruffle my hair.

Whoever had decorated the room and table needed to be fired. Everything was…gold. Gold leaf covered the entire ceiling above us, the columns on each side of the table, and the table itself. Even the flowers arranged on the table had been gilded, each petal covered in gold, smothering their natural beauty.

It was the most ostentatious and obnoxious display of wealth I'd ever seen. Tae's gaze met mine, and from the amusement flickering in his eyes, he was thinking the same. As usual, it was almost impossible to tell what was happening in Finvarra's mind.

The unseelie king sat at the head of the table, Tae on his right. I hesitated, glancing farther toward the center of the table, but Finvarra caught my arm in his hand. Our eyes met, and he jerked his head, gesturing toward the chair to his left.

Lutrin stiffened but took a chair farther down. Thankfully, it was several seats away from mine.

I didn't sigh, but it was close. The other nobles were paying close attention, and as soon as Finvarra sat, they took their own seats. Marnin sat at the other end of the table, his eyes flat and dead. He reminded me of a snake.

I would need lots and lots of wine for this dinner party.

Yet again, Marnin was relying on servants to serve each course. They appeared silently, lifting and replacing plates as Marnin's little court chatted among themselves. I poured myself another glass of wine, ignoring Finvarra's warning look.

"How long do you think you'll grace us with your presence, Your Majesty?" one of Marnin's cronies asked.

"As long as it takes to ensure everything is running smoothly in my lands."

"Do you doubt such a thing?" Marnin asked. The entire table tensed, and Finvarra leaned back in his chair, a wicked gleam entering his eyes. He opened his mouth, but all light in his eyes died as another servant appeared to take his empty plate, replacing it with dessert.

Finvarra caught the servant's arm. "Who hit you?"

She turned stark white. I opened my mouth, but she was already replying.

"No one."

Even a human without any extra senses would have heard that lie.

"Ah," Finvarra said. "So they're sitting at this table."

The woman began to shudder, and I kicked Finvarra beneath the table. He ignored me.

"What is your name?"

"Eratha, Your Majesty."

"You won't get into any trouble, Eratha." Finvarra's voice was achingly gentle.

She still shook her head. "Please."

"Was it Marnin?"

Marnin let out a choked noise. Finvarra just raised a hand, and no one dared make another sound.

More headshaking.

Finvarra continued to name names until Eratha's breath caught. "Versen," he repeated, and she shuddered.

"Ah," Finvarra said again, turning his attention to one of Marnin's loyal friends. "Tae, arrange for Eratha to pack her things. She'll be leaving this place."

Eratha burst into tears, and Finvarra glanced at her with a frown. I rolled my eyes. "She thinks you're firing her," I ground out.

His expression cleared. "No." He took Eratha's hand. "I would like to offer you a position in my household."

Her eyes widened. "But…my family."

"Your family is most welcome to join you. If they would rather not, I will have them moved to a comfortable home elsewhere. If you would prefer to stay here" —his voice was ice— "I will ensure you are never harmed again."

Eratha's mouth trembled, but the edges of a smile had appeared. "We've always dreamed of working for you, Your Majesty. But are you sure? I'm clumsy."

The temperature dropped several degrees. "Tae?" Finvarra said mildly.

Tae was already escorting Eratha from the room. Down at the other end of the table, Marnin was attempting to keep his expression blank, although he was practically vibrating with rage. I almost snorted. His blank-face needed some work. Next to him, his little friend Versen had gone still in the way of prey.

"I allow you to play your court games in my palace," Finvarra purred. "As long as you do not break my laws."

"No law was broken, Your Majesty." Marnin squared his shoulders.

I wished I could get to my feet and chant "Fight, fight, fight," but something told me that would be inappropriate.

"We do not harm innocents in this realm." Finvarra's voice got quieter, but the entire table flinched as one.

Versen swallowed. "With all due respect, Your Majesty—"

"Silence."

"She was a servant," Versen blurted. "Just a stupid, clumsy servant."

Finvarra slowly got to his feet. I longed for popcorn. This was going to be good.

"Where in my laws did I specify a woman may be harmed if her status is considered lower than the one harming her?"

Versen had turned a sickly gray color. Even Lutrin was

sitting silently, his eyes wide. Good.

Finvarra was a mean son of a bitch, but at least in this, we were on the same page. If *he* didn't handle Versen, I'd be waiting when the asshole least expected me.

"And you." Finvarra's gaze flicked to Marnin. "Your choice to defend someone breaking the laws of this land, instead of enforcing those laws, has been noted."

A dull flush traveled up Marnin's cheeks. Unlike his friend, however, he wasn't dumb enough to speak.

Guards had appeared, and they escorted Versen from the room. He didn't bother looking back at the table for support. None would be given to him since Marnin's *court* were all too busy studying their plates as if they held the answers to the universe.

Finvarra held out his hand. It took me a moment to realize he was waiting for me. Since he was clearly a man on the edge, I slipped my own hand into his and allowed him to pull me to my feet.

"We will speak of this tomorrow," Finvarra said. His voice was neutral now, without even the hint of a threat, yet several of Marnin's buddies looked like they were just about ready to piss their pants. My wolf paced inside me. Their fear was delicious. And she'd quite like to play with these men, to hunt them through the forest.

Finvarra leaned close as he escorted me from the room. Close enough that I had no doubt several of those men noticed as he murmured in my ear.

"Your wolf would find them bitter, rubbery, and filled with gristle," he said.

I couldn't help it. I grinned. Finvarra's eyes met mine,

and we stared at each other for a long moment.

I cleared my throat. He looked away, ignoring me as I tugged at his hand. Clearly, he wanted us to appear as if we were on the same team. "Besides," Finvarra said idly, and it took me a second to realize he was continuing his previous thought. "Those men have enough power to take down even the mouthiest, too-curious, sticky-fingered werewolf."

I glowered at him. Thankfully, we'd arrived at our chambers, and Tae turned from where he'd been staring out the window as I opened the door.

"They're going to retaliate," I stated the obvious.

Tae nodded at me from across the room. His brow was furrowed, and his hair looked as if he'd shoved his fingers through it over and over again.

"Oh yeah," Tae said as Finvarra sat on the sofa, his expression distant. "They're probably planning a meeting in their *hidden* temple tonight."

Finvarra shot him a warning look, but now I was intrigued.

"Hidden temple?"

I could see Finvarra deliberating about whether he'd tell me. He tapped his long, elegant fingers on the arm of the sofa, and my gaze dropped to his hand. It was a beautiful hand. Large and masculine, and—

Finvarra sighed, and I pulled my mind back from whatever strange path it had taken. "Marnin and his closest allies meet in the ruins of a temple deep in the forest," he said. "It's little more than a clearing with old rocks scattered around—rocks that are hidden with a ward created centuries ago. But it's still a place of power."

"Legend has it, Fin's ancestors used to meet there ten thousand years ago to discuss their war plans," Tae said.

I raised an eyebrow. "And now Marnin considers the place his?"

"His father raised him to believe he was blessed by a god called Tronin. And that he should have been the true king."

"So, they spend their time plotting in this secret temple thing because they consider themselves blessed by some ancient fae god who wants Finvarra's ass off the throne and Marnin's on it."

"That about sums it up." Tae's mouth twitched.

I filed that information away for later.

"Eratha told me some information you need to know." Tae addressed Finvarra. Clearly, I wasn't to be involved in that conversation. I was just fine with that.

A knock sounded, and my lip automatically curled. Lutrin. "Goodnight." I strolled toward my bedroom door.

I felt Finvarra's gaze on me. "Be careful."

"I don't know what you're talking about."

Two male snorts told me I wasn't fooling anyone. They knew I was going for a run. I scowled and stepped into my room, closing the door carefully.

Then I stripped off my dress and shifted.

I stretched, shaking off the last of my shift, and padded over to the window I'd left open. I could scent the guards, but they'd been warned a werewolf would likely be on the loose. Still, I heard several indrawn breaths as I jumped down three stories and launched myself into the night.

seven
Finvarra

I knew when Kyla returned. She'd run for hours—long enough that I'd begun to pace, unwilling to go looking for her and make it appear that the little wolf meant anything to me, and yet worried that she may have gotten up to no good.

If there was trouble to be found, I had no doubt she would find it.

Finally, I sensed her approaching. My power allowed me a small amount of what I called *recognition* if I focused. My senses couldn't tell *who* it was, but there was only one werewolf in this region.

For some inexplicable reason, I was waiting for her in her room as her paws hit the balcony rail, followed by her nose.

Her wolf was beautiful—a sleek, deadly predator. "How the hell did you get back up here? We're three stories high."

Kyla just let her mouth fall open. It could have been her version of a mysterious grin. It could also have been a way for her to threaten me once more with those long white teeth.

She watched me, clearly waiting for me to speak. I just raised my eyebrow.

She lowered her head slightly, her gaze on my face.

Given the size of her, it should have been threatening. But something about it struck me as…cute.

"Shift, puppy. Then we'll talk."

This time, there was no doubt that the show of teeth was a threat. But she turned, tail held high, and strolled slowly toward her bed and the robe lying over the end of it.

I turned and faced the wall, attempting not to think of the naked woman behind me.

Clearly, I was well overdue for female company if I was fantasizing about an irreverent, control-challenged werewolf.

I turned. Her eyes still glowed, the predator not entirely hidden away. But she wrestled with the wolf and won, tying the robe around her waist.

"What are you doing here?" she asked. "Shouldn't you be peeling the skin off Versen's bones?"

"Is that what you think I do to my enemies?"

She gave a bad-tempered shrug.

I just raised an eyebrow. "Why haven't I done that to you, then?"

"Probably only a matter of time."

God, this woman. "Shouldn't *you* be in a better mood after your run?"

Silence.

I studied her. "What is it?"

"I miss my pack, okay?"

And I refused to allow her to leave until she told me who she was working for and why they wanted my sword.

Kyla sighed. "Since you're in my room in the middle of the night, why don't you tell me why killing the seelie king is worth all this?" She crossed to one of the stuffed chairs by the balcony and sat on it as if it were a throne of her own, her head angled, eyes icy. The wolf on the hunt.

Clearly, she'd deduced the reason for Marnin's behavior. I hadn't been here. I hadn't checked in as often as I should, and while other regions in my lands could function easily—and well—without my oversight, this was not one of them.

I'd been so busy planning my revenge, I'd been neglectful of my duties. My father would be rolling in his grave if his body hadn't been burned.

"It's none of your business."

She smirked. "Cute. Since your thirst for murder is the reason you won't give up that sword, how about you tell me the truth?"

Where exactly did she find the audacity? "Regardless of what I want to do with the sword, the fact remains that it is *mine*."

She rolled her eyes.

"My parents were a love match." The words were out before I realized I'd said them. Kyla's eyes narrowed, and I turned, pacing to the balcony.

"What happened?" she asked.

"Taraghlan's father was involved with my mother before she met my father. They'd had a brief affair, but when she realized he was the seelie king, she'd ended it. He hadn't taken it well, and when he learned that she was to marry my father—the unseelie king—he threatened to have my father killed."

"He sounds like a little bitch," Kyla muttered.

"Indeed. Before that point, the two kings had cooperated,

for the most part. While we weren't exactly allies with the seelie, there was an uneasy neutrality between us. With that threat, it became war. My mother thought twice about marrying my father, but by then, it wasn't just about love."

"Marrying her had become a way for your father to piss off his enemy."

"Yes. They married, and the next century passed relatively easily. Neither king truly wanted war, and even the seelie king didn't want to throw his people away. My mother fell pregnant with me, and something snapped in the seelie king. Days after I was born, he had my mother kidnapped."

"That fucker."

Despite the topic, my lips twitched at Kyla's tone. I stared down at the gardens below us. As soon as my father had died, I'd ordered that no one change the flowers my mother had loved so much.

I sighed. "And so began a true war. My father would have done anything he could to get my mother back. She missed the entire first year of my life. And in that time… inexplicably, she grew to have feelings for her enemy."

"Stockholm syndrome."

I nodded. "I have heard of this. When my father found out, he vowed to cut out the seelie king's heart and hand it to her."

I glanced over my shoulder, and Kyla winced. "Anyone ever tell you just how unhinged that is?"

"It seemed perfectly reasonable to him. And six months later, he did it. My mother had convinced the seelie king to let her go. Apparently, she was wasting away because she missed me so badly. During the swap, my father killed the seelie king in front of his son. Taraghlan."

Understanding flickered in Kyla's eyes. "And so, your father killed one enemy and gained another."

"Yes. My father didn't see it that way. What could his enemy's whelp do to him? He was too busy punishing my mother. Their love was no more, and instead, he smothered her fire until she was little more than a ghost. He was both verbally and physically abusive, and his court did *nothing*."

"Not even his friends? What about her family?"

Turning to lean against the balcony, I shook my head. "Despite everything, some small part of my father must have held on to a ghost of that love for my mother. Or perhaps it was that she had become his possession. And men such as my father do not share their possessions with others. Either way, Taraghlan knew just where to strike. When he was old enough, he didn't bother trying to take my father's life. He sacrificed several of his most loyal warriors to create a poison that would kill her." My gut churned, vicious memories assaulting me until all I wanted was to drown them out.

Kyla's eyes glimmered wetly. "I'm so sorry."

"I don't know why I'm telling you this."

She shrugged. "Sometimes talking about things aloud helps you process them."

I frowned, my mind returning to Marnin. "If Marnin simply wanted to secede, and I could trust that his people would be safe and happy, I would consider his wishes."

Kyla gaped at me. "You would?"

"I'd take my mother's palace back." I smirked, and she

grinned. "But yes."

"I'm assuming that's not the case."

"No. While I haven't been here, I have plenty of spies in place, along with regular citizens loyal to me, who have kept me informed. Marnin has prevented any progress in Greleris. He disbanded the councils in each city—which voted on laws for their people—and insisted all laws be created by those he put in place of the council. You've seen how he allows servants to be treated. Those who serve are to be paid a good wage and treated with respect, and he has unwound any such protections for the least powerful among us. And he will not stop. Already, he has been encroaching on territory to the south, attempting to take land that is not part of Greleris. He's creating new weapons he believes I don't know about and attempting to sway other territories to his side."

"Did he succeed? With the other territories?"

"No. But what he has done here is bad enough." A low, simmering fury swept through me at the thought of the harm he'd done to the people of my kingdom.

She stretched out her legs. "So, what are you going to do about it?"

A simple question. I was beginning to learn that Kyla was a practical woman. "This was my fault. By ignoring these lands, I have allowed the evil here to fester."

"So now you have to clean that festering wound."

Despite my mood, I wanted to smile. "Yes. That's exactly what I need to do."

#

Kyla

We ate breakfast in Finvarra's chambers the next morning, which I appreciated. I was in no mood to deal with the staring as the unseelie watched just how much food I put away.

I was more appreciative of the fact that Lutrin wasn't invited to breakfast. I was still trying to figure out just how close he was to Finvarra. I knew he was his closest adviser, but I'd seen Finvarra relaxing around Tae enough that it was obvious Lutrin wasn't a friend. Finvarra still treated him with cool formality, while Lutrin kissed his ass at every opportunity.

Both Finvarra and I were quiet, while Tae kept up a steady chatter. At one point, Finvarra glanced at me, and I almost grinned at the painstakingly patient look on his face as Tae went on and on about some court gossip he'd heard.

Instead, I dropped my gaze to my plate. It felt like something had changed after last night. And it was… disconcerting to see Finvarra as more than just a royal pain in my ass. The way he'd spoken of his mother, the pain in his eyes when he'd talked about the abuse she'd suffered…

It made me see him as more than just the unseelie king.

It made me see him as a man.

And that was more than a little inconvenient.

The *king* I could deal with. I had all kinds of strategies up my sleeve to get me through the next few days. But then he'd had to go and ruin it by showing that hint of vulnerability. By letting me know that it wasn't just an ego trip that made him unable to let go of the sword.

Some part of me had expected him to defend his actions—to pretend that things weren't that bad here, and the summer palace his mother had so loved wasn't under immense threat from the way Marnin had taken advantage of Finvarra's physical and mental absence.

Instead, he'd acknowledged that he was at fault, and he'd vowed to fix it. That acknowledgment was small in the grand scheme of things. But...it was huge to me.

I hated that he'd brought me here. That I'd had to see beyond the arrogant, detached mask he wore so well. Instead, I'd seen a man who'd made laws to protect the innocent. And who took those laws seriously, ensuring even servants were safe from harm.

I'd seen a man who was constantly working, his brow furrowed as he read over paperwork or held meetings with the advisers he so despised.

I'd seen a man who loved his cousin. Who was torn between giving Tae the future he wanted—a future that didn't include a crown—and his duty to his people.

Something told me Finvarra would do everything he could to prevent Tae from having to sit on that throne. I wouldn't be surprised if he chose a queen in the next decade or so. After the way he'd spoken of his uncle's death and the dwindling line of succession, it was clear he knew something had to be done. So he would do his duty.

Would he...love her? Or would it be just another royal alliance?

Wow, that was so beyond my business, it wasn't even

funny.

"Kyla?"

I glanced up. Tae and Finvarra were both staring at me. Clearly, they'd both been attempting to get my attention for some time.

"What's up?"

"We need to leave soon for the meetings," Finvarra said. "You should eat more."

My instinct was to chafe at the order. Instead, I shut my mouth and nodded. His eyes narrowed.

"What's wrong?" he demanded.

"Nothing. Look, do I really have to go to these meetings? I'm not a member of your court. People will wonder why I'm there. I'll just be a distraction."

Finvarra gave me that humorless smile. "Nice try. If I have to be mindless with boredom, so do you."

"This is cruel and unusual punishment."

He just raised an eyebrow. "Perhaps it will teach you not to steal from those who are bigger and stronger than you. We leave in half an hour."

He got to his feet, ignoring my low curse. Next to me, Tae gave me a sympathetic smile. "I don't want to go either. But there's one good thing about not being important at these meetings."

"There is?"

"We can pass notes back and forth."

"Can we mock His Majesty in those notes?"

Tae's smile widened. "Oh yeah. Mocking His Majesty is mandatory."

"I can hear you," Finvarra called from the other room.

I just smirked and shoved another piece of bacon into my mouth.

Kyla

I'd expected the meetings to be boring. What I hadn't expected was for the unseelie men—and in Marnin's little court, it was exclusively men sitting around the huge mahogany table—to get so many things so ridiculously wrong.

Someone had placed an onyx stone in the center of the table.

"What does that do?" I whispered to Tae.

"Records the conversation. Records the entire room, really. A human I once knew compared the recording it plays to a hologram."

Ooh.

Tech didn't work in this realm, so the unseelie had evolved their magic to provide them with what they needed.

All I knew was I would love to get my hands on that stone, just so I could play this meeting for Danica, Evie, and Mere over margaritas—virgin for Meredith, who was currently hella knocked up. Because these guys had *no* idea what they were talking about.

So far, several people in Marnin's "court" had casually mentioned that werewolves could only shift beneath the light of the full moon, that black witches could transform into bats, and that the mages were more powerful than demons.

Where are they getting this shit? I scribbled, passing my note to Tae.

Tae glanced at one of Marnin's men who was in love with the sound of his own voice, droning on and on. Then he glanced at the notepaper, and his thoughts appeared on it, without a pen.

Now that was handy.

I'll have to show you a map to give you an idea of where we are. But though there are many internal portals in this region, finding a portal to one of the other realms requires several days of travel for most unseelie. That means that while the summer palace is one of the most well defended in the realm, those who choose not to travel often rely on secondhand information about the other realms—and the other factions in those realms.

That was similar to what Shemia had said.

Since I needed to write my thoughts down, I glanced around, but no one was paying any attention to us. I'd seen a few frowns when I'd strolled in, dressed in another formal gown. I'd expected Finvarra to make sure I was seated against a wall somewhere, but instead, he'd put me between Tae and himself.

Likely, it was another way to poke at Marnin, who'd turned purple at the insult. Lutrin hadn't exactly been impressed either. He'd kept his expression pleasantly blank, but I could scent his rage.

I scrawled another note to Tae.

Why doesn't Finvarra correct them?

Tae glanced down at the paper I slid him and smiled, writing this reply.

Why would he? If Marnin ever gets any stupid thoughts about challenging Finvarra, he won't, as the humans like to say, know his ass from his elbow. If he attempted to build alliances with other factions, they would laugh in his face—not just because many of them have already allied with Finvarra, but because Marnin remains so ignorant, they would find him offensive.

I thought about that.

So, even though Finvarra hasn't been paying enough attention to this part of his realm, he's still been able to rely on that lack of knowledge?

Tae nodded at me as the courtier droned on.

Marnin wouldn't be the first to rise up. To become unsatisfied with the territory he has and imagine himself as king. And he won't be the last. Finvarra will do exactly what he has done for centuries.

I shifted my gaze to Finvarra. Anyone who didn't know him would think he was watching with rapt attention. But I knew the expression in those gold eyes well enough now, after seeing it turned on me so many times. Finvarra was imagining strangling the man.

I suppressed a smile and replied to Tae.

And what is that?

Tae's expression turned cold as he glanced at my note, waving his hand so his words would simply appear on the paper.

Finvarra will ruthlessly suppress any challengers and make them beg for mercy before he is done with them.

I shivered.

"If you two are quite finished," that low, amused voice

said in my head. *"You're distracting me from this fascinating account of a skirmish within my borders."*

I ground my teeth. He knew I hated when he did that. Finvarra didn't even take his eyes off the man who was somehow still talking, but I could sense his satisfaction all the same.

We broke for lunch. And I ended up glowering at Finvarra over my food.

"It's the full moon. You don't know what it's like to sit there for hours," I snarled.

"You humans have a charming expression. Something about doing the crime and doing the time."

"I'm. Not. Human."

He sighed. "There is that."

Tae plucked an apple from the bowl in front of us. "Come on, Fin. Give her a break. I'm falling asleep, and I've dealt with hundreds of these."

Finvarra shook his head at Tae. "You've allowed the little wolf to charm you."

"Have a heart," I demanded.

Finvarra rolled his eyes. "Fine. Go run. Enjoy the full moon. But you'll be making this up to me tomorrow."

I sensed more mind-numbing meetings in my future. But at least they wouldn't be when my wolf was practically trembling with the need to run.

"Thank you," I said.

Surprise flashed through his eyes as they met mine. "You're welcome," he said quietly.

The moment stretched until Tae cleared this throat.

"I don't suppose…"

"No." Finvarra smirked. "You're not getting out of it."

Tae sighed, and I gave him a sympathetic pat on the shoulder, ignoring the way Finvarra tensed.

I was itching to run. "I'll see you guys tomorrow."

"You haven't eaten enough," Finvarra pointed out.

"Are you keeping track of how much I eat? That's weird."

"I know two servings aren't enough to keep you going."

"Ah, but I plan to hunt in my wolf form." I winked at him.

He just sighed and waved at me to go.

I scampered out of the room before he could change his mind. Within moments, I'd taken my dress off and dropped it on the end of my bed. Shifting, I trotted to the balcony and jumped down the three floors—to the amusement of the guard I could hear chuckling somewhere to my left.

I ran for hours, caught a few rabbits, and settled down for a nap in the late afternoon sun. By the time the sun set, I was already making my way back through the forest, my wolf coming alive beneath the full moon.

I stopped next to a lake, lapped at the chilly water, and howled at the moon.

It wasn't the same, running alone. I should be surrounded by my pack. We'd be nipping at each other's heels, play fighting, racing through the forest. Nathaniel would keep everyone in line with a single glance, and when we were finished, we'd shift, and someone would build a fire.

Often, we'd sit around and tell stories for the rest of the night—each more ludicrous and outlandish than the next.

I turned and ran until my muscles ached. Until my

wolf had taken over enough that I no longer thought about where I'd gone wrong in my life, or how I could fix all the mistakes I'd made. Until I was shaking with fatigue and I had no choice but to make my way slowly back toward the summer palace, unless I wanted Finvarra to come looking for me.

A werewolf's build was more like a bear than a standard wolf. The way my muscles were dispersed allowed me to haul myself up onto my balcony and into my room easily, where I shifted without a thought.

My wolf howled at me, and I froze.

I'd been so distracted, I hadn't noticed the foreign scents. I turned to jump back off the balcony, and something hit me in the face.

Fuck.

Pain exploded through my nose and across my cheeks. They'd broken my nose.

"Our friend has a unique power," someone murmured. "Super strength. Enough strength to hurt a werewolf."

I raised my head. Four unseelie men. They'd encircled me, pushing me back from the balcony. With a thought, I attempted to catalogue my weapons.

The dress over my bed. My purse. The lamps on the nightstands.

Useless, every one of them.

The leader stepped forward, and I recognized his scent. He'd been at dinner the other night. Clearly, he'd taken offense to Finvarra's punishment of Versen.

This was a message to the unseelie king. Retaliation. Maybe these men would make it look like I'd tried to run, and they'd set up my murder to look like one of the guards had just gotten too enthusiastic.

Us non-magic users. So fragile and all.

Or perhaps they'd just kill me and flee, leaving Finvarra to interrogate anyone who might know something. I'd still be just as dead.

I had one moment to consider my options. They were blocking both the door to the hall and the one to the balcony. But I was fast. I'd shift and dart past them.

And then they would chase me. Likely, at least one of them had the power to take me down.

My hand fumbled, and I reached for my purse, pulling out the stone Finvarra had given me.

"What have you got there?"

I attempted to throw the stone in the air, but one of them used his magic to pluck it from me.

"Well, this is pretty," one of the men murmured. "Almost as pretty as you, *little wolf*."

So they'd heard that nickname. And instead of coming to the obvious conclusion that Finvarra used it to annoy me, they'd clearly decided it was some kind of pet name or something.

One more thing to thank His Majesty for.

The unseelie tucked the stone into his pocket. And his friend punched me in the gut.

I folded, gasping like a fish on land.

Obviously, *he* was the one with the extra strength.

The leader leaned close to taunt me again. Close enough.

Baring my teeth, I swung my hand, claws slashing toward his face. Two of them caught him in the cheek, tearing through his skin and muscle, revealing bone.

He screamed. Clearly, Finvarra and Tae were elsewhere, or that scream would have—

The air shimmered around us. A silence ward. I was in deep shit. These assholes would kill me. I knew that much for sure. But I'd make them hurt first.

I shifted back to my wolf form. One of them cursed. The other one swung for me again. But I was faster now.

Almost fast enough.

One of the fae used his power to weaken my legs, and I tripped on nothing, sliding until my face met the wall.

Fucking *ow*.

A bag was shoved over my head. It was filled with some kind of powder that made my head spin. I clamped my mouth shut, attempting not to breathe it in, but it was too late.

"Fuck, she's heavy. Make her turn back into a woman."

"Shut up and lift your side."

It took two of them to carry me, and I was paralyzed but aware as they slammed my body into various walls, stumbled, and finally dropped me into another room.

This next part was going to suck. But I had to look on the bright side. I was relatively sure they wouldn't attempt to rape me in this form.

"Make her fucking shift," one of them was whining. If I'd been human, I would've grinned.

The bag was removed, but I was still useless, completely unable to move.

eight
Kyla

Nathaniel would go to war when he learned I was dead. Finvarra would have no choice but to meet the threat. Members of my pack would die.

I couldn't let that happen.

As much as the thought of being rescued by Finvarra left a bitter taste in my mouth, he was my only hope.

The leader held the stone up to my face. "What does this do?"

I snarled weakly.

The unseelie with the extra strength swung his leg back. His foot met my ribs, and something broke inside me. Agony exploded through every inch of my body, and the world turned white.

I wasn't sure how much time passed while I was lost in the pain, but when my vision cleared, all I could do was whine.

The leader just smiled. "Shift, bitch, and maybe we won't hurt you too bad before you die."

"She might not be able to shift," one of them muttered. "She's all limp and shit."

One of them cursed. "I don't like torturing animals."

"So just watch, then. Keep an eye on the door."

Staying as still as possible, I listened to them murmur about where they'd leave my body. They might have thought they knew werewolves, but I was currently burning through whatever paralytic was in that drug. I could move already, but not well enough to risk getting to my feet.

I had to wait it out.

The leader held up Finvarra's stone once more. "What do you think this does?"

His buddy shrugged. "It's ours now."

Oh, you idiots.

"We can keep this up all night," he said. "A dead wolf just isn't the same visual as a dead woman. We have instructions, bitch, and the sooner you shift, the sooner this is over."

And then the leader did the one thing I needed him to do. The one thing I couldn't do in my wolf form.

He grinned and chucked the stone a foot into the air, reaching out his other hand to grab it.

I was up and moving before he caught it.

The pain was all-encompassing. If I'd been in my human form, I would have screamed. But I didn't aim for the leader. Or the one who'd hit me.

I went for the man who'd used his power to trip me the first time. The one who'd prevented my escape. He was the first target.

He screamed as my claws found his gut. The next several moments were lost to blood lust. More screaming.

And then the room was filled with a dark, cold presence.

"What exactly is happening here?" an endlessly amused voice crooned. A man with far too much power appeared, gold eyes meeting mine. I snarled, and he went still.

Something that looked like fear flickered in his eyes. But…it didn't seem as if he was afraid *of* me.

Behind him, one of the men choked, and I turned my attention to where they were bound to the stone wall with what looked almost like thick black ropes, their bodies writhing as they attempted to escape.

I limped toward the leader and let loose a low, threatening growl. His gaze darted between me and the man at my back.

That man was talking once more. I ignored it, crouching, muscles trembling as I readied myself to lunge.

And my body was plucked out of the air.

"I don't think so," the man with the dark power said as I hovered next to him. He placed me back on the floor, and I snarled.

I'd miscalculated. He *was* a threat.

I waited until he'd turned away and leaped at him, aiming for his throat.

And he caught me with that power once more, his gaze furious. Planting me back down, he strolled toward me while the men on the wall howled for mercy.

He crouched, looking into my eyes, and went still in the way of a predator on the hunt.

He spoke a word. I showed him my teeth.

My head was still spinning, and he leaned closer, staring into my eyes.

This time, I understood him.

"Shift, Kyla."

Finvarra.

That was his name. But he wasn't my Alpha. I stared

back at him.

"Little wolf," he said warningly. "If you go feral here, it will be *war*. I won't allow a feral wolf to rampage through my lands. No matter who she is. Do you understand?"

There was a lie in there somewhere, but my wolf couldn't understand it. Finvarra just waited me out.

Finvarra.

And my name was Kyla.

Shift. Yes. Yes, I had another form. My mind was clearing as the remaining dust dispersed from my body.

Dust. Because those assholes had attempted to kill me.

Finvarra waited.

I concentrated. But I couldn't shift.

My whine escaped before I could suppress it.

Finvarra got to his feet, placing a hand briefly on my head. I snapped at his hand, and he ignored me, stalking toward the leader.

"What did you do to her?"

"I didn't source the powder," he said. "Ask Gariel."

Gariel trembled as Finvarra turned his attention on him. "What is it?"

"It's a paralytic. It was just supposed to keep her still. She burned it off much faster than I'd thought, but maybe it's stopping her from shifting."

Finvarra slid me a glance, but I couldn't tell what he was thinking. My wolf had thankfully returned to the background, allowing me back in control.

It was so, so incredibly dangerous for my wolf to take over like that. Especially after I'd been so close to staying wolf after my time in Lucifer's dungeon.

And these assholes had nearly cost me everything.

"So, you thought you would kidnap and kill my guest. May I ask why?" Finvarra's voice was almost…pleasant, but it was so cold in the room now, I was almost shivering, despite my thick coat.

"Revenge," the leader said.

"Ah. And you came up with this plan on your own, did you?"

Silence.

Finvarra smiled. "I assure you, I can hurt you much, much worse than whoever ordered you to play this little game with my wolf."

My lips pulled back from my teeth at the *my wolf* part, but I stayed silent. Finvarra had found a rhythm here, and from the way the third unseelie guy was trembling like he'd piss his pants any moment, Finvarra knew exactly what he was doing.

In the end, they told him everything. It wasn't Marnin who'd given them their instructions. But it was obvious he was behind it. He simply wasn't stupid enough to get his own hands dirty.

No, this had been orchestrated by a man named Bryric. A man who happened to be Versen's brother. He'd taken offense to the way Finvarra had punished Versen. And especially to the way he'd banished him from this realm. Unsurprisingly, Bryric hadn't appreciated having his own ties to power instantly severed.

I was dizzy and sore enough that I'd lain down while Finvarra interrogated the men. After a few minutes, he glanced at me and frowned.

Just moments later, someone knocked on the door.

"Enter," Finvarra said.

Several guards appeared. And I recognized those guards from Finvarra's castle. He was taking no chances. One of them glanced at me curiously, while the rest used Finvarra's dark magic as leashes, pulling the men off the walls and hauling them elsewhere.

When they were gone, Finvarra crouched in front of me.

"Can you walk?"

I slowly heaved myself to my feet. The room darkened slightly around the edges, and I couldn't help but let out a low whine at the pain.

"I will transport you."

I growled to let him know what I thought about that, and Finvarra let out a growl of his own. "You're a stubborn, obstinate woman."

That wasn't exactly news to me. I just turned, taking tiny steps, and waited until he opened the door.

The stairs were impossible. I attempted to take the first one and almost passed out. Finvarra cursed, waving a hand. Within a moment, I was on the landing above him, and he strode up after me.

"We don't have time for you to be a hero," he bit out.

Fine. I just followed him to his chambers, walking through the door as he opened it.

Tae gaped as we walked in. I was relatively sure my white fur was covered in blood, and I let my mouth fall open and even wagged my tail like a dog to show him I was okay.

His gaze jumped to Finvarra.

"What happened?"

Finvarra began to tell the story in his low voice, and I wandered over to the balcony, lying down and placing my head on my paws.

I was so tired.

Bone-tired in a way I'd never been tired before.

The men had stopped speaking behind me, and I had a feeling they were both watching me. I didn't even have it in me to snarl at them.

"What's wrong with her?" Tae asked softly.

"She can't shift back."

Tae's expression must have said everything he thought, because Finvarra let out a relatively impressive growl of his own.

"Apparently, the paralytic has interfered with her shift. Since her body burned through it fast enough for her to slaughter one of the men holding her against her will, I'm sure she'll be able to shift soon."

"And if she can't?"

Finvarra stayed silent.

Tae cursed. "You need to take her back to her Alpha."

"No."

"No? It's the full moon. You told me about how close she came to never being human again. Is that what you want for her?"

I almost growled at that, but I was more interested in listening to their little conversation.

"I was the one who managed to make her shift in the underking's dungeon."

"Because you had a bargain with her! What will you use this time?"

"Enough, Tae. She'll turn back. I'll keep a close eye on her. I know when her wolf is at the forefront."

"How? Her eyes are always the same color."

"I just know."

He *did* just know. And it pissed me off.

But I closed my eyes, letting the cool air play over my fur. After what I'd just experienced, I didn't want to sleep anywhere with four walls. This balcony was just fine.

They murmured some more, but I blocked them out, close to dozing.

Nathaniel would be pissed if he could see me now. If he knew how close my wolf had come to going feral once more. Of course, he would already be pissed after the way I'd shit all over his orders.

Loneliness clamped around my throat and squeezed.

Someone crouched in front of me. I opened my eyes.

Finvarra's expression was more serious than I'd ever seen it. "I need to check you for internal injuries."

I stared him down.

He just angled his head. "Let me put this another way. I'm *going* to check you for internal injuries."

I snapped at the air in front of his face, and he just sighed.

"Are you going to be difficult about this?"

I just held his gaze. I was hurt, tired, and I wanted to be left alone.

"Even werewolves can die from internal bleeding. One side of your rib cage looks like it has been caved in. I want you to see a healer."

The door opened, and I hauled myself to my feet,

lowering my head in a snarl.

The healer froze.

"Ignore her," Finvarra sighed. "She's hurt, which has made her even moodier than usual."

Tae choked on a laugh. "And you're tempting her to hurt *you*, you know that, right?"

Finvarra just looked at me. "Are you going to cooperate?"

I could scent the healer's fear. And it was making me hungry.

Finvarra sighed and turned to the healer. "She won't hurt you."

"I've never healed a werewolf before. To be honest, Your Majesty, I've never seen one. It will be difficult for me to examine her. Would you… Can you ask her to shift back?"

Finvarra tensed, and his expression turned cold. But it was Tae who let out a low curse. "She's not deaf, and she's not an animal. You can ask her yourself. In this case, she can't shift right now, thanks to the use of a paralytic."

The healer nodded. Since he didn't seem to be a threat and he hadn't done anything stupid to excite my wolf, like turn and run, I lay down once more.

Finvarra leaned in. "I can help you shift."

I glanced up at him. His face was very close.

"Your body has already burned through most of the paralytic. I can use my power to find the rest of it and burn it away."

I was a werewolf. I'd heal these injuries overnight. I closed my eyes, shutting him out, and he whipped out a hand, clamping it around my muzzle once more.

I yelped, pain exploding across my face. Finvarra immediately released me. I hadn't felt it last time, had been too filled with rage.

"Hit you there too, did they?" Finvarra's voice was low, and I realized he was barely containing his own fury.

"I'm sorry," he said to me. Across the room, I could feel the healer's surprise. Clearly, Finvarra wasn't known for his apologies. Tae had gone still in a way that told me it was likely he hadn't often heard those words come out of his cousin's mouth.

"I should have been here," Finvarra said. "And I should've known they would come for you. Please let me help you now. If not for yourself, and if not for me, for your pack. Because if you were to die from something stupid like untreated internal bleeding, you know what would happen."

War.

"I understand you're a werewolf," Finvarra gritted out when I didn't move. I had a feeling this was the most he'd negotiated with anyone in years. "And will likely heal these injuries yourself overnight. But it will be extended and painful. We don't know how long the paralytic will prevent you from shifting, and we both know you shouldn't be in your wolf form for too much longer after tonight's events."

That was a polite reference to the way I hadn't even recognized him.

Shame made me lower my head.

"We do this, and you'll be comfortable," he crooned. "You can go to sleep and relax. Otherwise, I'll simply hound you until you agree."

I heaved a sigh. Finvarra seemed to take that as agreement, because he moved closer to me. "I have a feeling the paralytic is masking the extent of some of your injuries. This may hurt."

I just looked at him, and the hint of a smile curved his lips. "Fine. I'll get on with it."

The unseelie king held his hands a couple of inches from my fur—one near my head, the other farther down close to my shattered ribs. He closed his eyes, and I studied his face.

Until the agony exploded through me. He'd been right. The paralytic was, indeed, masking the extent of my injuries.

My entire body seemed to catch on fire, and another useless, mortifying whine left my throat.

Finvarra frowned, his eyes still closed. "It will be over soon."

By the time he was done, I was back to lying on the floor, unable to move.

"Shift," he told me.

I was too weak. And so tired.

"Kyla," he said warningly. It was painstakingly clear that, unless I did exactly what he wanted, this man was going to nag me to death.

I took a deep breath and reached for my human form.

The shift took longer than it ever had, muscles and bones and organs rearranging, likely worsening that internal bleeding. By the time I was done, I was gasping, shuddering on the cool tile. Finvarra's expression was terrible, and he gestured imperiously for the healer.

To his credit, the healer got straight to work. Tae brought

me a blanket, which he laid over me as soon as the healer gave him the okay. Warmth was radiating from the healer's hands, and my eyes drifted closed.

"No," Finvarra said, and I opened my eyes to slits. His gaze was on my face. "You need to eat before you sleep."

I opened my mouth. Now that I was in my human form, I could tell him exactly what I thought of his orders. But Tae was already nodding. "I'll call for food now," he said. "You'll probably need a lot of it to finish healing, right?"

With a sigh, I just closed my eyes again as the healer completed his work. Finally, he stepped away. "You'll likely sleep for a couple of days. No physical activity," he told me. "Try to rest as much as you can."

"Did you hear that, little wolf? That means no more tearing out throats."

I glowered at him. "Why do you get to have all the fun?"

"Because I'm the king."

Tae snorted and strolled away as someone knocked on the door. Within moments, the healer was gone, and the scent of meat had seduced me enough that I allowed Finvarra to help me wrap the blanket around myself toga-style and carry me to the sofa.

"What are you going to do now?" I asked as I shoved another bite of steak into my mouth. Finvarra had decided to serve me an entire platter, preventing the need to go back for multiple helpings, and I'd worked my way through most of it. I could barely keep my eyes open, but they'd been right—I'd rest much better with something in my stomach.

"I'm going hunting," Finvarra said.

"Isn't that the kind of thing royalty usually outsources?"

Tae snorted, drawing my eyes to him. He was sitting on the other end of my sofa, picking at his own food. "Not Fin. He prefers to do his own dirty work."

My wolf approved of this, even as the thought of not being part of the takedown made my skin itch.

"I want to help."

Finvarra didn't dignify that with an answer. I narrowed my eyes at him, and he simply stared back, those gold eyes alight with a feral gleam.

Ah. The unseelie king was *pissed*. He'd hidden it relatively well since we'd left that room, but it was clear he was barely holding it together. I glanced at Tae, who raised an eyebrow at me.

It took you this long to figure it out?

I glowered at him. But it didn't feel as invasive when he spoke inside my head. Of course, not being able to speak back was a pisser. Maybe I'd cave and get one of them to teach me.

But it certainly wouldn't be tonight. Polishing off my food, I placed the platter on the table in front of the sofa, hitched my blanket tighter around me, and got to my feet.

"Uh-uh," I said when Finvarra stood. "I'm healed, I'm fed, but I'm not an invalid."

"Fine."

He sat again, and I glanced at Tae, who gave me a nod. He'd handle things from here.

But…

"Thank you for coming for me," I said.

Finvarra's eyes met mine. "Of course."

His voice was carefully neutral, and I nodded, turning

away and strolling toward my room. Of course he would come for me. I was his *guest*, and if I ended up dead, the political ramifications would mean one hell of a headache.

Still, it would have been nice to know that he gave a shit. Not just because of *what* I was. But because of *who* I was.

And clearly, that stupid paralytic dust had affected more than just my body. I loathed the unseelie king, and I always would.

I opened my door, wrinkling my nose at the lingering scents of those men. Finvarra's eyes met mine as I closed the door, and I nodded, turning away.

This was loneliness. That's all it was. I missed my pack. Missed my friends, the connections I'd made in Durham. And my stupid brain was attempting to replace them with Finvarra.

The tension left my body in a rush as I slid into bed.

As soon as I got home, I'd never think of His Majesty again.

#

Finvarra

"What are you going to do?" Tae asked softly.

We were standing on my balcony, and I created a simple silence ward with the wave of my hand.

My muscles were still tight, my gut churning. It was all I could do to contain my rage. It had taken every bit of my self-control to order my most trusted guards to get the information I needed from the unseelie who'd been stupid enough to attack Kyla. I wanted to do it myself.

I'd expected retaliation. Expected them to try to kill me, perhaps even Tae. I would turn them to ash, while Tae could more than handle himself. But instead, they'd targeted the little wolf. A woman possessing no magic to defend herself with.

If I went down to that dungeon...

Tae was still watching me.

"I'll allow this to play out," I said. "Marnin is expecting one of two responses. Either I begin ripping heads off bodies, or I ignore the situation completely. I'm going to do neither until I can prove he's behind this."

Tae nodded. "If you kill him without proof, any loyalty he's built here will ensure the people rebel."

Yes. And I didn't have the time or inclination for a rebellion. Not while my forces were preparing to wage war on Taraghlan.

"How are you going to prove it?"

I turned and leaned against the balcony rail, studying his face. "How would you prove it?"

He frowned, but his gaze turned distant as he thought over my options. As much as he loathed when I used real-world scenarios as teaching moments—preferring to pretend he wasn't my heir—Tae's problem-solving had always been exceptional.

"First, you need to know exactly who is loyal to him," he mused. "Then you need to figure out why."

Good. Tae likely wouldn't be pleased if I told him he was learning to think like me, but it was the truth all the same.

"Why do I need to know their reasonings?" I asked.

He sighed but indulged me anyway. "Because there's a big difference between someone being loyal to Marnin because of your…absence, and someone whose loyalty has been bought. There's also a difference between those who follow him because they're afraid of him and those who follow him because they truly believe he would make a good king."

I smiled. "Excellent."

I turned back, gazing down into the gardens below. My mother had loved those gardens. Had spent time planting flowers herself until my father had learned of it and forbade her from doing something so *beneath* her.

"So, how are you going to find out who is loyal?"

I kept my gaze on the gardens. I had vague memories of running through them with my mother. "I'm not. You are."

I could feel Tae glowering at me. I just shrugged. "I have meetings. And if I'm going to feign just enough indifference to unsettle him, while also keeping him off-balance with my displeasure that someone under my protection was harmed…"

It was a fine line to walk. But I could do it in my sleep.

"I'm not—"

"I wasn't asking. The guards are at your disposal."

"We need to talk about this."

"Another time."

"Fin." Tae's tone was pleading.

I turned, and he sucked in a breath. "Fuck."

I knew what he'd see. It had only happened a few times in my long life, but all of those occurrences had been triggered by a rage so deep, so unyielding, it was as if my body needed to display that rage to the world.

My eyes would be glowing, the gold having covered the whites. I could feel my teeth, incisors longer than usual, while my cheekbones would have jutted out farther. I'd shoved my power down deep, but it was leaking through, and Tae would be able to feel it, crackling along my skin.

We never spoke of it. Of the beast that lived beneath my skin. It was the same part of my father that had ruined my mother—his possession and jealousy turning on her instead of against his enemies.

That beast, the one I kept locked away, had ripped through each of the chains I used to ensure it stayed leashed. It had happened immediately, without a thought, the moment I'd stepped into Kyla's room, scented her blood— and several fae males—and known I had minutes to find her or I would be too late.

And then I'd felt it. The tug of that stone. And the relief had made my knees weak.

Tae seemed to be following my train of thought.

"How did you find her?"

"I gave her that stone during another investigation. When we needed to lure Fenrir. She used it to call me to her when Nathaniel finally gave up the book. And I wanted to kill her for the offense. For daring to call me as if I were hers to command."

Tae swallowed. "Why didn't you take it back?"

"It wasn't worth antagonizing the wolves, and I knew she wouldn't use it. She had no need to call me—it was just the possession of the stone she enjoyed. Another power game between us. In truth, I'd forgotten about it by the time she attempted to steal my sword. Besides, *I* created the stone. I can ignore its call, although it feels like an annoying tug on my senses."

"It wasn't Kyla who used the stone," Tae said.

"No. But she must have tried. If I had taken the stone back from her, she would be dead now."

"You would have found her."

"Perhaps. But she was already bleeding into her chest cavity when I got there. The paralytic weakened her enough that she likely wouldn't have lasted long enough for me to find her."

"Fin."

"They attempted to harm what is *mine*," I breathed, and Tae flinched. Beneath my clenched hand, the balcony rail froze.

"She's not yours."

"She is under my protection. And they came for her to taunt me." I smiled. "They have no idea what they have done."

Tae's eyes met mine, and to his credit, he didn't flinch. Far more experienced warriors than he had dropped to their knees when I'd reached this level of rage.

"This is why you want me to investigate."

"Yes. Because I refuse to rule as my father did. I won't tear my realm apart in the search for traitors. Won't reign solely through fear. When I know, without a doubt, exactly who was involved in this scheme, I will show no mercy. But if I rip into all of their minds, torture any whom I suspect were involved…I will be the tyrant Marnin is likely painting me to be. And that will cause further bloodshed."

And if I gave in to that *thing* inside me that howled for blood, screamed for retribution…there was a possibility I wouldn't come back.

"Okay," Tae sighed, shoving a hand into his hair. "I'll do it."

"Good." Turning away, I stalked back into the main room. Tae remained on the balcony, where he would likely brood away half the night. I kept my footsteps silent, used my power to ensure the door swept open without a creak as I moved into Kyla's room.

She slept naked, splayed on her stomach, and one long, sleek leg was thrown out from beneath the covers. I studied her, but other than her pallor, there was no sign of what had happened tonight.

Her eyes slitted open, and her wolf gazed back at me.

"Just checking on you," I told her.

She merely closed those eyes and snuggled deeper into her pillow. My lips curled. The woman would have thrown something at me for daring to sneak in while she was sleeping. The wolf merely ignored me.

Kyla was cagey, cunning, and likely planning some insane escape attempt. She'd also tried to steal my sword—and with it, any chance of revenge. Unfortunately, that didn't prevent my body from hardening at the sight of all that smooth brown skin on display.

I stalked silently from her room and back into my own. Somehow, the little wolf had gotten under my skin. I needed to remove this temporary…fascination with her.

I'd do whatever it took. Even if it meant finding a Kyla

look-alike to fuck.

I closed the door behind me with a curse. Unfortunately, the thought left a bad taste in my mouth.

Not for the first time, I wondered if I should simply forget that she'd attempted to steal from me and send her back to her pack. Her Alpha would punish her instead.

The thought made fury burn through my body.

No. She was mine. At least for now.

\#

Kyla

"Absolutely not," Finvarra declared, his nostrils flaring at my suggestion. "You heard the healer. You're to rest."

"I stay up here, and they think they've won."

"You were practically falling asleep during that meeting yesterday, and now you want to attend it to… What? Taunt them?"

I glanced at Tae, who was lying on the couch, throwing the stone I'd used to summon Finvarra into the air again and again. I almost grinned at the thought of him getting a magical nudge each time the stone left Tae's hands.

"Ah, yeah, that's exactly what I want to do."

Clearly, the action was driving Finvarra nuts, although he was ignoring it. For now.

"She's right, Fin," Tae said.

I loved it when Tae took my side. Unfortunately, Finvarra didn't seem as if he cared what his cousin thought.

I rolled my eyes. "We should show them their plan failed."

"And potentially risk them coming after you again?"

"I'm in more danger here alone. I was in my room when they took me."

Finvarra's eyes turned icy. "That has been rectified. I've adjusted the wards to ensure only those we give verbal permission to may enter."

Dammit, I was hoping that argument would be my way out of here.

"Just give her a few hours, Fin," Tae muttered, pinching the bridge of his nose. Clearly, our constant bickering was wearing on the man. "They'll see she's fine, and maybe it'll push them into making another move."

"That's what I'm afraid of."

I glowered at Finvarra. *That* was a lie. The man wasn't afraid of anything.

"Two hours," I said. That would give me enough time to show my new enemies exactly how well I'd shaken off their little scheme. And there was a chance I'd be able to scent some fear, maybe even some guilt.

Sure, Finvarra had plans to clean up his court. But if *I* happened to stumble across anyone involved in the attack…

My wolf stretched inside me. She was in complete agreement with my plan.

"One hour. And then you rest."

I rolled my eyes. "Fine."

Tae got to his feet, but not before I caught the flicker of surprise on his face. Clearly, he hadn't expected Fin to give in.

Truthfully, an hour would be more than enough time to rattle anyone in attendance who'd tried to kill me. Then I'd go back to sleep. My body was still healing, and I'd usually be asleep for another couple of days after a healer managed to repair that kind of damage.

But my wolf had woken me, and I'd realized I needed to be *doing* something. Something that would help me feel safe. Something that would ensure no one in this court ever made me weak again.

"We leave in ten minutes," Finvarra said, raking his gaze over my sweatpants and T-shirt.

"I'll get changed."

Shemia had been horrified to learn of my attack. I found her in my bedroom, laying a simple day dress on the bed.

"I thought you might prefer this one," she said. "It has some room around the ribs."

While I was healed, those ribs still twinged when I moved the wrong way.

"Thank you."

"You were very brave."

I glanced at her as I stripped, and she helped me into the dress, tying it loose enough that my ribs wouldn't complain.

"How did you hear about it?"

"His Majesty informed me of your injuries, so I could dress you appropriately."

I didn't know what to say to that. Shemia pulled out the chair of the vanity she'd summoned, and I sat, ridiculously grateful to no longer be on my feet.

"You were critically injured, and you still killed one of the men who'd hurt you," Shemia continued as I closed my eyes, her brushes tickling over my face. She was a Chatty Cathy today. "No one would dare attack you again."

My wolf preened, pleased that our enemies knew how dangerous she was.

"Hair?" Shemia asked.

I was guessing a ponytail was out of the question. I went for a loose braid, and Shemia nodded in approval, pulling a few strands out to fall around my face.

"Beautiful."

"Thank you."

I got to my feet. This was a stupid idea. But the thought of those bastards sitting around that table, smug in the knowledge that I was too injured to leave my room?

Intolerable.

Someone knocked on the door. "We're leaving," Tae called.

Shemia waved her hand, and the door opened. "She's ready."

He gave her his most charming smile. Shemia merely raised one eyebrow.

"Thanks again," I told her, following after Tae.

Both he and Finvarra were quiet as we made our way down to the meeting. Finvarra looked deep in thought, and I waited until we were mere feet from the door, darting around him so I could enter first.

I was hoping I'd catch a flash of emotion, the scent of guilt, anything to point to exactly who'd been involved. So I strolled into the room, sending the unseelie a vicious smile. "Good morning."

Several unseelie barely looked up from the conversations they were having. Unlikely to be guilty, but I allowed my wolf free rein as I continued walking.

Behind me, Finvarra stalked toward his seat, his expression cold. Everyone stood, waiting for him to be seated. Tae followed behind him, looking longingly at the carafe of coffee on the table.

Both of them had been alive for long enough that I could probably learn a thing or two from them when it came to resting "I'll kill you" face.

I kept my senses on high alert, my wolf ready to pounce at any hint of guilt. Unfortunately, thanks to the amount of threat Finvarra was radiating, all I could sense was fear.

Great.

Giving up, I took my seat at the table.

And so began another day of stifling any reaction to their idiotic, ridiculous, and all-around *wrong* intel about other paranormal groups.

By the time the first hour passed, my blinks were getting longer and longer.

"Samael is dealing with his own rebellion," one of the unseelie said finally, and that was enough to force me to pay attention. It was one of the few pieces of truth I'd heard. I studied the unseelie's face, memorizing it.

"Support for his reign is still not guaranteed," he said. "That makes it unlikely that the demons will make any difference if war is on the horizon."

I almost choked at that. If Samael seemed weakened in any way, it was because he'd chosen to—likely to encourage this kind of speculation. Yes, he was dealing with those who were still loyal to Lucifer, but Danica had told me at last count almost ninety percent of citizens were already Team Samael.

"You look amused." The unseelie addressed me. "Do you disagree with our spies?"

I *must* be tired, if my thoughts were showing on my face.

"What would I know? I'm just a wolf."

Finvarra glanced at me, and his eyes immediately narrowed. I sighed. I knew that expression.

"A short break," he said, getting to his feet. Everyone stood, and Finvarra jerked his head, gesturing for me to follow him.

Tae smirked at me, reaching for yet more coffee as he stayed at the table.

"What's your deal?" I muttered to Finvarra once I'd climbed the stairs.

"You need to rest."

Truthfully, I *wanted* to rest. It was his *tone* I had a problem with.

Pushing open the door to our rooms, I took a deep breath. "I understand you're pissy—"

"Pissy?" Finvarra mused, so softly I shivered. He closed the door and then turned to me, taking a single step closer. His hand darted out, catching my chin. I allowed it. "*Pissy* doesn't even begin to describe how I feel."

I gave him squinty eyes. "I understand. You're annoyed because you brought me with you, and within a couple of days, I was almost dead. And that would have resulted in a war."

His eyes glittered, and my breath caught in my throat as he stepped even closer, until his body was pressed against mine, the wall at my back.

UNENDING MAGIC

"When I realized you'd been taken…there are no words for the kind of rage I felt."

Right. Because if he went to war, he wanted it to be on his own terms. Seemed fair.

He slowly shook his head at my silence. "Not because of the political ramifications." He lowered his voice. "The thought of what your death would mean for my realm didn't cross my mind."

My mouth had gone dry. I licked my lips, and his gaze dropped. "What…"

"What was I thinking? I was thinking that I had failed you so inexcusably, I would never forgive myself. I was thinking I would rage through every inch of this realm until I found you, and if you weren't breathing, I would become a monster worse than anyone could ever imagine. I was thinking that you were clever and vicious, but you had no magic. And I had put you in that position, and the guilt would *ruin* me."

My eyes felt strangely hot, and it was as if there were a vise around my throat.

"Why?"

"Why?" The ghost of a smile curved his mouth. "Because you're stubborn, ornery, a thief, and a liar. You fill me with rage—often—and confusion—constantly. And yet I can't stop thinking about you. Every minute of every day. I'd planned to fuck a woman who looked like you—if I could even find one—just to try to get you out of my head."

He…he wanted me?

There had always been *something* between us, beneath the loathing. Both of us had refused to look at it, refused to crack open the door and look inside. And now Finvarra was throwing that door wide open.

Some of the warmth left his eyes at my silence, and he released my chin. I hadn't spoken, and he was assuming I didn't feel the same. Or that I did and would rather engage in our constant war than give in.

One of my hands lashed out, grabbing his shirt. Surprise flashed in his eyes, but I'd already flipped our positions, pressing him against the wall.

I glided a hand up to his neck, into his hair, and guided his mouth to mine.

His lips were a warm caress as he kissed me. Slow, gentle, achingly tender. His tongue slipped into my mouth, teasing, stroking, and I shivered, shifting closer.

In half a second, he'd reversed our positions, and I was pressed against the wall once more. I moaned at the feel of his lips, and he slid his hand into my hair, holding me steady for him as he plundered my mouth.

"I was wondering—whoa!"

Finvarra pulled away, and I peered around him to see Tae, his mouth open as he gaped at us.

"Now that's a sight I never would've expected to see. In fact, if someone had bet me that I'd walk in on you two in this kind of compromising position..." And on and on.

My face flamed, and I shoved down my instinct to bury my face in Finvarra's chest. Instead, I cleared my throat.

"I need some air."

nine
Kyla

If I'd thought things would be awkward between Finvarra and me, I was both right and wrong. Immediately after our kiss, he'd gone back to his chilly formality, and I'd gone back to fantasizing about stealing his sword.

And yet, I'd caught his gaze on me several times over the past two days. Unsurprisingly, his expression had been unreadable.

I knew he was planning something for Marnin. He hadn't told me what it was, of course. Because we didn't have that level of trust.

That was a pretty good reason for me *not* to be fantasizing about that kiss.

Tae found the entire situation far too amusing. But I'd barely seen him as he went about his business. From the way he'd been cozying up to one of Marnin's key players the few times I'd caught a glimpse of him, it was clear he was playing the irresponsible, unwilling heir, who only wanted to party and bed as many women as he could.

Tonight, Marnin had arranged for a ball to "honor the unseelie king." Thankfully, Finvarra had chilled with his determination to make my stay here as punishing as possible. He'd agreed that while I needed to show my face as his "guest," I didn't have to stay for long.

Now, I was standing in an ornate white gown, a glass of champagne in my hand, as Finvarra stood on a dais at the front of the room, dressed in unrelenting black—likely to match the glittering black crown on his head.

Finvarra's words had cycled through my head again and again today.

"I was thinking that I had failed you, so inexcusably I would never forgive myself. I was thinking I would rage through every inch of this realm until I found you, and if you weren't breathing, I would become a monster worse than anyone could ever imagine. I was thinking that you were clever and vicious, but you had no magic, and I had put you in that position and the guilt would ruin *me."*

And then that kiss. That fucking kiss that, despite all my best efforts, continued to haunt me. I found myself gazing into the distance at various times throughout the day, reliving that kiss.

I wanted him.

I didn't understand why. He likely couldn't understand why he wanted me either. Not for the first time, I cursed Selina.

I didn't *want* to see behind his cold mask. Didn't want to know that he protected people weaker than him. Didn't want to know how much he loved his cousin—and the guilt he tried to hide that Tae was his heir. Didn't want to know how fucking lonely the unseelie king was.

And yet, I did. And there was no way for me to unknow any of it.

"Thank you, Marnin," Finvarra said. "I can't tell you

how…enlightening it has been to visit this palace after all these years. Please—" he nodded at the musicians, who began playing a waltz "—enjoy the ball."

Tae appeared at my side, plucking the champagne from my hand and placing it on a nearby tray.

"Hey!"

"Save me."

I was in his arms and twirling onto the dance floor before I realized he'd moved.

"From what?"

He nodded over my shoulder and then shifted us smoothly into the next step so I could catch sight of the unseelie woman. Her expression was predatory as she stared at Tae, and my claws popped out.

"You need me to cut a bitch?"

He choked out a laugh. "Put those away before Fin loses his mind."

I complied, and he frowned down at the tiny holes I'd left in his blue jacket. "Women lose their minds over me," he told me seriously, although humor gleamed in his eyes. "It's a difficult life to live, but I do what I can for the good of the crown."

I rolled my eyes. "You're ridiculous."

"And you're a surprisingly good dancer. You'd be better if you didn't try to lead."

I showed him my teeth. "Did you expect any different?"

"Nope."

I couldn't help it. I smiled.

"Ah. There it is." He smiled back, but it was faint. Clearly, he had something on his mind.

"What's up?"

"You and Fin… I've kept my mouth shut about it up until now. I've been around a long time, and few things surprised me like seeing you guys attached at the mouth."

I refused to blush. But I practically squirmed as he raised one eyebrow.

"Don't get me wrong," he said. "The signs were all there. All that sexual tension hidden beneath rage and annoyance… It makes sense."

I sighed. "Say what you need to say, Tae."

His jaw firmed. "I think you should be careful."

My eyebrows shot up. "*I* should be careful?"

"I know you think Fin is this cold, arrogant, untouchable king—and he is all that—but he's been hurt and betrayed over and over again, throughout centuries. His last lover attempted to assassinate him. The lover before that was spying for his father. One of his childhood friends sold his secrets to the seelie, and the woman he once thought he would marry… Well, that's his story to tell. All I'm saying is, Fin's brain might know you're going to find that sword. But if his heart gets involved…"

I took a deep, shuddering breath. "I hear what you're saying."

"You're good for him, Kyla. Before we came here, I hadn't seen him smile properly for years. When you betray him… It will break him."

Cold dread settled along the back of my neck, and for a long moment, I couldn't speak. Tae sent me a sympathetic look. "You know, you can make this easier on yourself. Just tell *me* why you need the sword so badly. Fin doesn't need to know a thing."

I rolled my eyes at the shit-eating grin he sent me. "Believe it or not, I wasn't born yesterday."

And neither was Finvarra. No, he was born centuries ago, and in that time, he'd been betrayed again and again.

"Have a care with his heart, Kyla."

I attempted a smile. "I didn't think he had one."

Tae's own smile was sad. "That would be your first mistake."

The song ended, and Tae bowed theatrically, kissing my hand. "I've got things to do. I'll see you later."

I nodded absently, turning, my gaze automatically searching for Finvarra. The distance we'd put back between us over the past few days…

I didn't like it. I'd take his busybody ways over that formality any day. But Tae was right. That distance was a good thing. I couldn't blame Finvarra for protecting himself from me. He'd spent a long chunk of his life searching for that sword, and I'd attempted to break in to his home to steal it.

I was the bad guy here.

"You're stubborn, ornery, a thief, and a liar. You fill me with rage—often—and confusion—constantly. And yet I can't stop thinking about you. Every minute of every day."

I couldn't help it. Despite all the reasons why I should want nothing to do with him, I couldn't stop thinking about him either. It was damned inconvenient, but I'd never been the kind of person who buried her head in the sand.

Turning from the dance floor, I scanned the space. There were too many people in here for me to pick up his scent, but…

There.

He was speaking to a woman who was dressed in a gorgeous—if wildly impractical—gown, which shoved her boobs up to an impressive height. She had blond hair, blue eyes, and while her skin wasn't quite as dark as mine, it was the same tone.

"I'd planned to fuck a woman who looked like you—if I could even find one—just to try to get you out of my head."

Some strange new emotion shot through me. Something that made me want to rip into that woman. Taking a deep breath, I tamped it down.

Maybe…maybe it was for the best.

I was still in his realm for one reason and one reason only. If I didn't find that sword, we were all dead. And if I did…those portals were going to close. This was the one and only time I would ever visit the unseelie realm.

Finvarra's gaze met mine, and I immediately turned away.

Making my way around the crowd, I stepped through the open doors and onto the nearest balcony. It was cool out here. Quiet.

Relatively private.

I stripped off my dress and laid it over the balcony rail.

Gasps sounded behind me, and I ignored them. I was a werewolf. I didn't care about their false modesty. Within a second, I was launching myself off the balcony, changing in midair.

I hit the ground on four paws and disappeared into the forest.

I wished it had been the full moon. Then my wolf would have come out to play and I could have receded into the background. But while she was pissed, *I* was the one who had to deal with all these strange thoughts and feelings.

Seriously? This *is when you decide to be chill?*

I knew some werewolves said they had heard their wolf talk back to them. That had never happened to me. But I could usually get a good sense of her. She was all instinct, and if she'd buried herself, it was clear she couldn't see what to do.

Great.

I ran for a couple of hours. And then I caught the scent of a stag.

I wasn't huge for a werewolf, but I was downwind and in enough of a mood that I could take it down alone. I'd just imagine it was Finvarra as I tore into it.

"You'll end up impaled by those horns," Finvarra's voice said behind me.

The stag turned and bolted.

I watched the stag run, a low, threatening growl leaving my throat.

"I've been doing some research on werewolves," Finvarra said, his voice carefully neutral. I ignored him, padding toward the lake. Lowering my head, I lapped at the cool water.

"Wolves your size would usually team up to take down a stag that large."

I was fast and mean. Taking down that stag would usually be a piece of cake. Unfortunately, I was also distracted.

I ignored the unspoken question in Finvarra's words.

I wasn't going to stroke his ego by letting him know the sight of him with the woman who looked like me had made me furious enough to give in to my most reckless impulses. Or that I was *trying* to think before I acted for once. I was trying to protect His Royal Pain in My Ass.

"Shift, Kyla. We need to talk."

I slowly turned, displaying my teeth in a vicious snarl.

He just watched me, clearly unimpressed. "Or don't, and you can listen to me talk."

Fine. He wanted me to shift? I'd shift.

I reached for my human form and sauntered toward him, naked and comfortable with it.

To his credit, his gaze didn't flicker, but that muscle jumped in his jaw.

"You're a piece of work," he ground out.

I snorted. "Tell me something I don't know. If that's all…" I glanced away, and he stepped into my space.

"No, it's not all. You want to tell me what that was back there?"

"I'm a werewolf. We're not prudes like the fae."

"Not the getting naked part. Although the fact that half this court has seen your body makes me want to tear out their throats. The part where you *left* without talking to me. I thought we'd gotten past this shit."

I shoved both hands into his chest. He didn't even have the decency to stumble back a step.

"What exactly did you expect to happen? You tell me you want me, but your solution to that was going to be to fuck a woman who looked like me? You barely speak to me after we kiss, and then I walk in to see you flirting with a woman who could be my sister."

Confusion flickered across his face. I wanted to slam my fist into his jaw.

"Aurine? She looks nothing like you."

I glowered at him. "You've got to be kidding me."

He glanced away with a bemused frown. "I can see why you would be…concerned," he said finally. "But why would you not speak to me?" His eyes met mine once more, clear and open for a change.

"Yeah, because we've always communicated so well."

Humor flickered across his face now, and he caught my hand. He lifted his other hand, and my skin prickled as he created some kind of ward around the area.

"Aurine is my spy. She's seelie, but her mother was unseelie, and she spends most of her time gathering information for me. What you saw was her updating me."

"She looks like me."

He cupped my cheek. "I suppose she does. But I've never noticed it before."

I snorted, and he lifted his other hand, holding my face in place. "What I said about fucking a woman who looks like you…it was immature and stupid and beneath me. I'm…unused to this. To wanting a woman. It has been a very long time since a woman rattled me this way."

I sighed. "Look, Finvarra. I think we both know this isn't a good idea."

He ignored that. "Your wolf was possessive." His eyes glimmered with satisfaction. "I suppose I should be grateful you didn't attempt to rip out Aurine's throat."

Good god. "That's not what this was."

Finvarra smiled. It was one of the few times I'd seen him genuinely happy, and my breath caught in my throat.

"You looked beautiful tonight. I wanted to dance with you. And I wanted to do this."

His mouth crashed down on mine, and the forest around us, the unseelie realm, the sword...all of it just melted away, until I was engulfed in the scent of him, the feel of his lips making my head spin.

Finvarra slid one hand to the small of my back, pressing me close, until I could feel him, hard and thick against my stomach. He gripped my hair with his other hand, holding my head in place as his mouth caressed mine.

I buried my hands in his hair and dragged him closer, arching my back, needing *more*.

Finvarra stiffened, right as the back of my neck prickled. "Someone's coming," I murmured against his mouth.

He nodded, slowly pulling away. His eyes were molten gold. "Bad timing. We'll continue this later."

#

Finvarra

To say that Lutrin was displeased about the evolution of my relationship with Kyla was an understatement.

I'd escorted the little wolf to her bedroom last night before spending the next several hours considering potential strategies with Tae. However, my adviser hadn't been pleased to find me smiling at Kyla over breakfast the next morning.

Lutrin was smart enough not to say a word. But he'd

cleared his throat, reminding me I had another meeting to get to.

"Thank you, Lutrin. That will be all."

He'd given Kyla such a burning look of hatred, even Tae had tensed. Kyla had just licked her fork before baring her teeth in a wide, challenging grin.

"When are we returning to your castle?" Kyla asked.

"Eager to get back? *That's* interesting."

"At least in your castle, I don't have to wear heavy gowns every day."

She plucked at the bodice of the dress she was currently wearing. The dark green suited her.

"You don't have to wear them here," I said mildly.

"Then why am I?"

"Because Fin wanted to play nice for the first few days we were here, so he could see just what Marnin was up to," Tae said.

"And now?"

I gave her a slow smile. "And now I get to determine how exactly I'll deal with Marnin."

Kyla leaned back in her chair. I managed to refrain from asking if she'd eaten enough.

"Why can't you just have him detained, torture him a little, make him confess?" Kyla asked.

Tae snorted. I barely smothered a grin. "I can," I said. "But that comes with problems of its own. The moment I move against Marnin and those loyal to him, I make him a martyr. There will be unseelie in this part of my realm who will refuse to believe just how he has plotted to take my throne."

Tae poured himself some more water. "What Fin isn't saying is that he refuses to rule like his father."

"Tae."

He shrugged. "You could rule entirely with fear if you wanted. You could make an example of Marnin and ensure that even those who believe the lies he spread about you are too scared to act. But you won't."

Kyla frowned. "So, let me get this straight. You want to have Marnin arrested for plotting to overthrow you, but you're hung up on finding proof, because the people in this territory have been listening to his lies for so long and you don't want to have to put down a rebellion in a few years. You'd end up slaughtering your own people, which would make you a tyrant like your father."

My jaw clenched until my teeth threatened to crack. It took me a long moment before I was able to speak. "Yes."

"Hmm. You need to find a way to record one of his secret meetings and replay that shit for the entire kingdom."

"He's thought of that," Tae said. "If there's one thing Marnin excels at, it's staying hidden from unseelie magic. We know exactly where he'll gather his little friends, and we know at which time they'll meet. But the court uses ancient wards that are keyed to unseelie magic. If I, Finvarra, or anyone else with unseelie magic gets within a certain distance of that ward, they'll be instantly alerted."

Kyla smiled. And I immediately shook my head. "Absolutely not."

Unsurprisingly, she ignored that. "The black stone you guys use to record your meetings. Is that unseelie magic?"

"No." Tae frowned, glancing between us. "It's from the

middleground."

Her smile widened. "Put me in, Coach."

"Absolutely not," I growled.

Tae finally understood, and his eyebrows shot up. "It could work, Fin. She doesn't have unseelie magic. If she could get that stone close enough—"

"She doesn't have any magic at all. She dies, and we're at war with the wolves."

Kyla rolled her eyes. "I'll sign something. A release or whatever. Nathaniel will know I volunteered."

"You're not doing it."

Kyla and Tae just stared at me. Someone knocked on the door.

"No," I said, using a hint of my power to carry my voice out into the hall.

The knocking ceased.

"You're making life harder on yourself." Kyla smirked, peering down at her nails. "I could have your little rebellion stifled in the next twenty-four hours. Because I'm just that good."

Tae sniggered.

I just reached for my coffee. "Discussion over."

#

Kyla

The discussion was *not* over.

I spent the day in Finvarra's meetings, taking mental notes of anything I thought Nathaniel would find relevant or interesting. But my attention was entirely focused on convincing Finvarra to let me help him.

I had plenty of reasons to want this little visit wrapped up quickly. First, I hated this place with its grim formality. I loved the palace itself, but it had been ruined by Marnin and his little band of assholes.

If that wasn't bad enough, something had cracked open between Finvarra and me. Just days ago, our every interaction had been antagonistic. Now, that strange tension crackled beneath the surface whenever we were in the same room together.

After last night by the lake, I'd been careful not to be alone in a room with Finvarra again. He'd done the same. Clearly, I wasn't the only one who was unwilling to face up to *that* reality.

I'd found myself having…fun with Finvarra and Tae. Being in this place had turned us into allies, however briefly, and had taken the edge off the worst of my loneliness.

But I'd begun dreaming about the sword.

In some of those dreams, I managed to find it. I returned it to the demigod, saved the worlds, and had to live with the fact that the portals were closed.

But in most of those dreams…

I didn't find it in time.

Occasionally, dream-Kyla would tell Finvarra about why I needed the sword. In those dreams, he usually didn't believe me, or he somehow managed to protect his own realm while the rest burned.

Sometimes, he did believe me, but I'd waited too long and it was too late to return the sword by the winter solstice.

In those dreams, he raged at me, asking why I hadn't

trusted him.

Clearly, my subconscious was working through some shit.

The reality was, while I was here, I wasn't near the sword. There was no way Finvarra would have brought it with him. So I'd done what any self-respecting, if desperate, werewolf with impulse control issues would do.

When the meetings wrapped up, I watched who took the onyx stone. Within an hour, I'd followed the unseelie's scent, locating his room.

Tae had told me the stone was used as a formality, and the recordings were rarely, if ever, referred to. Apparently, the stone itself wasn't particularly valuable either. There were likely at least a dozen more floating around in this realm.

So I marked the door of the unseelie's room, wandered outside so I could match the balcony to the room, and suffered through yet another dinner with Marnin and his friends.

Something had changed among several of the men who'd sat at our table each night. They no longer watched Finvarra with malevolence in their gazes. No, the expression on several faces looked more like fear.

Interesting. As a werewolf, body language was my specialty. *Verbalizing* what I was seeing was often the problem.

So I reached for my wolf—although I kept her on a tight leash, noting the cold amusement she felt at my fear.

Would I always be terrified that she would take me over completely?

I buried that thought. Next to me, Finvarra stiffened.

He knew what I was doing, and he was…displeased.

My wolf looked at him, and I watched as he looked back, his expression blank, even as those gold eyes burned with warning.

And my wolf?

Was she…pouting? I could almost see her, head on her paws, despondent.

Good god.

She wanted Finvarra to be pleased with her.

Wanted him to stroke and appreciate her.

Well, that was an entirely unwelcome revelation.

"I don't know what you're doing." Finvarra leaned over, murmuring in my ear. His voice was so low, there was no chance anyone else would hear. "But I suggest you wrap it up and return Kyla to me."

My wolf was already gazing at the men we were sitting with. Several of them were…afraid.

The unseelie across from me… Lazirean was his name. His pulse thumped in his throat, and my teeth sharpened. That fear…delicious.

Finvarra reached for my hand beneath the table and squeezed. The feel of his skin helped me shove my wolf aside, but she'd shown me what I needed to see.

When I glanced at Finvarra again, some of the tension left his body, and he released my hand.

My wolf howled inside me.

I turned, focusing on each unseelie.

Four of them were no longer radiating that self-assurance, that "you-can't-touch-me" arrogance.

Ah.

They'd thought they were untouchable. They'd thought Marnin could protect them. And Finvarra had been showing them that was not the case. First, he'd made an example of Versen for what he'd done to Eratha. Then, he'd caught the unseelie who'd attacked me—and they were likely wishing they were dead.

Dad was home, and the kids were worried.

The unseelie began to stand, and I realized I'd plotted through most of dinner. Finvarra looked at my barely touched plate. I ignored him.

"I'll be right up," I said, and he narrowed his eyes. But Marnin had strolled over to talk to the king.

I slipped away the moment his attention shifted, but I felt his gaze slide back to me as I stalked out the door.

I smiled. Too late.

I'd been keeping a close eye on the unseelie in charge of the onyx stone. His name was Cyprinan, and he wasn't considered important enough to dine at the royal table, but I'd overheard one of his friends talking about visiting a gambling den tonight.

Cyprinan's room was a floor down from mine but five balconies to the left.

Wandering out of the summer palace, I strolled toward the forest. I could feel the guards' attention briefly resting on me, but they'd seen this all before. They knew I came and went, often returning in my wolf form.

As soon as I found enough cover in the forest, I slid off my heavy gown, rolled it into a ball, and shoved it beneath a bush. Thankfully, I'd gone commando underneath since that was the way I rolled. I shifted, stretching out my paws and cracking my back.

My wolf wanted to run. We were on the same page there.

Later, I told her. Instead, we waited until the guards changed their shift. They wouldn't know I'd only been out of the castle for twenty minutes or so—a much, much shorter "run" than usual. And several of them nodded at me as I trotted toward my balcony.

I let my mouth hang open in a wolf grin, and one of them let out a low whistle.

"Those are some teeth."

I winked at the guard, and he burst out laughing. Then I was scrambling up to my balcony. This next bit was the most dangerous. I was counting on the fact that most of this court spent their nights drinking and gambling and wouldn't notice me touching down on their balconies.

I shifted once more, then climbed over the edge of my balcony, peering down. The room below me was dark, and I dropped soundlessly onto the balcony.

No shouts sounded from the guards. I'd watched them closely enough to know most of them were half asleep in this place.

Climbing up onto the edge of the balcony, I crouched, preparing to leap. There were only a few feet between the balconies—something I could jump in my sleep. But I had to stay silent, hidden in the shadows.

I leaped, landing silently once more. There were plenty of downsides to being a werewolf, but even I could admit that this was one of the perks. I didn't hesitate, just kept my wolf close to the surface and leaped again and again until I was outside the unseelie's door.

Cyprinan's balcony door wasn't warded. And why would it be? He wasn't anyone *important* to Marnin. That made it particularly delicious that Cyprinan would be part of Marnin's downfall.

His door wasn't even locked. I opened it, and the handle let out a high-pitched squeak that seemed to echo across the night. I froze.

Below me, one of the guards coughed. I waited another few moments, but no one had noticed me breaking in.

The door was quiet as I cracked it open, scanning the darkened room. Empty. I slipped inside and went wolf again, so I could find the freshest scent.

He'd only spent a few minutes in this room after the long meeting, and his scent was still relatively fresh. No one else had been in the room, and it didn't take long for me to narrow down several places to search.

Shifting back to my human form, I winced as my stomach rumbled. I definitely should've eaten more at dinner.

I searched the bathroom first, switched to the small writing desk, and finally found the stone in the bottom drawer of his bedside table.

A moment later, I was walking out the door. A few minutes after that, I threw the stone up onto my balcony and hauled myself up behind it.

I grinned. It wasn't easy, being this awesome. But someone had to do it.

I'd left my own balcony door open—Finvarra had

warded the shit out of our rooms. My sweats were waiting on the bed, and I pulled them on, shoved the stone into my pocket, and strolled into the main room.

Finvarra was sitting on the couch, his shirt rolled up to bare his forearms as he scowled down at whatever boring papers he was reading. Tae sat across from him, reading a document of his own.

Finvarra lifted his head. "Why was your wolf out at dinner?"

"She notices things even I don't." *And for some reason, she craves your approval. She wants you to like her. To stroke her. It's fucking weird.*

Finvarra studied me for a long moment. I raised one eyebrow and crossed my arms, waiting him out.

He began lowering his head, returning his attention to his paperwork.

Then he stiffened.

"Where. Is. It?"

Tae looked up and winced at the threat in Finvarra's voice. I just blew them a kiss.

The unseelie king slowly got to his feet, and the temperature in the room plummeted. I angled my head, my claws shooting out.

"You stole the stone." Finvarra's voice was so soft, I shivered. Obviously, he could sense the magic somehow.

I swallowed, forcing bravado into my voice. "You want to wrap this shit up, and so do I," I said. "So why don't we work together, and we'll be out of here in the next day or two, with Marnin rotting away in one of your dungeons."

I had the stone. What I didn't have was the location of

the secret meeting. I could probably learn that location, but it would take me days.

Tae heaved a sigh. "Clearly, she's going to do it anyway, Fin. And she's right—she's our best option."

"Stay out of this."

Tae went still. Then he got to his feet. "You want me to be prepared to take that crown? These are the kinds of decisions I would be making. And I wouldn't let my feelings get involved."

I snorted at that. Tae winked at me. "Well, I'd try not to."

"Why?" Finvarra's voice was low as he addressed me, ignoring his cousin.

"Because I hate what they're doing here. In your mom's palace. And I'm tired of wearing these stupid dresses."

It wasn't just that, but some of the tightness had left Finvarra's expression at the mention of his mom.

"If you're determined to do this, you'll wear this." Finvarra stalked into his room, returning a moment later with a gorgeous amulet.

"Why?"

"It will shield you from magical attacks."

I swallowed. He almost sounded like he cared.

"I can't. I'm going wolf."

His expression shuttered. "I don't like it."

"It snowed last night. My wolf is white. It's the best way for me to stay hidden."

A muscle ticked in his cheek. "I can't go with you. I get close…"

"I know. They'll sense your power. I've got this. Just

tell me how the stone works."

Tae strolled forward and slapped Finvarra on the shoulder, sending me a grin. "It's similar to the stone that called Fin. You just throw it a foot or so into the air, and it will activate."

I'd need to shift to my human form. That would be the most dangerous part.

"I've got this."

Finvarra still didn't look happy. His Royal Control Freak couldn't stand not to be part of this little mission himself.

Poor guy.

He flashed his teeth at me, as if reading my mind. My heart beat faster in my chest, but I just raised an eyebrow.

"If you're determined to do this, then let's get it over with."

"Why yes, I will save your ass," I said. "You're welcome."

Ignoring that, Finvarra stalked toward his desk, pulling out a blank sheet of paper. He stared at it for a long time. Perhaps he was losing his marbles in his old age.

Ink bled onto the paper, spreading across the page. Within a moment, I was standing next to Finvarra, peering around his body. I went still as the blank paper turned into an elaborate map.

Sneaky unseelie.

The map was intricately detailed. But it only showed the castle.

"I thought you said they'd be meeting outside."

He flicked me a glance. "Watch."

I turned my attention back to the map, and my wolf came to attention as the ink lifted *above* the map, Finvarra's magic turning it into a perfect 3-D rendering. More ink appeared, rising from the map and filling in around the castle. The forest.

"Whoa."

Finvarra glanced at Tae, who reached over and pointed to a spot on the map while Finvarra held his hands steady, obviously keeping the ink in place.

"Here," Tae said.

I brought the clearing into my mind. "This is close to a lake," I murmured, and Finvarra nodded.

I'd run across the clearing the night of the full moon—right before I was attacked. I blocked that thought and focused on what I remembered of the clearing itself.

"I can hide here, here, or here," I said, "depending on which spot is downwind at the time." Unseelie couldn't scent nearly as well as a wolf, but I was taking no chances.

"Then we're in agreement," Tae said, but it sounded more like a question as he glanced at Finvarra.

The unseelie king turned and studied me. There was nothing remotely human in that expression. No, he was evaluating me as a possible tool. Carefully weighing the potential risk and reward, my strengths and weaknesses.

Grinding my teeth, I waited him out.

Finally, some of the life returned to his eyes. "Don't get killed."

"I won't," I promised. "I've got this."

ten
Kyla

According to Finvarra's spies, Marnin's meeting would be within an hour or so. I'd need to go now so I could be waiting in position.

While the stone was magically recording everything we needed, Finvarra would be gathering his most trusted guards and taking out the trash. Hopefully, by the end of the night, the summer palace would once again be in trusted hands.

"You're sure about this?" Tae asked.

Finvarra had already left, after giving me a scorching look I hadn't been able to read.

"I'm sure. See you soon."

I shifted, using my mouth to pluck the stone out of Tae's hand. He grinned at me.

"Fin's going to owe you for this, you know."

Oh, I knew. Unfortunately, I was pretty sure there was no real way for me to leverage that little fact. If there was one thing being in this palace had taught me, it was that he was willing to sacrifice almost anything to take Taraghlan down.

Trotting to the balcony door, I waited for Tae to open it, then launched myself down into the garden and toward the forest as usual. The guards were quiet behind me. Nothing to see here.

My biggest concern was accidentally swallowing the stone. The round, polished edges made it difficult for me to hold it in place, and I found myself walking most of the way toward the clearing.

The next part would be the most dangerous. It was possible Marnin had a sentry waiting to make sure his meeting place was safe. I took a deep breath and let my wolf mostly take over.

Surprisingly, she was…fine.

There was no power struggle. It felt almost like before I was taken—before I spent so much time in Lucifer's dungeon. I let her take just enough control to improve my senses, to notice the things I would otherwise miss, and she didn't attempt to take more.

If I'd been in my human form, tears would have been rolling down my face. I'd missed this. Missed being a partner with my wolf. Missed being a team.

I crouched, staying close to the ground. Processing information through my wolf was easier tonight as well, and for the first time in a long time, I felt…hopeful that we'd work it out.

No scents. No wards or sign of any other magic. Slowly making my way around the clearing, I circled it, checking for hidden traps.

There.

To my right was one of the tiny wards Evie called "stealth wards." I had no doubt that if I'd walked past that rock, Marnin would have been immediately notified that someone was here. Keeping an eye out for any other wards,

I kept moving.

I found two more. By the time I'd set myself up downwind, behind a fallen log and several shrubs, I was glad I'd taken so much time to scope this place out.

Shifting to my human form, I threw the stone into the air, caught it, and placed it in the hollowed-out log, carefully hidden from each side but visible enough that—according to Tae's instructions—it should capture everything we needed. I had to actively prevent myself from messing with it and attempting to give it a better "view." Apparently, it didn't function like a human camera. It just needed to be within distance of the clearing to do its job.

Technically, I could get out of here now. But my wolf was insistent that we stay. And since she didn't have that feral edge that warned me she wanted to go on a rampage, I trusted her instincts. So, I burrowed down beneath the bush, creating just enough space for myself to hide.

It wasn't exactly comfortable, and even my wolf form was chilly. But my adrenaline would keep me warm.

Just minutes later, Marnin's people began filing into the clearing. He waved a hand, and several stone statues appeared in the clearing, along with the remains of what must have been the temple Finvarra had told me about.

Someone had worked some serious magic on this place to guarantee those ruins weren't visible unless he willed it. Likely another way to ensure people wouldn't be hanging around the area.

I stayed completely, utterly still. Sixteen men entered the clearing in total. One of them held up a hand, and the entire area was enveloped in a silence ward. Thankfully, I was within the ward.

No one wasted any time on pleasantries. The other fifteen unseelie watched Marnin expectantly.

"We all know why we're here," he said. "The unseelie king is no longer the best choice to lead us into the future."

The irony. These guys were as backward as it got.

I had a relatively good view from where I was crouched, peering between a gap in the foliage. Standing to Marnin's right was one of his most loyal cronies, an unseelie named Rechiar. I could also see two of the unseelie I'd watched earlier today. The ones who'd seemed extra afraid when Finvarra had walked into the room. One of them was Lazirean—the one who'd almost been trembling with fear.

"He's the most powerful unseelie king to have ever ruled," his friend said.

Marnin slowly turned his head. "Do you no longer have what it takes to ensure we secede from this kingdom, Hilfron?"

Hilfron shook his head. "That's not what I'm saying."

"That's not what I'm saying, *Your Majesty*," Rechiar said. Marnin shot him an approving look.

Hilfron bowed his head, dutifully repeating the words. But it was clear he was spooked. "I'm merely concerned about the…power imbalance," he said delicately.

In other words, he knew damn well Finvarra would be smiting some peeps. Honestly, I was looking forward to it.

"Do you think we haven't made arrangements for such a thing? Do you truly believe I wouldn't have put my people in place over the past several decades? All waiting for this moment when the unseelie king would be distracted, fraternizing with wolves, going to war alongside the demons, and giving all his time and attention to the *sword*."

From the conversations I'd caught between Finvarra and Tae, I had no doubt they were keeping a close eye on exactly who had been put "in place." Finvarra had played a long game, allowing this little rebellion to play out. But it was only recently that he'd realized precisely how much support Marnin had gained.

He'd given Marnin just enough of a rope to hang himself.

Even at his worst and most distracted, the unseelie king had been ten steps ahead of this guy. It was impressive.

"We have no time for cowards and nonbelievers," Marnin said softly, and a ball of dread settled into my stomach.

Oh shit. The guy was nuts. He could feel everything he'd plotted for slowly disappearing as his allies saw Finvarra again and realized what they would be up against. It was one thing to plan to rebel against a king who wasn't here. It was another to see all that power every day and realize just how dangerous he was.

Lazirean seemed to realize just how much danger they were in. Because he lifted a hand. "All of us recognize you as the king of this territory," he began, "Hilfron simply—"

"Hilfron simply *nothing*," Marnin howled, spittle flying from his mouth. There was no sign of the sly, smooth man I'd met when we'd first arrived here.

His hand lit with fire, and I rolled up to my feet. My wolf's instincts were always to protect, and while Hilfron wasn't innocent, his crimes were for Finvarra to punish.

I was too late. Marnin's flames met Hilfron's ward, and everyone went silent as it began to eat away at that ward.

Hilfron turned ashen. "Please," he begged. "*Please.*"

The sky darkened. The temperature dropped. And I loosed the breath I'd been holding.

Finvarra was here.

The flames disappeared. Tae stepped into the clearing behind the unseelie king, and the silence ward fell. The new ward was steel-colored. Like the bars of a cage.

Marnin went still. And I watched the moment he realized all his hopes and dreams were dust. Finvarra's guards were stalking through that ward, although one of Marnin's friends attempted to make a run for it, hitting the ward with his face. He bounced back, landing on his ass.

Clearly, it was one-way only.

Chaos broke out.

One of the guards went down. Finvarra threw a protective ward over him and waved a hand, dark tendrils of his power forcing Marnin to his knees.

Marnin knew better than to target Finvarra. But he knew exactly how to cause him the most pain. With a glance at Rechiar, he jerked his head at Tae, who was still directing the guards who were making their arrests.

I saw the moment Rechiar made his decision. He raised his hand.

No.

Tae was distracted. He was—

"Kyla!" Finvarra roared.

I was already launching myself at the unseelie.

He spun, but it was too late. I hit him with my considerable weight, and we both went down. Rechiar screamed as my claws dug into his gut, his other hand aiming that deadly power at me.

Tae and Finvarra were already there. Tae hauled me off Rechiar while Finvarra smiled coldly across the clearing at Marnin.

"Attempting to assassinate my heir," he tutted, and Marnin's face drained of color. He was all out of moves. His little rebellion was done, and whatever plans he'd made to take Finvarra's throne were dead.

I shifted to my human form and surveyed the clearing. The remaining unseelie were all on their knees.

"What will you do with them now?" I asked Finvarra as he stepped toward me, handing me a cloak from one of the guards. His expression was still cold, remote.

"They will be given a trial. And the stone will be used, so there will be no doubt of just what they were planning. You saved countless lives here today."

I wrapped the cloak around myself. "Just another day at the office. You yelled my name. I figured you were pissed."

"I thought Marnin would hit you. Tae, at least, had enough power to ward."

"Tae couldn't see Rechiar aiming at him."

Finvarra sighed, running a hand over his face. "It was a stupid, impulsive thing to do. Thank you."

I burst out laughing. "You're welcome."

Tae wandered over, swiped the stone from where it was sitting in the log and slung his arm around my shoulder. "I guess I owe you one."

"Oh, I'll definitely be calling in that favor at some

point."

He just pressed a kiss to my cheek. "Deal. Don't do it again."

I rolled my eyes. My stomach rumbled, loud enough that Finvarra went still.

"I'm on it," I told him. "I'll eat as soon as I get back to the castle. Don't worry, I'm not planning to snack on your people."

One of Finvarra's guards was approaching, close enough that he flinched, obviously hearing me.

"Thank you for that," Finvarra growled.

I smirked, strolling back toward the palace. "You're welcome."

eleven
Kyla

We returned to Finvarra's main castle two days later. While that strange tension still crackled between us, it was as if being back here had reminded us of just who we both were.

He'd gone back to being his usual cold, disinterested self, and I'd gone back to plotting. All three of us had been silent as we ate breakfast, lost in our own thoughts.

Clearly, Finvarra was struggling with everything that had happened with Marnin. I'd also stepped in and helped—blurring the lines between captive and asset.

Then there was the fact that he'd left the guy in charge in the palace his mom had adored, and Marnin had not only broken that trust, he'd shit all over it, attempting to turn anyone with any power against Finvarra.

Not to mention, every time Finvarra looked at me, he likely saw a woman who had come to his realm to steal from him. I couldn't blame him for wanting nothing to do with me. Because the truth was, no matter what happened between us, I would betray him again.

Nothing had really changed. Even if we gave in to the sexual tension between us, I still had a job to do. I wasn't leaving this realm without that sword, and I needed to do it sooner rather than later.

Tae's words continued to haunt me. Finvarra was a grown man and responsible for his own feelings. But at the same time, it was clear the constant betrayals he'd experienced over the centuries had left their mark.

The thought of being yet another person who wounded him…

It sucked.

If there was one person who was even less pleased than either Finvarra or me by the sexual tension brimming between us, it was Lutrin. Finvarra had sent him ahead of us, so he would return to the castle in time for our own arrival. Lutrin wasn't trusted with information about Finvarra's secret portal.

And from the way he'd just marched in here, he was *pissed*.

The adviser was currently standing in front of us, his attention on Finvarra. "You…you didn't tell me about your plan with Marnin, Your Majesty."

"It was an impromptu decision," Finvarra said.

Lutrin's gaze flicked toward me, then back to Finvarra. "May I ask…do you no longer trust me?"

"Nonsense," Finvarra soothed. "We had less than an hour to act and needed to move quickly. There was no need to call you back from your travel."

A hint of relief entered Lutrin's gaze, but he still looked…put out.

He should, because while I didn't know Finvarra all that well, by now I knew when he was lying.

Finvarra nodded at us, getting to his feet and stalking

out of the room.

Lutrin smiled at me. "After the attack in the summer palace, I saw the need to increase security. You'll now have two guards with you at all times."

I opened my mouth, but he was already headed for the door, practically running. Coward.

If there was ever a man who deserved evisceration, it was that guy.

Tae raised his hand, and I felt the silence ward go into play. "You can't kill him." He grinned at me from the other end of the table, throwing an orange into the air and catching it.

"I *can* kill him," I said. "There will simply be repercussions."

Tae sighed. "I'm sorry he's being like this. I'll talk to Finvarra."

"Don't bother."

He began peeling his orange, offering me half. I shook my head.

"I have something for you," Tae told me in a low voice. "I'd forgotten it was still here, but Finvarra hasn't ordered me *not* to give it to you."

I grinned. "Tell me more."

"Meet me in the stables."

It suddenly hurt to breathe. My grin fell. "No."

The ghost of a frown crossed his face. "Uh, okay. How about the eastern edge of the garden? Near the wall."

I nodded, slowly getting to my feet. "I'll go get some fresh air."

Finvarra's gardens were beautiful. They weren't overly

fussy—someone had let them grow a little wild. The eastern edge was one of my favorite spots to sit, on a bench near the weeping willows.

All I needed was access to my favorite romance series, and I'd spend hours out here.

Tae appeared, striding toward me. He handed me a tiny, eight-sided device about the size of my palm. I frowned. "What is it?"

He glanced around, and I slid the device into the pocket of my hoodie. "Think of it as a way to use FaceTime between realms."

I went still. "Seriously?"

"Yeah. I mean, it doesn't actually connect to a phone or anything like that. But your face will just kind of appear like a hologram in front of the person you're attempting to contact. Things can get awkward if they're in the middle of…you know." He grinned.

I could talk to Evie. And Danica. I doubted Nathaniel wanted to talk to me, but at least I could contact my friends. A lump formed in my throat. "I don't know what to say."

Tae shrugged. "I know it's been hard for you here. And you're probably lonely. I just thought it might help."

"How does it work?"

"You just think of the person you want to contact. Hold them in your mind and say their name."

I'd thrown my arms around him before he finished speaking. "Thank you. Thank you so much."

Someone cleared their throat. I stepped back to find Lutrin grinning at us. Finvarra stood next to him, one eyebrow raised. But his eyes had turned feral.

Tae froze. "Hi," he said. "Well, uh, I'll just be going." He turned and walked away. I rolled my eyes. Way to make things look suspicious, bro.

I ignored Lutrin. I had no doubt he'd brought Finvarra here with some ridiculous story about me colluding with his cousin. My eyes met Finvarra's.

"Was there something you wanted?"

"No." He turned and walked away. Lutrin gave me a smug look, and I gave him my middle finger.

Finvarra knew there wasn't anything between Tae and me. He wasn't an idiot. More importantly, he had work to do, and Lutrin had brought him out here, likely with some outlandish lie.

I took a deep breath. We were having this out. Tonight. As soon as Lutrin was no longer around.

But first, I was going to talk to Evie.

I took the yellow device up to my room, stepped into my bathroom, and locked the door.

"Evie Amana," I said, picturing her in my mind.

The box heated in my hand, and a strange orb appeared about a foot in front of me.

A moment later, Evie's face was in the middle of that orb, and she was staring at me, her eyes wide.

"Fuck, Kyla. I was afraid you were dead. Where are you?"

I grinned back at her. "Still in Finvarra's realm."

"How... What?"

"A friend helped me out and gave me this cool device. Is anyone with you?"

"No, I'm in my office. Just let me lock the door."

A moment later, she was sitting back at her desk. "This is so weird. Your face is just floating in front of me."

I laughed. "Yeah, it's wild."

"Tell me everything."

I took a deep breath. And I did. When I was finished, she was silent for a while.

Finally, she angled her head. "Things I've learned about Finvarra… He's not as much of a dick as I thought, even though he's still holding you against your will. Oh, and he kisses like a god."

"I didn't say that," I muttered.

She gave me a wicked grin. "Oh, you didn't have to."

"Can we get back to the point?"

"Hmm. Tell me more about the kisses. God, I can't believe you were interrupted. Twice."

"Evie!"

She rolled her eyes. "Fine. It just so happens, I've been doing everything I can to try to contact you. Finvarra didn't make that easy. We've been getting everything in place here. The demons are ready to march, but…we're heavily outnumbered."

My stomach clenched. "Any sign of Gabriel yet?"

"No. He's staying hidden—likely waiting us out. As much as I'd love to assassinate him, that would be too easy. I'm guessing we'll meet him on the battlefield. Any sign of the sword?"

"No. I was away from the castle. Finvarra took me with him… It's a long story." But fresh determination had filled me at the thought of our people, outnumbered by the seelie and the mages. Evie was organizing our allies, and I was here, flirting with Finvarra.

"I may be able to help," she said. "We managed to find someone who used to be in Finvarra's court. He left, thanks to some scandal years ago."

"And?"

"And since you're already there, you should check for the sword in Finvarra's father's study."

Of course. Of course he'd hide it in the room no one would go near after his father's death—Finvarra included.

I swallowed. "Any chance you know where that is?"

"Nope. But I know Finvarra is too smart to put it in a safe or down in his own dungeon. If you get into the study, you can at least poke around and see if you can find it. The good thing is, you can see wards, so you'll know where to look."

"I can see wards, but I can't break them."

Evie waved her hand. "We'll cross that bridge, yada yada. You find it, and then we'll figure out how you're going to steal it."

God, it felt good to be working as a team again. I grinned at her. "Thanks."

"No problem."

I wanted to ask about Nathaniel and the pack, but her eyes widened. "Nate is here. Gotta go."

She waved her hand, and her face disappeared. Obviously, Nathaniel was still pissed enough that if he learned Evie was helping me, he'd put a stop to it.

It was only the middle of the day. I couldn't go for the sword until later. So, I might as well attempt to soothe Finvarra's ruffled feathers. He was in his library when I found him, a whiskey in his hand, a stack of paperwork in his lap.

"Yes?" He signed something, doing his best to ignore me.

"Uh, what you saw in the garden."

He lifted his gaze, and his expression was inscrutable. "It wasn't you colluding with my heir, so you could talk to your friends?"

I swallowed. "Do you know everything?"

"Yes." Not a glimmer of humor flickered across his face. And for some stupid reason, it made my throat tighten. I blamed fucking Lutrin for this shit.

"Okay, well, bye."

I turned to walk away, and then Finvarra was there. He leaned against the wall, his huge body blocking my way. I swallowed.

"Can I help you?"

"Did you enjoy talking to Evie?"

"How do you know I was talking to her?" Had he magically bugged my bathroom?

"Process of elimination. Of course you'd speak with her first. You've got some plan together that involves *my* sword."

This man. "And how do you know that?"

"I didn't. But your heart rate just increased, and your pupils dilated."

Ugh.

"Let me guess, you talked all about how cruel and wicked I am, and how you're the innocent victim in all this."

I gave him a sly little smirk I knew would make him

want to strangle me.

"No, actually, we talked about your kisses."

It wasn't often that I'd seen Finvarra genuinely surprised. But I enjoyed seeing it now. His eyebrows rose, his eyes widened almost imperceptibly, and...

I leaned closer. "It sounds like *your* heart just sped up."

His eyes darkened, and I almost caught my breath as his gaze dropped to my mouth.

"My kisses? And why would you be talking about *that?*"

This was straying into dangerous territory. "You may be...deficient in every other metric," I said. "But you get a passing score when it comes to your kisses." I shrugged. "I guess it comes with the territory when you're older than dirt."

He stared at me. And then he threw back his head and laughed.

Now my breath really did catch. His eyes met mine, and god, they were so bright.

"A passing score, hmm? Sounds like I need to work harder."

I opened my mouth, but he'd already shifted us until I was the one with my back against the wall. I tensed, ready to reverse our positions.

"Uh-uh," he murmured against my lips, and my entire body went hot. His hand slid to my rib cage, thumb stroking below my breast, and I arched my back. He let out a low, approving sound and ducked his head, pressing long, hot kisses to the side of my neck, my throat.

This was the stupidest thing I'd ever done.

But I couldn't bring myself to *stop* doing it.

Ever since I'd met this man, some secret part of me had wanted him almost as much as I loathed him. Clearly, he felt the same. Maybe we just needed to roll around in the sheets and get each other out of our systems.

He lifted his head. "Will you come back to my rooms?"

"We can't—"

"I know. Nothing changes."

We were on the same page, then.

I nodded, burying my hand in his hair. But something tugged at my gut, and my eyes flew open.

The library was disappearing, becoming blurry at the edges. Finvarra's arms clamped tightly around me, holding me in place, and I barely breathed as his bedroom solidified.

"What was that?"

"Within my realm, I can travel short distances using my power."

I swallowed. That was how he'd gotten to me the other night with the stone. But…

"You've appeared in my realm that way, too."

He gave a faint smile. "That stone helps. Otherwise, the amount of power required can be crippling, depending on how far away from a portal I am." He studied my face. "Is this really what you want to talk about now?"

I grinned. "I guess not."

Was I seriously doing this? With Finvarra?

"Yes," he told me.

Frowning at him, I opened my mouth.

"No, I can't read your mind," he said. "But I can read the doubt on your face. If you don't want this, you can leave now, and we'll pretend it never happened."

No. That wasn't what I wanted at all.

His mouth found mine once more, and Finvarra pushed me back, until I was lying on the ocean of his bed, staring up at him. He reached his hand down, his thumb caressing my lower lip, and I opened my mouth at the silent demand, allowing him inside. My tongue teased him, and his eyes lit with cool fire.

He surveyed my body, his expression almost…smug. I wasn't even naked yet, but something about the way he looked at me—as if memorizing every inch of my body—made me want to burrow beneath his covers.

The unseelie king raised that eyebrow, reading my discomfort. Daring me to attempt such a thing.

My wolf responded with a snarl. Finvarra laughed, clearly delighted.

In the blink of an eye, all of our clothes disappeared. I'd never get used to the casual display of his power. I thought I knew what he could do in my own realm, but it seemed as if that power was near limitless here in his domain.

One look at him, though, and any thoughts of power or realms disappeared. The man was a work of fucking art.

It should be illegal to be so large—with muscles carved as if from stone—and yet move in such a sinuous, graceful way. He paused, allowing me to stare, and I drank him in—from his alien gold eyes and pointed ears, to the arms that looked like they could snap me in half, the abs I wanted to *lick*, the huge thigh muscles.

But…unsurprisingly, my gaze got stuck on his cock.

It was long, thick, and perfectly proportioned—just like

the rest of him. He fisted it, and a thrill shot through me.

He wanted me just as badly as I wanted him.

Today's power games would end in a draw.

But there was always tomorrow.

Finvarra leaned over me. I attempted to drag him closer, but he slowly shook his head. "If you think I'm going to fuck you without tasting that perfect pussy, you clearly don't know me as well as you think you do, little wolf."

My cheeks blazed, but my thighs clenched, my core heated, and he gave me a knowing look.

His hand shot out, pushing my legs apart. Since I wasn't an idiot, I let them fall open, although I had to close my eyes at the sight of his pleased expression.

"Uh-uh. Look at me."

Taking a deep breath, I complied. Finvarra kept his gaze on me and leaned closer, blowing lightly on the insides of my thighs. I blinked. How could such a tiny sensation make me need to suppress a moan?

He sent me a wicked grin and followed up with a trail of kisses along my sensitive skin. One thigh. And then the other.

My breath caught, and I let my legs fall open even wider. He gave a pleased hum against my thigh, moving higher, until he was staring at the wet heat of me.

His eyes met mine. "Fucking perfect."

He'd dropped his head before I decided how to respond, his tongue caressing me in one long swipe. My hips bucked, and he grabbed them, holding me still for him. His tongue danced along my clit, and I sucked in a breath, letting it out on a long moan as he used that clever mouth to circle and *suck.*

My body tensed, already on the edge. I writhed, breaking out in a sweat.

Finvarra let out a rough growl, pulling my legs up over his shoulders so he could get even closer. And then he buried his face against me, dragging his tongue over my wetness.

"More," I demanded.

He laughed, and I almost came from the vibration. But then he was slipping one finger inside me, crooking it in a "come here" motion, and continuing that same wicked dance with his tongue.

I shot my hands out and grabbed his hair, holding him close as I ground up into him. He growled again, picking up the pace, adding a second finger.

"Come for me," he demanded, keeping me still with his other hand while he drove me wild.

I arched, gasping, tossing my head from side to side. I could feel the edges of my climax. *Knew* it would be amazing.

I let out a garbled sound as pleasure shot through me, enveloping every inch of my body, my climax coming in waves that went on and on. Finvarra didn't stop until I was wrung out, pushing weakly against his head.

He smirked at me. "Delicious."

Grabbing my legs, he used them to drag me to the edge of the bed, holding me in place for him. Within a moment, he was pushing inside me, just enough to tease.

"More."

"I'm in control here. It'll be your turn later. When I'm done."

I bared my teeth at him, and he thrust deep, letting out a tight laugh when I let my head fall back with a moan.

His thrusts were measured, going an inch deeper each time.

Keeping his precious control, while I lost mine.

I don't think so.

"If you won't fuck me properly…"

I slid my hand teasingly down to my clit. His eyes fired, and he pushed it away. But that muscle ticked in his jaw, and then he was pounding into me, finally unleashing himself the way I wanted. The way I *needed*.

He glowered down at me.

I snarled back.

He flicked my clit, still thrusting deep, hitting that spot that made me tighten around him. I clamped down, and he let out a rough curse.

My climax washed over me, the edges of my vision darkening, until all I could see was his face and the pleasure in his eyes as he watched me let go.

#

Finvarra

Kyla gave me a wicked look and lifted a strawberry to her mouth. That was all it took, and I'd hardened like a human teenager. From the amusement in her eyes, she was well aware.

Tae stepped into the room and gagged. "I can't believe I'm going to say this, but I liked it better when you two were at war."

Kyla smirked. "We're still at war. We're just enjoying a short cease-fire."

Her words burrowed deep, and I nodded at Tae. "Exactly."

Unfortunately, while I'd imagined I could fuck the little wolf once and move on with my life, my body had disagreed. We'd spent the past several days tangled on various horizontal surfaces throughout the castle—and a few vertical ones, too.

Kyla's eyes met mine, and she gave the breakfast table a considering look. Just like that, I wanted to throw Tae out and lock the door.

She was enjoying herself, the little minx.

Both of us were choosing to avoid talking about why she was here, but nothing had changed—she still wanted to go home, and I still wanted to know why she was after my sword.

In the meantime, we were enjoying each other in ways I certainly hadn't expected.

Tae heaved a sigh and narrowed his eyes at me. "I need to talk to you after this."

I just nodded, thoroughly entertained by the woman in front of me. I found myself checking her food intake, almost obsessed with confirming she'd eaten enough. She was a grown woman—one who'd been a wolf for years now—and yet I still had to bury the instinct to make sure she had more than enough food. Some strange part of me needed to ensure she would never again be weak.

"I'm going for a walk in the garden," Kyla announced, getting to her feet. "You two enjoy your little talk. Tae, I'll see you later."

I watched her prowl out of the room before I turned my attention back to my cousin. I was glad they'd become friends. Tae needed someone right now, and they both shared the same irreverent humor.

Tae lifted a hand, enveloping the room in a silence ward. "I would like to know what you plan to do with Lutrin."

"Is that a question because you're interested in my decisions as ruler? Or because you're attempting to protect Kyla?"

"I don't see why it can't be both."

"Hmm."

"Finvarra."

"I'm leaving Lutrin for now. It benefits me to have him right where he is, distributing false information."

"Not all of that information is false."

I shrugged one shoulder. "And any truthful information he gleans can't hurt us."

"Why play the game at all?"

"You know why. Lutrin has a direct line to the seelie king. And the more desperate he becomes—the more he panics at the thought of not knowing my every move—the more of my people he attempts to sway to his side."

Tae sighed. "Don't you get tired of playing these games?"

"I've been playing them for centuries. If I allowed myself to feel the exhaustion, the citizens of this realm would be bowing to someone like Marnin. Never forget, Tae. Anyone can betray you."

His gaze darted to the door Kyla had just walked

through, and I turned away.

It was time to remind myself of the truth that was etched on my bones.

Anyone can betray you.

#

Kyla

I was considering doing something stupid.

But…I could no longer justify not telling Finvarra why I needed his sword.

And no, it wasn't because I was getting dicked by him.

At first, it had been an obvious choice not to tell him. He couldn't be trusted.

In my mind, he'd been an arrogant, entitled king who would always believe he knew best. And all those things were still true. But I'd seen him with his cousin. Seen him make decisions based on what was best for his people. Finvarra could be reasonable.

The prophecy said I needed to do this alone. And I would. But…I could tell Finvarra why. Could convince him to let me take the sword to save the realms.

He sure as hell didn't want the unseelie realm to burn.

So, I was going to do something that didn't come easily to me. I was going to trust the unseelie king to be reasonable.

I kept my footsteps quiet as I wandered toward his library, a smile curving my mouth. Yesterday, he'd taken me up to the mezzanine I'd pondered when I'd first arrived. Then he'd laid me in front of a fire and gone down on me until my voice was hoarse from moaning.

"There are…concerns, Your Majesty," Lutrin said.

I scowled. Obviously, Finvarra was busy working, so I'd have to come back later.

"Concerns?"

"Yes. About the wolf."

Since I was the only wolf in town, I went very still.

"And what kinds of concerns would those be?"

"Ah, some of the senior advisers and courtiers are talking. Especially after Marnin. They don't understand why you haven't yet punished the wolf for her theft attempt."

"I'm holding her here against her will," Finvarra said, his voice distracted. It was clear he was in the middle of something.

"They want to know why she hasn't been punished properly. And why she hasn't been interrogated."

Finvarra heaved a sigh. "If she doesn't tell me what I need to know, she'll be moved from the tower to a cell in the dungeon. Now, if you've finished attempting to tell me how to rule?"

His voice had gotten very quiet, *dripping* with threat.

But my heart had already cracked.

"Y-yes, Your Majesty. I apologize for overstepping."

I pulled myself together long enough to dart into the closest room as Lutrin stepped into the hall.

My eyes were hot, my hands shaking. And for some strange reason, it felt as if someone were sitting on my chest.

I sucked in a deep breath and pulled myself together. This wasn't unexpected. Finvarra was behaving entirely true to form. I was the one who'd somehow decided to give him qualities he didn't have.

Turning, I snuck back up to my bedroom, a pit opening up in my stomach.

His dungeon. After everything he knew about me—about what I'd been through at Lucifer's hands—he would do that to me.

I was *weak*. So fucking weak to feel this sense of betrayal. I'd promised myself I wouldn't get attached while we were rolling around naked, and yet the first chance I'd gotten, I'd managed to forget exactly who and what Finvarra was.

Stalking into my bathroom, I wiped the tears from my face and stared into my eyes. Eyes that would never be the same after those dungeons.

Evie had told me where she thought the sword was. I needed to act natural around Finvarra for the next day or two while I scoped it out. And then I needed to do what I'd come here to do. Already, I'd wasted enough time here.

"Little wolf?"

Fuck. Leaning down, I splashed cold water on my face.

"A minute," I called. Drying my face, I glanced in the mirror. My eyes were overly bright, but I would just have to act as if nothing was wrong.

All while I fantasized about murdering Finvarra.

His gaze met mine, and I wished I could act half as well as he did. His eyes lit up, and I was in his arms an instant later.

"I missed you." He nuzzled my ear.

"What were you doing?"

"Meetings." His voice turned cold.

"Ah." I attempted to keep my voice light. "And now

you've come to me for some entertainment."

He slowly pulled his head back, until he was looking me in the eye.

"Is that what you think you are to me?"

I tried out a smile. Clearly, my acting needed some work, because those gold eyes narrowed.

"What's wrong?"

"Nothing."

"Kyla."

He so rarely used my name. I *hated* that he was using it now, when he was pretending to give a shit about me.

"Evie and Nathaniel had a fight," I lied. "I've just been chatting with her. That's all."

"Ah."

I wandered toward the window, gazing down at the expanse of land beneath me. If I didn't cooperate with Finvarra, he would take the sight of those lands away from me without a second thought.

He wrapped his arms around me from behind, and I almost stiffened. When he nuzzled my ear, I wanted to stab him. Then the world melted around us once more, and I closed my eyes, dizzy. When I opened them, we were lying on Finvarra's bed.

Finvarra pulled me close. "How did the Alpha wolf convince you to return with him?"

"There was no convincing about it. My wolf knew he was Alpha, and she was more than happy to fall in line."

"But the woman?"

I was silent for a long moment. "The woman wasn't as convinced. But…things were getting desperate. And

Nathaniel wasn't lying when he told me I would end up killing someone."

My mind threw me back to that meeting, and I distracted both of us with the memory.

"Hello."

I was in a forest. Why was I in a forest? And who was this man who spoke to me in that low, compelling voice?

I'd escaped all the other men—both human and wolf. I'd killed more than a few of them. This one would be no different.

"I wish I could allow you your freedom. You've led the packs on quite the chase. But you'll be caught, eventually. If not by me, then by another Alpha."

I showed him my teeth.

He looked at me. I dropped my gaze.

What was this? I attempted to raise my head once more, but I couldn't. The man radiated authority. Seemed to exhale dominance. My heart rate tripled.

"You don't need to be afraid." *He sighed, stalking closer, and I stepped back, keeping my head low. I would wait until he thought he had caught me, and then I would slip past him. My wolf was very, very fast.*

A hand clamped around the back of my neck. I lashed out automatically, but the man easily dodged my claws.

He looked into my eyes. *"No,"* *he said.*

I went limp.

This was horrifying. I would rather die than become some male's plaything, purely because he'd been lucky enough to be more dominant than I was.

He sighed, and I could even feel my wolf's surprise

when he sat down, resting his back against a tree. He pulled me down with him.

"My name is Nathaniel," he said. He reached out a hand and slid it down my ribs. I snapped my teeth, and he clamped his other hand around my muzzle.

"I thought so," he said. "Half starved. If I hadn't found you, you would have made your way into the closest town and eaten your fill."

I turned my gaze away, staring into the forest.

He just laughed. "Werewolves need a pack. Now, I'm not going to promise to make you my mate or treat you as a queen or any of that nonsense. You won't receive special treatment because you happen to be a female wolf, and you'll be expected to follow orders and to learn how to control your shift. But what I will give you is a pack. A family. Somewhere to belong. You're headstrong. You won't like following my orders, but that's okay. You'll do it anyway."

I looked up at him. He'd tamped down his Alpha-eyes so we could have this discussion, although it wasn't really a discussion when I couldn't talk back.

My growl was long, low, and filled with threat.

He just tapped me on the nose as if I were a misbehaving puppy. I snarled.

His eyes narrowed. "Shift."

I couldn't. I'd forgotten how. Panic screamed through me, dark and vicious. His gaze softened. He could likely smell it.

He clasped my chin with his hand, wrapping it around my muzzle once more, keeping my mouth closed. He stared deep into my eyes again.

"Shift."

And I did.

Finvarra was silent for a long moment. "I'm guessing there were other wolves who attempted to take you."

"Yeah. You said it when we first met. Myth given life." I snorted. "Since female werewolves are so rare, the moment those packs learned I existed, they began the hunt. By the time Nathaniel found me, I was being cornered, with packs on three sides. At first, they'd sent wolves who'd promised me all kinds of things. Not because they wanted to help me, but because having a female werewolf in the pack meant bragging rights. Nathaniel…he gave it to me straight. He wasn't promising me anything stupid. And I could smell his sincerity—knew he wasn't lying."

"You never…"

I frowned. Then it hit me, and despite the betrayal still roiling through me, I laughed, turning in Finvarra's arms. "No, I never rolled around in the sheets with Nathaniel. Ew. It would be like boning my brother."

Finvarra seemed satisfied by that reaction, and I eyed him. "Are you…jealous of Nathaniel?"

His eyes were very gold, almost as if they glowed with a light of their own. "Why would I be jealous, when you're in *my* bed?"

I gaped at him. That sounded a lot like jealousy. From someone who was prepared to throw me in his fucking dungeon if I didn't give him what he wanted.

Men.

"While I *am* pretty spectacular and tend to leave

brokenhearted men wherever I go, Nathaniel has never been one of them."

He smiled at that, pushing a lock of hair behind my ear.

"You know, you're going to have to let me go at some point." I tried one last time. "I have shit I need to do."

"I will. Just as soon as you tell me why you were trying to steal the sword from me. I know you well enough now to assume there's some larger plan at play. And it's unlikely you're working alone."

I attempted my own smile. "How do you know it was the sword I was after? Maybe I'd planned to clean out your royal jewels. And wow, that sounded dirty."

He just gave me an amused look. "You won't leave here until I'm confident you've told me everything." In a panther-quick move, he rolled me onto my back, leaning over me. "And in the meantime, I have you right where I want you."

He pressed his lips to my racing pulse, and I stiffened.

He was right. He did have me right where he wanted me. I'd almost told him why I needed that sword, right before I'd heard that the bastard would shove me in the dungeon.

How long would he give me before he tired of me and sent me down for some quality time with the Naud chains?

Maybe…maybe I could talk to him. Could explain why it was so important.

And if I was wrong? I would be betting the survival of *worlds* on Finvarra's ability to trust. The lives of everyone I loved would be in the hands of the man who'd been betrayed so many times, he no longer knew how trust even worked.

Finvarra wasn't going to let down his guard. And he

was right. He'd removed me as a threat, completely.

It was time to strike.

#

Kyla

I'd known better than to get emotionally attached to Finvarra. But my heart ached like I'd been stabbed in the chest.

There was no going back from this.

But this was about so much more than my own happiness. This was about saving the realms and everyone I loved.

I choked out a sob. Then I pulled myself together and made my way to Finvarra's father's old rooms.

They weren't locked. Why would they be, when no one came in here? While Taraghlan had kept his sword in an armory behind layers of dungeons, traps, and monsters, Finvarra had gone for a much more subtle approach. He'd given this room no true security and likely hadn't been seen stepping into it for centuries. No one who knew anything about his family history would imagine he'd use his father's room for anything—especially something this important.

And there was no ward shimmering in front of me. I checked every inch of the door, including the intricate handle. Letting my wolf peek out, I used her senses to search for any hint of magic. Thankfully, hanging out with Danica and Evie had given me a good idea of how wards could be hidden. When I was positive it was safe, I cracked open the door and slipped inside.

The furniture was covered in white dust sheets. It was clear that after his father's death, Finvarra had simply yielded this part of the castle to his ghost.

I wondered if his mother's rooms were the same. If he'd shut any memories of her away, or if he occasionally walked through those rooms.

And that was certainly none of my business.

Keeping my footsteps silent, I moved into the bedroom. Evie hadn't known exactly where the sword was hidden, but I padded toward the closet. Might as well get started there.

"I knew you'd do this."

I slowly turned my head. Finvarra stood in front of the door, flanked by several guards. Behind him, Lutrin smirked at me, victory written all over his face.

I didn't attempt to play dumb. There was no reason for me to be in here. "You left me no choice."

Finvarra was already shaking his head, his expression blank. My heart panged. I hadn't seen that expression since the first few days after I'd arrived here.

"You could have trusted me."

I gaped at him. "Oh please. We both know that's not true."

Surprise flashed across his face, followed by that remote expression once more. He wasn't even really here anymore. He'd retreated behind that mask he wore.

"Your Majesty."

Finvarra slowly glanced at Lutrin. The adviser froze at whatever he saw on his sovereign's face, but he swallowed and continued talking.

"If I may… I would be happy to take the traitor off your

hands while you decide what you'll do with her."

Fucking Lutrin. Finvarra's eyes met mine. Surely, he wouldn't. He knew Lutrin was a—

"Fine," Finvarra said. He looked at me for a long moment, opened his mouth as if he wanted to say something, and then turned, stalking away.

The guards approached, and I shifted, snarling at them. I didn't want to hurt Finvarra's guards. Even if they were looking at me like I was a piece of shit. But Lutrin? He was fair game.

My wolf crouched, readying to rip out his throat. Finvarra should have known better than to leave him down here with me.

Lutrin's smile widened, and he glanced at one of the guards. The guard reached into his pocket, and I snapped warningly at him.

But the attack came from behind.

I sneezed, and a moment later, I'd shifted back to my human form.

"Wolfsbane." Lutrin smirked at me. "Hideously expensive and almost impossible to find, of course. It only blooms under the full moon in the middleground every few years. But the good news is we don't need much of it to stop you from shifting. And to drain you of that unnatural strength."

He jerked his head, and the guards attacked as one.

Even naked, weaponless, and without my strength, I held my own. For about ten seconds. The wolfsbane continued to weaken me until I stumbled, practically running into one of the guard's swords.

The guard's eyes widened, his mouth dropping open, and I caught the regret that flickered through his eyes.

I knew this man. Had joked with him multiple times.

Slumping to my knees, I felt blood slipping from my side.

"Just a flesh wound," Lutrin announced. "She's a werewolf. She'll heal it." He leaned closer to me. "I have a special place I'm taking you. You'll be broken afterward—completely useless. But you'll tell us what we need to know."

For the first time, true fear slid through me. Wherever Lutrin was taking me, he was keeping it from Finvarra.

I kept my face blank, refusing to cry. But Lutrin grinned at me anyway, and the guards hauled me up, carrying me out of the room.

twelve
Kyla

I'd assumed I was being dragged down to the dungeon. But the horror that had been waiting for me was much, much worse.

The magic in the room began reaching for me before Lutrin pushed me inside, immediately jumping back, his pulse thundering. He was no longer scared of me. No, it was whatever was in this empty room that had made him almost breathless with fear.

I sat on the cold stone floor and shivered. The wolfsbane had managed to do what nothing else had ever done.

It hadn't just removed my strength. It had silenced my wolf completely. I was completely, utterly human.

But I could still feel the walls of the room around me. Could sense tendrils of filthy magic slipping toward my body, readying to strike.

I took a deep breath, turning and crawling for the door.

But it was too late.

The nightmares… The memories… The worst moments of my life.

They came so quickly. One after the other.

And I was trapped, with no way to pull myself free.

#

There was Joel—both of us pretending he hadn't been

turned. But I was stupid then. And he could hear my racing heart. Could smell the sweat on my skin.

His eyes gleamed at me, no longer human, but filled with the same arrogance. Only it was worse this time, because he had all the power. He was either going to kill me or ruin my life.

"Oh, Kyla," he crooned. "You're so smart, baby, but you can't play with me anymore. I'm invincible now. And we'll be together forever."

I took a single step back. And I begged.

"No, Joel. Please. I don't want—"

He'd turned before I realized he'd moved. So fast, my mind couldn't process what I was seeing.

His fur was black, his eyes were wild, but all I could see were his teeth, so sharp and white.

And then he struck.

I'd turned to run, but he took me down in an instant. Those teeth burned like fire as he buried them in my shoulder. His paws hit my back, and my ribs snapped.

I screamed.

And then there was no more pain.

For a while.

I woke sometime later to a tongue on my face. Was Joel…hungry?

Our eyes met. He was still in his wolf form, and he stepped back, using his muzzle to nudge something toward me.

A dead man. Joel had gone hunting. Did he expect me to…eat the body?

I closed my eyes once more, ignoring his demanding

growl. I could feel death calling to me like a lover, ready to embrace me.

Despair clawed at me. Despair and something darker. A deep, unrelenting fury that made me more conscious.

My eyes opened to slits. I was lying in the dining room. And just feet away, the closet door was open a few inches.

In the closet, I could see my bright-red backpack. The bag I'd packed in preparation to leave.

I'd been at the airport. So close to freedom I could taste it. And then my flight was delayed.

Joel's friend's mother had called. They were missing. And like an idiot, I'd returned here, waiting for the news that he was dead.

Joel growled, and the slick, wet sound told me he was eating the body.

I looked at the backpack. At the future I'd lost. At the freedom I'd thrown away.

And I closed my eyes.

#

In the room, I struggled against those dark tendrils, making it to my knees. The door. I just had to get to the door.

#

I woke.

And I felt stronger.

This wasn't supposed to happen. I should be dead.

"Kyla?"

Joel's voice practically dripped smug satisfaction.

Somehow, against all odds, I was still alive.

I cracked my eyes open. My throat was so dry, my lips

split open when I attempted to speak.

Joel was grinning. "It's okay. You survived, baby. You'll be a wolf now. We'll start our own pack, you and me. My god, I thought it was a myth. Females don't survive. Except, you did."

He'd known he was killing me, and he'd bitten me anyway.

An icy, endless fury crawled through my body. I rolled onto my stomach, pushing myself to my knees.

Joel held out his hand.

I ignored it.

"Are you…upset?"

"You killed me."

"You're alive," he growled, and I glanced up at him. His eyes had turned wolf. "You should be thanking me."

"Thanking you?" I let out a low laugh and slowly got to my feet.

And then he struck.

His hand lashed out, knuckles meeting my cheek. He moved so fast, I hadn't been prepared.

I dropped to my knees, head spinning, stomach churning.

"I am your Alpha," he hissed. "You will respect me, Kyla Hill. Or you will learn consequences."

Every inch of my body went cold. My heart slowed.

Werewolves could live for hundreds of years.

Hundreds. Of. Years.

And I wouldn't tolerate one more day of this shit.

I'd rather be dead.

A strange sensation began to crawl up my spine.

No, no, no, no.

"It's okay." His voice was soothing once more. Joel had always kept me off-balance with his lightning-fast switches between adoration and disgust. "You're shifting into your wolf. Let her come."

I didn't want to. But I was prey in this form. So, I relaxed into it.

At first, there was pain. Agony ripped through me, and I gaped.

"It only hurts the first time," Joel said.

I ignored that. Pain disappeared, becoming tingles of sensation that danced across my skin.

I dropped to all fours. Except I wasn't on my hands and knees. No. I was staring at huge white paws.

"You're so beautiful," Joel crowed. "Made just for me."

I looked up. And our eyes met.

He exuded dominance. I could feel it itching at me, like an annoying mosquito buzzing around my head.

His eyes widened when I didn't drop my gaze.

"It can't be," he breathed. "Kyla, stop."

I took a single step closer. He swallowed. "It's okay to be angry. We'll figure it out. Together."

He was reaching for his gun. I opened my mouth and displayed my teeth.

He shifted, and a moment later, I was staring at a huge black wolf.

He lunged at me, but I was smaller. Faster. And when I looked at him, he couldn't meet my eyes.

My claws slashed. I launched myself toward him, still clumsy in this form. But my teeth found flesh.

And I ripped out his throat.

\#

Finvarra

"You put her in the nightmare room?"

Lutrin frowned at me. "But of course. You said to punish her, Your Majesty."

My fault. I'd known she hated Lutrin. Had thought to punish her by allowing him to take her to the dungeon. But I hadn't specified my orders, and he'd gotten his revenge after all.

Bitter regret pushed aside the worst of my rage.

"She will be incoherent by now."

Lutrin smiled. "Ah. You wanted to be able to question her. I will see to it that she is removed and given the truth serum."

I ground my teeth. I would deal with *Lutrin* later. "I'll free her myself. Leave."

He seemed to realize exactly what he'd done, because he began trembling. "Your Majesty…"

I just looked at him.

"I'll get the serum." He practically ran from the room, almost bumping into Tae as he stepped inside. Of course he'd been listening.

"You pushed her into this," he accused.

I had. I'd known exactly what I was doing when I'd told her I had her right where I wanted her. And I'd known her tears weren't from a fight with Evie. She'd been crying because she was still planning to steal my sword. I'd simply pushed her into it a little quicker—making things easier on both of us.

Tae was still waiting for my response. "She was always going to betray me, Tae. I just made it happen faster."

He shook his head. "Instead of talking about it, you decided to force her into moving. She got under your skin, and you couldn't handle it. And because she's as emotionally constipated as you are, she took the shot."

"You want to psychoanalyze me? Do it on your own time. I have a traitor to interrogate."

His mouth dropped open before he snapped it closed. "I hope this is worth it, Fin. I really hope you know what you're doing here."

#

Kyla

"Kyla."

I frowned, turning at Nathaniel's voice. He sounded tense in a way I didn't often hear.

Ian stood next to him. My brother. A smile began to spread across my face. He'd found me. He did care.

But…

No.

That was disgust I could smell. And even if I hadn't been a werewolf, I wouldn't have missed the way he wrinkled his nose, the way his mouth thinned. He looked at me as if I were a monster.

Because in his mind, I was.

I waited for him to say something. Anything.

His eyes narrowed.

And I flinched.

Next to me, I could sense Danica's shock.

But I was too focused on Ian to even glance at her.

He knew. He knew I was a werewolf. And I knew my brother well enough to know he hated me for it.

Maybe...maybe he just needed to talk to me. To see I was still the same person.

I sucked in a breath and pasted a smile on my face.

"Ian—"

He shook his head. "Not only are you a werewolf, but you're colluding with filthy demons?"

Not only *was I a werewolf.*

Because that was bad enough. And yet I was a monster who hung out with other monsters.

"These are my friends, Ian. This is Danica, and this is—"

"I don't care."

I stiffened, and Nathaniel moved close. It had likely been difficult for him to allow Ian into his territory without fully being prepared. Now he wasn't going to tolerate my brother speaking to me that way.

For a moment, I wished everyone could just disappear. So I could just talk to my brother. So I could explain.

"Watch how you speak to her," Nathaniel said, his voice low and dripping warning.

"Kyla is my sister."

"And she's my wolf."

Ian swallowed, and our eyes met. "So that's how it works? You've completely turned your back on us?"

The grief and sadness mingled with fury, and I let out a low growl.

Ian paled at the sound, but I was already stalking toward him.

"You accuse me of turning my back on you? Where were you when Joel was preventing me from seeing my friends? When he declared we were moving two hours from my office, and I had to quit my job? When I didn't get to say goodbye to Granddad before he died? Where the fuck were you then? Oh, I know. You were best buddies with Joel's friends, and you didn't want to piss any of them off."

Nathaniel snarled. And I felt him begin to shift. Danica's strange power gathered around her, Vas spread his wings, and Virtus…

He let loose a roar that almost shook the ground.

Fucking great.

The look Nathaniel sent me told me, without words, that he was pissed. Both at me—for not warning him about my brother, and for *me—for having a brother who would turn his back on me publicly this way.*

It was one hell of a look.

Ian took a step back, and my wolf could scent his fear. She delighted in it, while I just felt sick.

"Why did you come here?" I asked.

"To find you. I've searched for you since you went missing."

"Why? To see if you could tolerate being around a werewolf?"

Nothing. I forced a laugh. "These are my friends. That's the future underqueen who you just insulted. She's guarded my back for the past several weeks. Oh, and she gave me a job."

"Kyla—"

"Leave, Ian. There's nothing for you here."

Ian glanced at the people I'd gathered around me. Our eyes met, one final time, and he nodded.

Then he turned and walked back to his car.

I watched him go, and something broke inside me.

I jolted awake. The room. I was in a room. I had to get out of here. This place would *kill* me. It would—

#

The dungeon was cold. Even in my wolf form, I shivered. But it was the cuff around my neck that chilled my bones.

The stench of death and rot and mildew wound toward me, stuffing itself up my nose. Where was Danica?

Was she okay?

I attempted to shift, but my vision darkened at the edges, my body unable to take its human form with the cuff around my neck.

Days passed.

Thinking of Danica hurt.

Thinking of the life I'd had hurt.

Thinking of my pack…

So I began to push that part of myself away. I knew it was dangerous. But it was the only way we would be able to live through this.

Of the two of us, my wolf was the survivor. She was the one who would keep us alive, who would make our enemies beg.

I roused myself long enough to watch as the human woman appeared occasionally, bringing meat.

The mage spoke occasionally, and my wolf fantasized about his death. She'd never liked him, and she planned how we would kill him slowly. How we would hear him beg.

That thought was strange enough to shake me from my misery. My wolf didn't play with her food. She was a quick killer, interested only in survival. Was she changing down here, too?

Then the woman with the green eyes came once more. Only this time, she brought something that smelled of witch.

Black witch.

She attempted to place her dark spell in my cage. In my territory. I readied myself to rip her hand off at the wrist.

"No," my wolf whispered. The shock of hearing her for the first time made me go still. "This strange thing smells like pack."

The human woman placed her black magic in the corner of my territory. I allowed it, but I showed her my teeth. A warning.

She spoke, and I ignored her words, my wolf already focused on the link it could feel between us.

#

Oh god, oh god, oh god. I managed to make it to my feet. Because I knew what was coming next. It was so stupid. So fucking small in the grand scheme of all the bad shit that had happened in my life.

And yet that one memory had the power to break me.

But I could feel it come for me, and I dropped to my

stomach. A howl ripped from my throat.

#

Her name was Nessie. She was sixteen hands, a chestnut, and my best friend. She had a bone-rattling trot, a smooth canter, and a big, swooping gallop.

I'd worked at the stables for years—something my therapist had suggested after my parents died when I was a teenager.

I'd spent thousands of hours mucking out the stables, hauling hay, and grooming in return for time in the saddle. And Nessie was my favorite.

High-spirited but never mean with it, wild-hearted but never dangerous. We'd ride for hours in the forest near the stables. When my parents died, she taught me that it was okay to be happy sometimes, even if my heart was still broken. When Grandpa died, and I didn't get to say goodbye, I found comfort in Nessie and the routine of riding. Even when Joel took everything else, I still found a way to get to her.

Right after Joel turned me…after I gained enough control to be human for a few moments, I'd gone a little crazy. I'd thought…I'd thought if I could just get to Nessie, it would prove everything would be okay.

The horses scented me before I opened the stable doors.

They were going nuts. Nessie…

Nessie reared, her eyes rolling, her terror saturating the air.

If I didn't leave, she would hurt herself.

They would all hurt themselves.

Because I wasn't Kyla anymore.

I was a monster.

\#

I let out a choked sob. That wasn't all of it. And the room knew.

\#

Months later, when I'd been with Nathaniel's pack for long enough that I no longer struggled for control...

I went to a witch.

A witch who gave me a charm and swore it would hide my scent.

I didn't go back to Nessie.

I'd already frightened her enough.

Instead, I went somewhere new. At night, when no one could see me.

A black horse was grazing in a paddock, visible to me only because of my new vision. My heart tripped in my chest, and I took a step closer.

Horses were prey animals. And they were smart.

Either the horse caught my scent, or it knew I wasn't human by the way I'd moved.

It bolted.

\#

I was hyperventilating now. Small. Lonely. Desperate. Willing anyone to save me from this horror. It was almost amusing, how my worst memories—the ones that cut and bled—weren't the ones anyone would expect. The trauma of being turned into a werewolf was nothing compared to Nessie being frightened of me.

Of suddenly being a predator to the horses I'd loved so much.

I could feel another memory coming, and this time, I let out a choked scream. I didn't even know who I was screaming for. I was so fucking stupid, thinking I could pit myself against the unseelie king.

I'd walked right into this, the moment I'd walked into his arms.

thirteen
Finvarra

The nightmare room had been my grandfather's creation. It wasn't enough to punish his enemies' bodies. To make them bleed and scream. He wanted to break their minds. To show them all of their worst memories, turned into nightmares, over and over again.

And now Kyla…

She stole from you. Betrayed you. Lied to you. Would have stolen your only chance at revenge.

And I didn't fucking care.

I'd also goaded her into taking action. I'd felt myself *enjoying* her. Felt myself wondering what would come out of that smart mouth next. Felt myself letting down my guard. Becoming *weak*.

And I knew the little wolf. Taunting her about having her right where I wanted her?

It had been guaranteed to make her take action. She couldn't help herself.

The nightmare room.

She would never forgive me.

I fisted my hands and stalked down the hall, ignoring the guards. This was what I'd wanted. I'd wanted to see her betray me again. Now, I could finally get to the bottom of why she was here. I had an excuse to use truth serum.

Even if the thought made me want to roar.

The nightmare room was below my dungeon, through a hidden passage few knew of. My grandfather had created the room as a particularly sadistic way to deal with his enemies—and to break the spies he found in his court.

The walls whispered as I stepped inside, the magic pulling at me. The nightmare room had tasted me before, and it wanted me yet again.

But I was king now. My father wouldn't be shutting me in here again.

No, instead, *I* was the one who broke minds by using the room.

Bile burned up my throat as my eyes found Kyla, curled on the stone floor.

She looked so tiny, so fragile.

She was in my arms within a moment, and I stared down at her beautiful face.

Her dark hair was limp, her lips almost bloodless. She cracked open her eyes, and even they seemed drained of color. Those eyes glittered at me with malice. But I could see the fear.

I'd gotten what I'd wanted. The wolf who feared nothing and no one…feared *me*.

Her eyes rolled back in her head. The nightmare room was still working on her. I strode out, carrying her up the stairs and directly into one of my cells.

Lutrin had already set up what I needed, a single metal chair waiting—the threat of Naud chains hanging from it.

I gritted my teeth, steeling myself against what would

come next.

Placing her in the chair, I crouched in front of her.

"Kyla."

Her eyes opened once more. A quick glance around us and her lip curled.

I *hated* when she gave me that look. Something she would know perfectly well.

"I'm going to give you another chance to tell me why you keep attempting to steal my sword," I said.

She laughed hoarsely, and I fought to leash my temper.

"I don't want to hurt you."

Her laugh turned choked, until she cut it off abruptly.

"Lies are beneath you, Unseelie King."

So be it.

I'd heard Lutrin approaching, the truth serum in his hand. I turned to him, but it was Tae who stepped up behind him, his eyes wild.

"Don't do this."

"*She* broke *my* trust."

"You set her up."

I didn't answer that. He just swallowed, his face pale. "If you do this, Finvarra, there's no coming back from it."

I glanced at the wolf, who was ignoring all of us. "So be it."

I crouched in front of her once more. "Do I need to use the Naud chains and collar to prevent you from shifting, or will you behave?"

"Finvarra!" Tae stepped into the cell. Kyla ignored him, her gaze on me.

Lutrin shifted his weight behind me, and that drew her

attention. She smiled at him. "Someday, I'm going to rip out your throat. You won't even see me coming."

He paled at her words. But his gaze slid to Tae and me, and he squared his shoulders, opening his mouth.

"Leave," Tae ordered him.

Lutrin glanced at me. I nodded.

Kyla's gaze shifted to Tae. He was staring at her pleadingly.

"Please, Kyla." His expression was grim. He knew the stubborn wolf well enough now to know his logic would fall on deaf ears. "Please, just tell us why you want the sword."

A bitter smile curved her lips. "It won't be enough for him." She gestured to me, her eyes still on Tae. "He won't believe me. So, let's get this over with."

If I'd thought that meant she would cooperate, I would have been wrong. No, it took both of us to hold her down— Tae only cooperating because I threatened to use the chains, and he'd watched her eyes turn stark at my words.

Her teeth clamped down on my hand, semi-shifted. Ignoring the pain, I squeezed her jaw, Tae pinching her nose until she was forced to open her mouth.

The spell took hold instantly. Even werewolves, who retained some natural defense from magic, were not immune. My ancestors had made sure of that.

"Why do you keep attempting to steal my sword?"

Kyla's head dropped, and when she spoke, her voice was *different*. Lifeless.

"You must return the sword to its true sheath or the realms will burn."

I stiffened. Next to me, Tae let out a hoarse laugh. I

ignored him, focusing on the little wolf.

"That sounds like a prophecy. Who gave it to you?"

"Selina."

The witch who had allowed me to track Kyla when she entered my own realm.

"What do you know of the true sheath?"

Kyla bit at her lip until it bled. I just waited her out. Finally, the serum overtook her will.

"Demigod. Guatemala."

Frustration prickled down my spine. "This would be a lot easier if you stopped fighting the serum and just told me what I needed to know."

She lifted her gaze, and the hatred in her eyes was so encompassing, my chest clenched.

Gone. She was gone. She was right *here*, and yet she was gone. Never again would she smile at me. Never again would she let me touch her.

Her smile told me she knew what I was thinking. The bitter fury on her face told me I was right.

"You want to know? Fine."

It all came out. I'd already known the demigod was the source of the mages' power, but Kyla ground out the reasoning behind sending him to sleep. The sheath he wore, the way he'd asked for his sword, and the timeline.

"Winter solstice. How do you know?"

"Etchings on the cave wall," she muttered.

"So you decided to do this all alone."

"Selina said I had to."

"Selina betrayed you."

She flinched. Then she let out a bitter laugh. "Yeah.

Obviously, it's going around."

"I didn't betray you," I hissed. "*You* did this. You could have told me why you needed the sword at any time."

"And you would have handed it over, I suppose? Would have given up your revenge based on my word. Tell me, when would you have gotten tired of me and thrown me into your dungeon?"

She laughed again at whatever she saw on my face. Tae had begun pacing restlessly.

"What happens when the demigod goes back to sleep?" Tae asked. It was a rhetorical question, but Kyla was forced to answer anyway.

"The portals opened because when he woke up, there was enough power in our realm to sustain them. When he goes back to sleep, it's more than likely the portals will close."

Tae swallowed. Then he glanced at me. "Surely, she's done now."

Kyla ignored the question, her gaze on the stone floor.

"Yes," I said. "You may return to your bedroom," I told her.

She ignored me, and I fought not to kick out at the wall. "Or fucking stay down here. I don't care."

She let out a hollow laugh. Within a moment, she'd shifted, returning to the form that made her feel safest. The wolf wouldn't look at me, prowling past both of us, out of the cell.

Tae turned to me. "You're a cold, heartless bastard."

"I'm protecting my people."

"Yeah? From where I'm standing, you're just like your

father."

He knew exactly where to hit. I ground my teeth, but he was already stalking out.

My gaze had already found the empty metal chair. But all I could see was the horror in Kyla's eyes when I'd drugged her.

I was the betrayer here. And she was the one attempting to save my life, along with everyone else's.

She was impulsive, impetuous, and occasionally immoral.

But she'd come here hoping to prevent the realms from burning.

#

Kyla

I lay on the floor of my bedroom and stared at the wall. I could still feel the truth serum. Could feel it making me face all the truths I'd kept inside for so long.

My eyes burned with the need to cry. To release just a tiny sliver of the pain that was poisoning every inch of me.

But I refused. I wouldn't fall apart here. Not in my enemy's castle while he strolled around somewhere below me, smug with the knowledge that he'd broken me. He'd won.

I should never have fallen for his charm. Should never have surrendered to his touch. Should definitely never have fucking *felt* something when he gave me that crooked smile.

I was a stupid woman.

But I wasn't a victim.

I would get out of this place.

For a moment, homesickness shoved into my chest, as sharp and cold as a blade.

I was impulsive, and I was arrogant. I should have told Nathaniel what I was doing and why.

How could I even trust that Selina had told me the truth about needing to steal the sword alone? She'd already broken her word to me. Was she using me for her own plans once more?

It didn't matter. I'd figure that out later. For now, I needed to pick myself up off the floor and work on an escape plan.

I choked on a sob. It was dry, my eyes still unable to form tears. But the sound was enough to shock me into action.

I sat up, right as my door opened.

I almost shifted, ready to rip out a throat or two. But that was... "Virtus?" I gaped at the griffin. He just angled his head, although his paws lifted as he danced in place. Clearly, he was pleased with himself.

"How the hell did you get in here?"

He stared at me and, as usual when talking to the griffin, whatever he wanted me to know appeared straight in my head.

No one kept track of his movements. He went where he pleased. If he wasn't with the wolves, they assumed he was visiting Meredith and Vas, or even in the underworld with Danica and Samael.

Instead, he was here.

He was here because Evie had gotten worried when I

was supposed to contact her and didn't.

My heart fluttered at the thought of the unseelie getting their hands on him. "You need to get out of here. I…I underestimated Finvarra before. But he's an evil bastard. If he catches you, I don't know what he'll do to you."

Virtus just stepped closer until he was nuzzling my face. I closed my eyes, something squeezing in my chest.

He smelled like pack. Like *home*.

"You know where the sword is? You saw Tae with it?"

Of course. It had to be removed from Finvarra's dad's study. I hadn't expected the unseelie king to give it to Tae, which was likely why he'd done it.

I smiled. Finvarra could prepare for any number of things, but Virtus was *different*.

"Okay. Let's get the sword and get out of here. It's time to save the worlds."

fourteen
Finvarra

The reason the nightmare room was so monstrous?

It recorded the memories it brought to the surface.

And that had allowed both my grandfather and father to *change* those memories and make their victims relive them. An excellent way to make their enemies question their own minds. To make them insane.

Unfortunately, whoever sat on the unseelie throne was also tied to the nightmare room. My father had warned me of the consequences, but I'd never planned to use the room.

It didn't matter.

I sat at my desk, teeth clenched as the magic that tied me to this castle—and the nightmare room—assaulted me with the memories it had dragged from Kyla's mind.

Over and over again, it showed me the moments that had almost broken her…and how she had survived each one.

By the time the room was done, I was almost vomiting, a silence ward thick around my rooms.

I'd done that to her.

To Kyla.

To my little wolf.

Who was just trying to save the realms.

I needed to talk to her.

After what the nightmare room had shown me, I understood Kyla on a deep level. So much had been done to her without her consent. She'd never wanted to be a werewolf. She took orders from Nathaniel every day, and even though her wolf responded, the woman remembered a time when she owed her allegiance to no one and nothing but herself.

I'd violated her consent once again.

To see the horror in her eyes as she'd come close to *begging*. The grim resolve and the wasteland of her eyes after I'd used the truth serum...

It wasn't often that I admitted I was wrong. I so rarely *was* wrong. But this time, I was wrong in the worst possible way.

Her face flashed in my mind, her eyes laughing down at me as she pushed my hair behind my ear, a grin on that beautiful face.

Stalking into the bathroom, I splashed water on my face, unable to even meet my own eyes in the mirror.

I owed her an apology. I pushed open the door to my rooms and stalked toward Kyla's bedroom. More than an apology. I owed her an explanation. I'd work with her to save the realms. I'd fucking *crawl* if she asked it of me.

"Your Majesty."

"Not now."

"But, Your Majesty—"

I turned, and whatever the guard saw in my eyes made him pale. Tae appeared behind him, out of breath. "Fin. It's bad. I had the sword, but this fucking *griffin* appeared and stole it."

I whirled, striding into the closest room—an empty sitting room. My stomach sank as Kyla shot past the window, on the back of the recently healed griffin.

I could *feel* archers aiming at her, and I projected my voice over my entire kingdom.

"Hold your fire!"

The sword was slung over one delicate shoulder, and she leaned forward over the griffin, likely cheering him on. He turned toward the portal.

Kyla didn't bother looking back. Didn't even turn her head, although I was sure she could feel my eyes on her.

No, she just shot her middle finger into the air and sailed through the portal, back to her own realm.

Where she'd always belonged.

#

Kyla

Arriving back at my pack felt a lot like returning with my tail between my legs. Sure, I may have flown in on Virtus, a legendary sword slung over my shoulder and a don't-fuck-with-me scowl on my face, but that meant nothing in the face of Nathaniel's "I'm not angry, I'm disappointed" look.

Sighing, I jumped off Virtus and strode over to my Alpha to face the music.

"I guess you're pissed, huh?"

Nathaniel just watched Virtus, who was having some secret conversation with him. Nathaniel's lips curved, but the smile dropped from his face when he glanced at me.

"I'm not just pissed, Kyla. I'm confused."

I opened my mouth, unsure *what* I was going to say, but Liam appeared, out of breath. "Dominance fight," he managed to get out.

Dominance fights were common in a pack our size, but Nathaniel liked to keep an eye on them whenever he could.

Nathaniel nodded. "I'll be right there."

Liam walked away, and Nathaniel glanced at the sword still slung over my shoulder. He let a hint of his power out. Oh yeah, pissed was an understatement. I dropped my gaze automatically.

"Give me the sword."

I ground my teeth but handed it over.

"Let me be very clear," he said, and I had to fight the urge to slam my hands over my ears. "You will not take this sword to Guatemala alone. Do you understand?"

"Yes." I took a deep breath. "I'm guessing you have some kind of punishment in mind."

"Of course." Nathaniel turned and strode away, not giving me another glance.

I took a shuddering breath. Around me, the pack was whispering, as if I couldn't *hear* them.

"Yes, I went to the unseelie kingdom. And yes, I stole the sword that'll save all your lives. You're fucking welcome."

I hadn't done it for the glory, but their stares and gossip? That was some bullshit right there.

The breeze carried Evie's scent toward me, and I turned. She grinned at me, and something in my chest relaxed. At least one person didn't think I was a piece of shit.

"You got it."

"I got it."

"I want to hear all about it. But I have to go. I'm meeting Aubrey."

"Any news from him about Selina?"

Her expression turned bleak. "No. I'm worried about her."

I didn't bother telling her about Selina's betrayal. It would only eat away at her the way it was eating at me, and there would be more than enough time for that later tonight.

Virtus strolled up to us, and Evie grinned at him. "You kicked ass," she told him.

"You sent him?"

"I told him what was going on. I couldn't go, 'cause, you know…act of war. But Virtus is the most neutral party. And he knows Finvarra's castle like the back of his paw."

I leaned down and nuzzled him. And now Finvarra would never trust him again. "I'm sorry."

He looked me in the eye. Finvarra would understand.

"I don't think so, buddy. But it's okay. You don't want to be friends with that fuckhead, anyway."

He nuzzled me and wandered away.

I glanced at Evie. "I need to go see Danica in the next couple of days."

"Tell her I say hi and I'll see her soon."

I studied Evie's expression. "You haven't told her yet, have you? About the portals."

"No." Blue-green eyes filled with tears, and I pulled Evie into a hug.

"Do you want me to tell her?" My life couldn't get much worse. I may as well break another one of my best friend's hearts while I was on a roll.

"No. No, please. I want to tell her."

"Okay. I won't say a word."

Evie pulled back and wiped at her face. "She's the queen of the underworld. She's connected to it. I don't think that realm would even survive if she couldn't access it anymore. And at the same time… There's this part of me… the part that's so used to feeling abandoned—" Evie's voice cracked, and my own eyes filled.

"That part needs your sister to choose you."

"Yeah. It's not logical, and I would never actually want that for her. I guess it's all mixed up. The thought of never seeing her again, Kyla… I don't know if I'll survive it."

"I know." I felt the same. God, the whole situation was so fucked. Was this what life was about? Just one gut punch after another?

"I need to go. Aubrey will be waiting." She attempted a smile.

"Look after yourself. I'll see you soon."

The area had cleared out, the rest of the wolves making themselves scarce. For the first time in a while, I had no idea what to do next.

If it were up to me, I'd take the sword directly down to Guatemala.

Unfortunately, Nathaniel had nixed that plan.

The answer was obvious. I *could* find the sword. Because I might not be able to go to Guatemala alone, but I could take someone with me. But, there was no way any of my pack members would go with me.

Something strange fluttered in my chest. Was it…panic?

It felt almost like a sense of impending doom.

Frowning, I stalked toward my house.

My place came into view, with its wide porch, the swing I loved, and the cozy rooms. All of a sudden, it seemed too small. Stifling. Crowded with memories from another woman.

I turned and stalked back into the forest, staying to the marked path for now. I wasn't aiming for anywhere in particular, but the sound of laughter reached my ears long before the cabins came into view.

If I'd been in my wolf form, those ears would have pricked. Instead, I moseyed down the path and leaned against a tree.

After everything that had happened, I'd forgotten to check in on the people here. These were the people we'd rescued from the HFE labs. Nathaniel had negotiated with the FBI, and he'd chartered a plane, taking anyone with the tiniest drop of paranormal blood with him.

Unfortunately for the FBI, that had been most people. HFE was all about experimenting.

Even Finvarra had ordered some of his people to build the new cabins. Although, knowing the unseelie, there hadn't been any physical labor happening. No, they'd likely used their power.

A group of kids ran by. One of them saw me out of the corner of her eye and froze. Alert.

I held up my hands.

"I'm not going to hurt you."

Angling her blond head, she took me in. Her friends returned, surrounding her and watching me.

She looked human, but she sniffed at me and smiled. "You're a wolf."

"I sure am."

"You're a *girl* wolf."

"That's right."

"I'm a girl wolf too."

One of the boys snorted. "You can't even shift." His face darkened. "None of us can."

HFE had given these kids just enough wolf genes to improve their senses, just enough to long to run, but not enough to shift.

Fury rolled through me, and the little girl stepped back.

"I'm not mad at you," I said gently, crouching. "I'm mad at the people who were mean to you."

She nodded. "I'm mad at them too. Mama says I'm allowed to be."

I could feel eyes on me, and I lifted my gaze. Across the clearing, a woman was standing outside her cabin, her eyes on me. I lifted my hand in a wave, and after a moment, she lifted hers back.

"Amanda. Dinner."

The little girl sighed. "Will you come visit again?"

My throat tightened as I surveyed the cabins, the people going about their business, the kids—no longer caged.

"Yeah," I said hoarsely. "I'll come visit again."

She smiled, and the kids dispersed. I continued watching for a long moment.

I'd forgotten. That the world sucked sometimes, but that it was also beautiful. That no matter how bad it got, somewhere, some kid was still being called in for dinner.

I'd planned to go to Meredith's and drink until I couldn't feel anymore.

Now, I'd go see her because I missed my friend. And because when life was hard, you had to cling to the ones you loved. Or else you'd have nothing to fight for.

Naomi nodded to me as I stepped back onto the path. I nodded back, but both of us continued walking. I made my way back toward the street, hoping someone had taken pity on me and brought my car back. I wouldn't exactly blame them if they hadn't, but I also wasn't above a little grand theft auto.

It was parked outside Nathaniel's, keys on the front seat, doors unlocked. It wasn't as if anyone was going to come into wolf territory and attempt to steal our cars. Sliding in, I drove on autopilot until the emotions were once more buried behind a numb shield.

Vas was outside chatting with Orin when I pulled up, sliding neatly into the spot they'd begun reserving for friends and family.

Both men grinned at me as I stepped out of the car, and it was almost startling to see someone look at me without censure in their eyes.

"Kyla." Vas wrapped an arm around my shoulders. "I heard you've been a bad girl."

I elbowed him, and he rubbed at his chest with a grin. His wings were hidden, but I could feel the feathers brushing up against my body as I hugged him back.

"*I* heard you've been in the unseelie realm," Orin said. "How long was it anyway?"

"Too damn long," I muttered. "I went after I headed

down to Guatemala."

"That's right." Vas grinned. "You certainly have been busy."

I winced. He just laughed. Orin nodded at me, taking his keys from his pocket. "Glad you made it back okay."

"Thanks."

Vas pulled me inside. "Mere, Kyla's here."

I took one look at Meredith and laughed, delighted. Time passed slightly differently in various realms, but I hadn't thought I'd been away that long. Yet, at some point, Meredith had begun to show. Now, she had the cutest little bump.

"Get over here," she said, pulling me in for a hug. "I was worried."

Guilt pricked me. Of course she was. Because I hadn't given anyone any warning. I'd just disappeared. Maybe Nathaniel had a fucking point.

"You look like you need a drink."

"Yes, please."

She wasn't yet waddling, but it was coming soon. Vas and I shared a grin as she rounded the bar, and Meredith looked up in time to catch it.

She pointed a finger at us, but her lips trembled as she returned her attention to the bottle of whiskey she was pulling down off a shelf.

"I'll do that," Vas said.

"We've had this discussion," Mere said in a singsong voice. Orin took a seat next to me and shook his head.

"It's always like this," he whispered.

I hadn't realized how much I needed this. How much I

needed just to be around some normalcy.

I took the drink Mere slid me. "How are the renovations going?"

She beamed. "Great." She nodded at the blue plastic hanging in front of the left wall. "Things are really coming along now. But no distracting me. How are you? What happened in the unseelie realm?"

I sighed and filled them all in.

"That son of a bitch," Vas said. A glass fell off the bar, and we all jumped. His wings had obviously spread with his fury.

"Yeah, well, at least we have the sword."

"What can we do?"

"Nothing. Evie said we're preparing for battle against the mages. I'd hoped I could slide in there and shove the sword into the sheath, but the reality is… Gabriel is still a threat, and he'll have that cave guarded. Not to mention, Nathaniel won't let me touch the sword."

"Can you blame him?" Meredith asked gently.

I narrowed my eyes at her. She reached out and grabbed my hand. "Nathaniel was so, so worried, Kyla. We all know why you did it. And we're so fucking lucky that you're *you*. That you're so fearless. But the rest of us… We're not fearless. We were all so afraid that something would happen to you."

"I'm not fearless," I muttered.

Vas rounded the bar and patted me on the shoulder. "You seem to think you're disposable. All we're saying is you're not. And people are probably going to be pissed at you until you understand just how much they love you."

Ugh. I couldn't even argue with them, because they were being too sweet.

"Now I'm even more depressed."

They both laughed. Mere glanced at her phone. "Vas got tickets for the theatre. Samael has a box. You want to come?"

"No. No, you guys go have your date night. I just wanted to stop in and say hi."

Finishing my drink, I hugged each of them goodbye, pasted a smile on my face, and wandered out to my car.

With nothing to do, nothing else to steal my attention, the only thing I had left to focus on was Finvarra.

I drove home, my mind whirring. Nathaniel's lights were on when I parked outside his house, and I could hear the sounds of pack. Laughter, teasing, arguments…

I'd wanted to be back here so badly when I was running by myself on the full moon. And yet, now all I wanted was to be alone.

The nightmares I'd seen in Finvarra's room…they'd been given new life. Some of them, I hadn't had in years, and yet they'd always lurked, ready and waiting.

Now, I knew if I went to sleep, they'd be waiting.

I could forgive Finvarra for many things. After all, I wasn't perfect.

But I could never forgive him for that.

Or for the way he'd watched with those cold eyes while I'd been *forced* to tell him what he wanted to know. The way he'd threatened the Naud chains—all while knowing exactly how close I'd come to losing my humanity forever the last time my wolf had been suppressed.

I stopped a few feet from my home. Turning away, I stripped off my clothes and left them in a pile. With a thought, I was wolf once more, and I padded into the forest.

I ran for hours. When I was finally exhausted, I made my way back toward the cabins and picked a spot outside, beneath the stars.

Curling up, I fell into a deep sleep.

I woke to rain. At first it was light, just a drizzle. I curled up beneath the tree, tail over my face. The drizzle turned to true rain. In the distance, thunder rumbled, followed seconds later by lightning.

My wolf didn't mind the rain. But I would need to find a leafy shrub or a hollow under a log if I was going to get a decent sleep.

A scent reached me moments before strong arms lifted me up. Nathaniel.

I let out a warning growl, which he ignored. I'd expected him to take me back to my house, but he was heading in the opposite direction. Evie was waiting with a stack of towels on his porch, and he placed me back on my feet, both of them silently rubbing away the worst of the water.

I could just shift, but…I needed to be wolf right now.

I curled up, planning to sleep on the towel beneath the covered porch, but Nathaniel was lifting me into his arms once more.

Evie yawned and followed us up the stairs. Nathaniel dumped me on his bed, and Evie slipped in the other side. They left a Kyla-sized hollow between them, and I tucked myself into it.

Nathaniel's eyes met mine, and he stroked my ear.

"It will be okay."
I just closed my eyes and nuzzled close.

fifteen
Finvarra

Just months ago, the werewolf Alpha had come to me with a request. He wished for me to give him the book that had caused so much pain and suffering, so he could follow Kyla and Evelyn into Taraghlan's castle.

I'd sat in my library and thought through my options, pleased with the idea of Nathaniel being forced to grind his teeth while he asked for what he wanted.

Now, I was in the exact same position.

Unsurprisingly, I didn't care for it.

"You want me to *what?*" Nathaniel eyed me in the way he did when he was imagining tearing out my throat. Usually, I enjoyed watching his boring lethal fantasies play out in his eyes. Today, I didn't have time for it.

I kept my face expressionless. "Like it or not, we will soon go to war. As allies. The mages are currently consolidating their power. My spies have reported that more mages have been given access to magic than ever before. And they will fight next to Taraghlan's seelie army.

"I have studied that army's capacity for centuries. I know exactly how much power the light fae have, how many men are in each of his legions. I know how many legions are in his military and how they will choose to attack on the battlefield near the demigod. I know that, even with the demons, the unseelie, and the werewolves, we will be outnumbered so severely with Taraghlan's men that the field will be stained with blood."

Nathaniel's eyes brightened, his wolf peering out at me. I stared back at it.

"How is his military so large?" he asked.

"The seelie kingdom is more populated than mine." I shrugged. "And Taraghlan favors the use of brutal methods I refuse to engage in."

"What kinds of brutal methods?"

"The kinds that involve using his least powerful people as little more than cannon fodder. Putting them on the front lines and using his power to take away their fear."

"So they will charge to their deaths, but at least take us with them."

"Yes."

"And your answer is to kill Taraghlan. For the good of the *war*."

Nathaniel's words were lightly sarcastic, but I shook my head. "No. I will kill Taraghlan for all he has cost me and my family. But all of us will benefit from that death immensely."

"I'll consider it."

I watched the Alpha, but his expression was carefully neutral. He had been alive for a fraction of my life-span, yet he'd already mastered his emotions enough while negotiating that I truly couldn't tell what he was thinking.

"There's one more thing."

He bared his teeth, and the mask disappeared. Ah. *There*

was the protective fury.

"You want to talk to me about Kyla."

I stretched my legs out, forcing nonchalance. I hadn't missed the white fur clinging to his jeans this morning. The dark monster inside me knew this man considered Kyla a sister, but it didn't care. He'd spent time with her, while I'd been forced to pace restlessly, simmering in self-loathing.

I wrapped my discipline around myself like a blanket.

"Yes," I said. "I want to talk to you about Kyla."

#

Kyla

Two days later, I was finally able to sleep in my own bed again. I was still shuddering awake each night as nightmares found me, but I'd conquered those dreams before. Now I just had to conquer them again.

My biggest problem was that Nathaniel wouldn't engage with me about the plans for the sword.

If I didn't know him better, I'd think he didn't even care. Since I *did* know him, I also knew he was planning something he was keeping from me. And that really pissed me off.

He knew I had to be the one to sheathe the sword. I might be…annoyed at Selina, but I trusted her that much, and I knew Nathaniel did too.

Evie wasn't taking any new clients as we prepared for war, and Nathaniel had refused to give me any responsibilities regarding the preparations. So all I could do was pace and plan for the action I couldn't take. It was more than a little depressing.

"Kyla."

A dead weight pressed on my chest, even as a vast chasm opened inside me. A hot ache burned up the back of my throat, and I slowly turned.

Finvarra stood in front of me, just a few feet from my house. In *my* territory. The unseelie king looked so normal, so composed and unemotional, I wanted to rip out his throat. He gave me a faint smile, as if he were reading my mind.

"What are you doing here?"

"Speaking with Nathaniel. I miss you, little wolf."

"Like I give a shit."

"Why didn't you tell me why you needed the sword?"

The words weren't accusatory, but they rubbed my fur the wrong way all the same. How *dare* he?

"I was going to," I hissed. "And then I heard you speaking to Lutrin about how, if I didn't give you what you wanted, you'd move me from the tower to your fucking *dungeon*."

"Ah."

"Ah? You know what, Finvarra? I've got your sword, and that's all I wanted from you. So get the fuck out of my life."

"You little liar. You wanted more than that."

I curled my lip at him. "I can get fae dick anywhere."

His eyes turned icy. "Fuck, you're a piece of work."

"Right back at you."

"I was playing with Lutrin," he ground out. "He has been betraying me to Taraghlan for decades."

"Surprise fucking surprise." My wolf had hated him

from the moment I'd met him, and *she* had excellent instincts. About everyone except Finvarra. She still wanted to curl up next to him. "You still let him put me in that room of horrors."

"I wasn't aware that you'd been put there. The moment I found out, I had you removed."

"Yeah, so you could shove a truth serum down my throat." Talking to him was just making me angrier. "You know what? I don't have to deal with you any longer. In fact, I never have to deal with you again. I've got your sword, so you can go eat a bag of dicks."

"You *don't* have my sword. *I* have my sword."

My mouth dropped open at that, and Finvarra's gaze slid down to my lips, his eyes darkening.

"What are you talking about?"

Amusement flickered in those strange eyes. "A little deal I made with both Samael and Nathaniel. I have two days to kill Taraghlan with the sword, and then it gets returned."

"Of course, because why wouldn't you procrastinate *saving the realms* when you can get your revenge?"

All amusement disappeared. "Our attack needs to be planned," he ground out. "If Taraghlan is alive, he will lead the seelie, and we will have to fight them, along with the mages. If I kill him, his successor may still choose to ally with our enemies, or they may be able to be reasoned with."

"I bet that sounded like a great justification in your head when you came up with this plan. But I see right through it."

His cheeks whitened. Because he was grinding his teeth so hard. Perfect.

"You want him dead just as much as I do. He allied with

your enemies. Risked everyone you love."

I just shrugged. "Go get your revenge, Finvarra. I'll work on saving the worlds."

"You're coming with me."

"Aw, look at you with your little imagination. It's cute. Really."

"Kyla," a low voice growled. I spun.

Nathaniel leaned against a tree, his arms crossed. His eyes met Finvarra's, and something passed between them. The hair on the back of my neck stood up as Nathaniel returned his attention to me.

"You asked about your punishment."

Evie stepped into the clearing on the other side, her eyes narrowed as she strode toward us. Her curls were down today, and they swung back and forth as she beelined for her mate in what was likely an attempt to prevent whatever he was about to do.

She wasn't going to make it in time.

I shifted my attention back to Nathaniel. He leveled me with a hard look. "You want to go save the world alone? Without your pack? So be it. You will go work with Finvarra to kill the seelie king."

I stared at him. "Are you…serious? You hate Finvarra."

The hint of his wolf slid into his eyes, and I dropped my gaze. Behind me, Finvarra stiffened.

"You don't want to be a pack member, Kyla. Or at least, you only do when it suits you."

"That's not fair. The prophecy said—"

"We could have helped you. *I* could have helped you. Even if you had to perform the specific task alone, your pack would have had your back. But instead, you went after the sword without anyone to help. Again. In the process, you've hurt yourself. You're not sleeping, you're barely eating, you won't talk to anyone."

Evie sucked in a breath, and I could practically feel the rage radiating from her. "She didn't hurt herself. *Finvarra* hurt her." She glowered at Finvarra, and her hands sparked warningly. "Kyla was literally saving the worlds."

Nathaniel nodded. "That's right. So, she can go and save them some more. With Finvarra."

"Why?" Evie demanded. Their gazes met.

Hunter and Ryker appeared, Xander and Naomi following them. Ah, so all the dominants were here to watch my humiliation. This was like a fucking intervention.

Only I didn't even get to be drunk or high for it.

Ryker shook his head at me, while Xander looked vaguely amused. Naomi's expression was blank, while Hunter's eyes were…sad.

More people I'd disappointed. Great.

"Because like it or not, I'm her Alpha," Nathaniel sighed, running a hand over his face. "And this is what's best for everyone."

"It's not best for Kyla," Evie snapped. "Out of sight, out of mind, is that it?"

Nathaniel reached out, and Evie ducked beneath his hand, wrapping her arms around me. "I won't let this happen," she murmured.

"It's okay," I said back. The last thing I wanted was to cause problems in her mating. I'd never shied away from accepting the consequences of my own actions, and

I wouldn't start now. Even if those consequences felt as if they were stripping the skin from my body.

Evie's face was wet. I glanced at Nathaniel. His expression was tortured as he watched her. His eyes met mine, and that cold, determined light entered them once more.

"Pack your things," Finvarra murmured in my ear, invading my personal space as usual. "And be back at my castle in three hours."

Evie stiffened, her body taking on a strange glow.

Her eyes met Finvarra's, and they'd gone witchy.

Uh-oh.

I glanced at Nathaniel, but he'd already stepped forward and hauled her away.

"It's okay," I called to Evie. "I'll get this done and be back soon."

Finvarra leaned close once more, likely to say something smug. I lashed out, my claws extended, and they whistled inches from his face as he jerked back.

Without a word, I stalked out of the clearing and toward my car.

My mind raced. My next little errand was one I'd sworn I would never do.

Funny how your morals go fuzzy when your life turns to shit.

I parked outside Hannah's house, but I couldn't make myself get out of my car. I'd always loathed the black witch. My wolf could scent her foul magic and longed to take a bite out of her. Still, with Selina gone, and the pack banned from helping me, Hannah was my last resort.

Her words echoed through my head.

"You will lose everything one day. When you are ready, you will come here and allow me to feed on your misery, and I will give you the advice you will need. Eventually, if you're not an idiot, you may find happiness in the place you least expected it."

Well, she had plenty of misery to enjoy. I was an all-you-can-fucking-eat buffet.

I'd pushed the reality of what was to come out of my mind. But if I was successful in shoving that stupid sword into the demigod's sheath, the portals were going to close.

I'd never see Danica again.

Evie would always be my friend, but ultimately, she was mated to the Alpha now. Nathaniel had made it clear where he and the pack stood, and I refused to mess up Evie's relationship on top of all the other things I'd fucked up.

"You will lose everything one day."

Well, Hannah wasn't wrong. Here I was with no family, no pack. The world was ending, my lover had let me be tortured, and now I had to go work with him.

I got out of the car.

As usual, Hannah stepped out of her house immediately. It was difficult to know if her power had told her I was coming, or if she'd just happened to have been sitting by her window.

With her curly white hair, the apron tied around her waist, and twinkling light-blue eyes, she looked like she'd been baking cookies.

Then she smiled, and even the most innocent child would have run at the threat in that smile.

"Wolf."

"Witch."

Her smile spread. "I can taste your misery from here."

I glanced at my car. Hannah laughed. "Come in, then. I promised a trade. And you could certainly use it."

She wasn't wrong. I loped up the path leading to the front door of her mint-green bungalow. She stepped back, allowing me to walk in front of her. I wasn't worried. My wolf was at the front of my mind, and she knew exactly what kind of threat this witch presented.

I made my way through the antique furniture the witch favored, sitting on the armchair that would give me the most room to move if I needed to.

My wolf was displeased. I couldn't blame her. Werewolves had no magic of our own. Sure, we could see magic and were immune to some, but that certainly didn't make us invincible.

Still, I'd studied *this* witch enough that I knew it took her some time to cast her spells. And it took me less than a second to rip out a throat.

"You're considering whether you could kill me before I could kill you," Hannah said, sitting across from me. "I won't offer you tea or coffee. Something tells me you wouldn't drink it."

I waited her out. Finally, she sighed.

"Relax, wolf. Even if I wanted to kill you, I value my relationships with the demons, wolves, and, of course…the unseelie, far too much."

"And just what relationships do you have with the unseelie?"

"None, yet. But when you use the information I give you, that relationship will be solidified."

I narrowed my eyes at her. "The other witches must truly be becoming a threat if you feel the need to ally with so many other factions."

"Yes, well, many would have suggested we leave you to destroy one another in your little wars, but that would be utterly *boring,* wouldn't it?"

"Yeah," I said. "Boring. One-line it, Hannah. Now."

"The seelie king favors his left leg."

"Seriously? That's all you've got?"

She smiled. "That's all you need. His knee was crushed in battle two centuries ago, and the healing wasn't performed correctly. The king is too proud to have the bone re-broken and the injury seen to."

What a fucking waste of time.

"Anger isn't as delicious as misery, but both are filling," Hannah mused.

"Cool, cool. Enjoy it, 'cause it's the last snack you'll be getting from me."

"Well, we both know that's not true. Enjoy your time in Finvarra's castle. Ah, to be a fly on *that* wall."

Since I couldn't think of a single good comeback for that, I stalked out of her house.

Favors his left leg.

A crushed knee.

If only the witch could remove my misery as she dined on it. Then I'd let her eat her fill for the next hour until I had to go.

A white blur appeared in my peripheral vision, and I

glanced up.

Virtus.

He landed, picking up his front paws and placing them down again, one by one. Despite my misery, I couldn't help but smile.

"Yeah, you're already flying everywhere like a boss. Good job. What are you up to?"

He stared at me, and I angled my head. "Are you sure your wings can handle that?"

He stared at me again, this time silently. I laughed. "Fine. I was going to go see her anyway."

Virtus strolled toward me. And this time, he told me how he wanted to spend as much time with Danica as he could. How worried he was about the portals closing.

"Yeah. I get that."

I stayed quiet on the way to the underworld portal. But the silence sucked. With no one to talk to, I was forced to think. And thinking was the last thing I wanted to do. Because when I thought, Finvarra was all I thought about.

Approximately a decade later, we finally flew through the portal. The demons just nodded at us, well used to visits from both Virtus and me.

Virtus had an even better nose than mine. He unerringly found Danica behind the castle. Except…

The sky was filled with wyverns.

Demons trained with them, and I could see Bael and Lilith ordering them into formation. But even Virtus seemed wary, and he gave them a wide berth as we landed next to Danica.

I gaped at her. "You *fixed* them. They're not attempting

to kill anything that moves anymore."

She smiled and ran her hand down the wyvern closest to her. It nuzzled into her hand.

"Selina managed to find me some witchweed. Just a little mashed up in their food and..."

I hissed. *"Selina?"*

Danica gave me wide eyes. I filled her in, and she gaped at me. "Selina betrayed you? And left a note?"

"She sure fucking did. I just spent far too long in Fin's castle."

"Fin? Sounds like you really settled in there."

The backs of my eyes burned. "He used a truth serum on me, Danica."

She went still. And then her wings appeared, her eyes firing. "Then he's *dead*."

Despite the situation, I smiled. If a best friend didn't vow to kill the man who broke your heart, was she even your best friend?

"I'll take care of him," I said. "I want my face to be the last thing he sees. How do you think Aubrey would feel about holding *two* fae thrones?"

She just wrapped her arm around me. "I'm sorry, Kyla. I know you guys had a weird little...something."

"Well, that weird little something is over. It's like my mother always used to say, 'When a man magically roofies you, it's time to pack your shit and get out.'"

She grinned at me. "Your mom didn't say that."

"Well, she should've." And talking about Finvarra just depressed the hell out of me. "Tell me about the wyverns."

"If you're sure. But whenever you need to talk, I'm

here."

"I know."

"Okay, so usually witchweed has to be combined with a spell. You have to calibrate the dose perfectly to make sure you don't take away too much. For the wyverns, we managed to take away enough of their memories that they seem to think they're younger than they are."

"You removed time for them."

"Essentially. I mean, the time still happened, obviously. Their bodies are still scarred. But their brains don't remember what they've been through. There are some ethical questions there, but since it came down to either this or putting them down, we figured at least we would give them a chance."

I studied the wyverns as they flew above our heads. The one next to Danica eyed me, clearly confused by my scent, but it didn't seem like it was about to attack me.

"I need you to do something for me."

"Name it."

"Nathaniel is making me work with Finvarra again. They did some kind of side deal, and I have to go with him to kill the seelie king."

Danica's mouth dropped open. "What? When?"

"Now."

"Absolutely not. I'm coming with you. And what the hell is your Alpha thinking? I expected better of him."

"You and me both," I muttered. But my mind replayed the memory of him carrying me into his bed just nights ago so my nightmares couldn't find me. I swallowed around the lump in my throat. "As soon as Taraghlan is dead, we need to be ready to go to war. The mages will know we're coming for them. Flores will be the battlefield."

"We'll be ready. You just focus on doing what you need to do. We've got this, Kyla."

"I know. Thanks."

I hugged Danica. Evie was next, and I was running out of time. Thankfully, Virtus was more than happy to be my ride back to the pack. I texted Evie, and she agreed to meet me at my house.

I filled a suitcase while I waited. I wouldn't be wearing anything Finvarra had to offer me, that was for sure.

"Knock knock." Evie's brow creased when she took in my suitcase. "I can't believe this is happening."

"It'll be okay. I'm in the acceptance phase now. And even though I have to go with Finvarra, I also get to see that prick Taraghlan die, so there's the silver lining."

Her mouth trembled. But she slumped onto my couch, clearly still pissed.

"Don't go too hard on him, Evie. I don't want this to impact your relationship."

"We've agreed to keep pack stuff separate. He knows I'm pissed at him as a pack member."

"I need to ask you to do something for me."

"Name it."

"This isn't going to be easy. Finvarra… Shit happened between us."

"I figured that. Someone can't betray you unless you trust them first."

"Yeah. When all this is over, I'm taking some of that witchweed and I'm ditching a healthy chunk of the past few weeks."

She gaped at me. "Kyla…"

"It's okay. I've written a letter to myself. I just need you to give it to me, and to reassure me that everything went according to plan."

I handed her the piece of paper.

She opened it and read it aloud.

"Dear future Kyla, Trust me, this was for the best. Love, past Kyla. PS: You're a bad bitch."

She looked up.

I shrugged. "I mean… I *am*."

"Are you sure about this?"

"Working with Finvarra for this is going to be torture, Evie. I'd literally rather be cut open a thousand times. I don't know who I'm going to be at the end of it, and I don't know if you'd like that person. I don't think *I'd* like that person. I had an okay life before this. I was in a good place with my job, my friends… I didn't have nightmares… And this will allow me to get back to that place again. When I ask you what went down with him, you'll just tell me we bickered, but we managed to deal. And now the realms are closed, and I never have to see him again." My eyes stung. "I know it's a cop-out. Know you probably think it's weak…"

"Stop it. I know you, and you're a fucking fighter. But you don't have to fight alone. And if this is what you need from me, this is what I'll do."

I blew out a breath. "Thank you."

sixteen
Finvarra

"Working with Finvarra for this is going to be torture, Evie. I'd literally rather be cut open a thousand times. I don't know who I'm going to be at the end of it, and I don't know if you'd like that person. I don't think I'd like that person. I had an okay life before this. I was in a good place with my job, my friends… I didn't have nightmares… And this will allow me to get back to that place again."

"That's all she said?" I asked.

Virtus angled his head. We had a deal, but he wouldn't betray Kyla any further. I'd only convinced him to do this because he wanted to be able to see Kyla when she was in my realm.

Truthfully, I knew she needed him.

Apparently I hadn't had any idea how much.

She didn't think she would like the person she would be after she spent any more time with me.

"Tell me the rest of it."

Virtus sighed. But the words appeared in my mind.

"When I ask you what went down with him, you'll just tell me we bickered, but we managed to deal. And now the realms are closed, and I never have to see him again."

She was going to forget everything. Take every part of me away.

I let out a hollow laugh. I couldn't fucking blame her. Honestly, her plan was brilliant. If I could, I'd do the same thing. Only, I didn't have the luxury of forgetting even a second, thanks to the political situation in my realm. Any hint of weakness, and my enemies would strike.

But if I could?

Her face flashed in my mind. Those lush lips, high cheekbones, and brilliant blue eyes. And the way she'd looked at me in complete horror just days ago.

Oh yes. I would forget her without a second thought.

Virtus shifted on his feet. "Fine," I told him. "You may stay."

He turned and wandered out.

#

Kyla

Making my way to Finvarra's had been the hardest thing I'd ever done. Thankfully, Virtus showed up and escorted me from my car. He'd offered to give me a ride, but I was carrying a massive suitcase, so I'd refused.

"He let you come back, huh? You should go."

Just like all the other males in my life, Virtus ignored me. I sighed, hauled my suitcase through the portal with me, and made my way back to the castle, strolling past guards who'd arrested me just a few days ago.

Not one of them would meet my eyes.

The castle seemed strangely empty. With no other

instructions, I took that to mean I was staying in my old bedroom, and I meandered up there, ignoring the few guards and servants who gawked at me.

Throwing open my door, I dumped my suitcase on the floor and strode to the window. I *loathed* that I was back here as if nothing had changed.

My skin prickled, and I ignored the dark presence standing in the doorway behind me.

Finvarra merely waited me out until I rolled my eyes and turned, surveying him.

The bastard looked perfectly fine. If anything, his gold eyes were steely, shoulders back. He looked at me as if I were a faint acquaintance.

I kept my expression blank. Two could play at that game.

"You're needed in the war room."

"Why?"

"As ordered by your Alpha, you're to work with me to kill the seelie king."

"I don't know what you want me to do. I don't know the guy."

"Regardless." He turned, clearly expecting me to fall into step with him. Instead, I trailed behind him, keeping my distance.

I'd never been inside the war room. The first thing I noticed was its size. I'd never seen a table this large—it probably could have sat a hundred people easily. About half that many were already seated or standing around, pointing at maps and reading documents. The second thing I noticed was Lutrin was nowhere to be seen.

Although that didn't mean anything. He was probably lurking around a corner somewhere, wolfsbane clutched in his fist. Who knew how much longer Finvarra would want to use him to pass false information to the seelie king.

Finvarra gestured for everyone to take a seat. I turned to stalk farther down to the middle of the table, and he clamped his hand down on my shoulder.

I slowly turned my head, and my wolf prowled to the front of my mind, eager to pounce. Turned out, she was no longer despondent.

No, she understood that this man was the reason we had been helpless. The reason she had been too weak for me to even feel in that nightmare room. And she wanted to rip his throat out just as badly as I did.

Finally, we agreed when it came to the unseelie king.

Finvarra pulled out the seat next to his, gesturing for me to sit down. The room had gone so quiet, it was as if no one even breathed.

Another power play. I'd let him win this one, solely because the sooner this meeting was over with, the sooner we would go to war, and I could return to my pack.

I slipped into the seat and ignored him, glancing at an unseelie who wore a black tunic covered in medals. Something told me this guy knew what was up.

I caught the wave of Finvarra's hand out of the corner of my eye. "Update us, Torvit."

The unseelie bowed his head. "So far, everything has gone according to plan, Your Majesty. Our spies have confirmed Taraghlan has returned to his castle, after meeting with Gabriel and several mages beneath him.

During this meeting, he agreed to provide Gabriel with a third of his forces if he attacked the wolves and demons simultaneously."

My stomach swam. "When is this attack due to take place?"

Torvit glanced at Finvarra. The unseelie king must have nodded, because he returned his attention to me. "Three days from now. Taraghlan instructed them to target the women and children."

The room did one slow spin around me. I needed to get home. Needed to warn them. Needed to protect my pack.

"Sit. Down," Finvarra ordered.

I stared at him. I hadn't realized I'd moved. Something in his expression softened almost imperceptibly. "Your pack will be safe. We are attacking Taraghlan tomorrow. Two days before he would go after the wolves."

"And what about HFE?"

"They wouldn't dare wage war against the demons and wolves without Taraghlan as backup. Not without careful planning. The moment they learn he is dead, they will change their plans."

"At least let me warn Nathaniel!"

"He has already been warned." Finvarra flicked his gaze past me and nodded at Torvit.

I let out the breath I was holding and sat, loathing Finvarra more with each passing moment.

As much as I wanted to rip out Taraghlan's throat myself, I also wanted to be at home. Protecting my pack. Where I belonged.

"We enter at these points." Torvit was indicating

coordinates on a map. "There are portals here and here, but they are well guarded. Our people have infiltrated the guards on this portal, so this is where the first teams will enter, before traveling to the other portals and taking out the guards. It will be quick and quiet."

"I go in with the first offensive," Finvarra said.

A muscle ticked in Torvit's jaw. "That is far too dangerous, Your Majesty."

"Oh, I don't think so," I said. "I'm sure His Majesty can handle anything that comes his way."

Finvarra slowly turned his head, and his gold gaze slammed into mine. He knew what I was saying. What I was hoping for.

If all went according to *my* plan, Finvarra and Taraghlan would kill each other, I'd sweep in and grab the sword, and everything would be right in the world.

"I'm glad you feel that way," Finvarra said, "because you're coming with me." He gave me a cold smile. "Don't worry, I'll keep you safe."

That might have been the most ironic thing I'd ever heard.

At the same time, Nathaniel would kill him if…

Would he? Evie's bitter words ran through my head on a loop.

Out of sight, out of mind.

The rest of the meeting passed in a blur. All I could think about was the disappointment in Nathaniel's eyes.

I was desperately, achingly alone.

Unseelie began filing out the door, and I got to my feet.

"Why isn't Tae here?" I muttered.

I could feel Finvarra's gaze on me, but I focused on pushing my chair back in and stalking toward the door.

"His father only has days to live. Besides, he is safer if he stays out of sight for now. How did Lutrin get you down to the nightmare room?"

I stared at him. "Excuse me?"

"You heard me."

"Your guards didn't tell you?" I let my gaze wander to them as we walked out of the room, and they shuffled on their feet.

"No. I want you to tell me."

"Why? So you can exploit more of my vulnerabilities?"

His eyes narrowed. "You have some audacity to say that to me."

I just gave him a sly little smile and leaned close. "You want to know how he got me down there? Why don't you go talk to your good friend Lutrin?"

"Lutrin is gone."

For a wild moment, I thought that meant he'd killed him. But oh no.

"You're keeping him alive, aren't you?"

Silence.

I just shook my head, turning to head back toward my room.

"You need to eat."

"I'm not hungry."

"Funny, I didn't think you were that stupid."

"I should clarify. I don't want to eat with *you*."

He just waved his hand as if he couldn't care less. "Food will be sent up."

And then he was gone.

seventeen
Kyla

During the battle in the underworld, I'd been stuck in a cage, slowly losing what little humanity I'd had left.

In the moments before *this* battle, I was practically trembling with the need to take out my rage on the people who would attack innocent women and children in an attempt to break the pack's spirits.

Next to me, Finvarra wore silver armor that gleamed so brightly, it was almost white in places. I'd examined it when he wasn't looking, and it looked thin enough to snap. Yet it seemed to shift in place as he moved, automatically covering his most vulnerable spots. He'd attempted to make me wear the same armor, and I'd refused. My biggest weapon was my wolf, and I couldn't exactly pause mid-fight and ask the bad guys to wait a moment so I could remove my armor and let my wolf free.

While Finvarra had accepted that, he'd insisted I wear the amulet—the same one he'd offered me the night Marnin had been arrested. It was a dark gold—eerily similar to Finvarra's eyes—with a green stone in the center. Apparently, it would offer me some protection from direct magic strikes.

I wasn't an idiot. I'd taken the amulet.

It had been interesting watching Finvarra during the entire process. While he overruled his people occasionally—the fact that he'd insisted on heading straight to the castle as soon as the guards were under attack was a good example of *that*—he also listened intently when they spoke, asked advice. And unlike Marnin's conspirators, the command of Finvarra's forces was a relatively even split, both male and female unseelie giving the orders.

I hated that he'd surprised me once again.

Cool, he's not a complete misogynistic dickwad. He's still the asshole who allowed you to be mentally tortured.

There was that.

I hated that I had to see his face. We were barely speaking, but we'd need to work together if we were going to get to Taraghlan. So, for now, we were putting our mutual hatred and disgust aside and hissing at each other in low, furious voices.

Okay, not all of our hatred and disgust had been put aside.

"You want to saunter into Taraghlan's throne room and take his head?" Finvarra ground out. "That's not a plan."

"You're overcomplicating things. From what we've seen, he's a coward, so it's not like he's going to come out into the open and attack you directly. We're going to need to go to him."

"So, what's your suggestion, then?"

"We bypass the guards on the gate and sneak in through the basement level."

Instant understanding flickered across his face. "There's another way in."

I nodded. "We didn't use it the first time because the last thing we wanted to do was get stuck in his castle. But I spent a lot of time with that map, and I saw the set of stairs."

"Where do those stairs exit?"

"Inside the castle, near the entrance. I've been in the throne room before. We can figure it out from there."

"Fine."

"Fine."

Finvarra called Torvit over and gave him the updated plan. I waited, my wolf antsy. When Torvit nodded and wandered away, I glanced at the unseelie king.

"What's your plan for after Taraghlan is dead? You can't just leave his realm without a king."

An amused voice sounded behind me. "*I'm* the plan."

I whirled, and Aubrey held out his arms. I practically dove into them, catching the flicker of surprise on his face before those arms closed around me.

"I was going to ask how things were going here," he murmured. "But that reaction tells me everything I need to know."

My eyes burned, but I pulled myself together and lifted my head with a grin. "Can't a girl be happy to see you?"

His gaze darted over my face, but he obviously got the hint because he nodded. "Have you heard from—?"

"Selina?" My voice was bitter enough that his eyes narrowed. "No. And I doubt I'm going to."

"Kyla…"

"As touching as this little reunion is, it's time to get into position," Finvarra said.

I ignored him, angling my head. "You're not coming in

with us?" I asked Aubrey.

"No. The plan is for me to be the liberator after the unseelie attack."

It made sense. Despite Aubrey's popularity, the people would be unlikely to follow him if they knew he was working with their enemy.

"Are you sure you want to go in?" Aubrey asked, giving me a long look.

Behind me, I could practically hear Finvarra planning to kill not one, but two seelie kings today.

"I'm sure. I had to sit out the last battle, remember?"

Aubrey frowned. "Don't remind me."

I gave him another quick hug, just to annoy Finvarra. From the grin Aubrey gave me, he was well aware of what I was doing, but he squeezed me back.

"Be careful."

I gave him an unconcerned grin and turned, strolling back to Finvarra. Around us, the first wave of the attack had already formed into neat lines, readying themselves to jump through the portal.

I could feel Finvarra's gaze on me. "Are you ready?" he asked.

Keeping my gaze on the portal in front of us, and the unseelie who'd begun to sprint through, I just nodded.

I could practically feel Finvarra weighing his next words. I *loathed* that I had to work with him. But the sooner this was over, the sooner I could get back to my life. That thought was the only thing keeping me going right now, and I repeated it over and over again.

Kill Taraghlan and go home.

Kill Taraghlan and go home.

Kill Taraghlan and go home.

"Kill Taraghlan and go home?" Finvarra mused, and I realized I'd been mouthing the words.

I ignored him some more. Thankfully, he got bored with poking at me and turned to speak to one of his generals.

"We're going," he said when he returned. "Now." He grabbed my upper arm with his huge hand, practically dragging me toward the portal. I snarled, but a moment later, pain had engulfed every inch of me, and then the portal spat us out, right where we needed to be.

It was carnage.

Finvarra hauled me with him, and I allowed it, ducking my head to avoid a flash of fire. The sky lit up with lightning—someone using their power to attack. God, I hoped it was someone on our side.

People would die today. A lot of people. History would be made. At the end of the day, either Finvarra or Taraghlan would be dead. If we got lucky, Aubrey would be sitting on the seelie throne, and it would be the first step toward true peace between the realms.

If we weren't lucky, all of us would be dead.

It had taken me a moment to get my bearings, but now I knew where I was going, and I tugged at Finvarra's hold.

"This way."

Taraghlan's guard had abandoned his post by the tunnel, and Finvarra's hand lit with magic, guiding our way. I'd warned him about how Evie had needed to avoid using her power down here, and he'd simply shrugged, pointing out that Taraghlan already knew we were attacking.

The grisly remains of the scorpions had been removed, although the stone was stained with blood and gore. As soon as we were through the first couple of chambers, I stopped and got my bearings.

"Okay, this is where Nathaniel and Evie went right. I went left."

We hurtled down the corridor until we reached what had looked like a dead end. I shoved my hand against the wall, pushing the hidden door open, and surveyed the intersection. "I went that way last time, but I remember looking at the map and seeing the other exit…"

Finvarra just nodded, strolling to my left. My wolf stretched inside me, and he glanced over his shoulder as if he'd felt it.

"What is it?"

"I can hear movement and voices above us."

"Good."

A few minutes later, he angled his head in a way that made it clear his sensitive fae ears had picked up the same sound. We'd reached what looked at first glance like another dead end, but Finvarra simply raised his hand and blew the wall apart.

I coughed at the dust, waving one hand in front of my face. By the time I managed to peer through the dust, he was gone.

Oh no, he didn't.

If he thought he was going to have all the fun in this place, he was wrong.

I took the stairs two at a time as I sprinted up behind him. The fucker was fast. I couldn't even see him above me.

But I found plenty of evidence he'd passed. Any guards who'd attempted to stop him were currently lying dead at various points along the stone stairs.

By the time I got to the top of the staircase, Finvarra was waiting for me. I didn't bother snarling at him, just waited as he pushed open the stone wall and strolled out into the mayhem.

The staircase had ended at the entrance of Taraghlan's castle. I knew my way from here, although obviously, Finvarra did too, as he was already wandering toward the throne room—his movements relaxed, as if he had all the time in the world.

I pulled my largest knife, slipped my iron knuckles over my left hand, and stalked behind him.

Any guards who turned and ran were spared. Any who attacked were dead in an instant. Within moments, they realized exactly who was in their midst and just how hopelessly under-powered they were in comparison.

Watching some of Taraghlan's most trusted guards desert him was particularly delicious.

My wolf warned me of the attack before the seelie got close. I ducked, shoving my knife into his gut and kicking the back of his knee. He slumped to the floor, and one of Finvarra's people was there instantly, slapping chains on his wrists.

"Aubrey wants as many kept alive as possible," the unseelie said. And I realized they'd managed to fight their way through the bloodbath and into the castle while we'd been sneaking in. No wonder this was Finvarra's elite team.

I headed toward the throne room. Taraghlan's guards

had lined up, three-deep and ready. Just a few feet away, Finvarra moved like a whirlwind, using his sword to conserve most of his power, slashing again and again, until blood hung in the air like mist.

I ducked beneath a sword and slashed out with my knife, slitting a throat.

Blood sprayed, and I let my wolf take over, guiding my movements.

Ducking around one of the unseelie, I lifted a sword from the floor. Heavier than I was used to, but nothing I couldn't handle. Swinging my wrist, I smiled.

The seelie who attacked me was fast. But I was a wolf.

I was behind him, kicking him into one of the unseelie before he realized I'd moved. The unseelie cursed at me, and I shrugged as he buried his knife in the seelie guard's gut.

And there was Taraghlan, surrounded by guards. Although those guards were thinning as they fought off Finvarra's people. Soon, Taraghlan would be forced to fight too. In the meantime, he was letting Finvarra grow tired with the continual onslaught.

Taraghlan's eyes met mine and immediately flicked away. He didn't see me as a threat, and he knew he couldn't kill or catch me. At least not until Finvarra was dead and his amulet ran out of power. So Taraghlan would wait until Finvarra was so tired he could barely use the power. Could barely lift the sword that could finally put an end to Taraghlan's brutal reign.

Fuck that.

If Taraghlan succeeded, not only would he join with the

mages to fight our attempts to send the demigod back to sleep, but he would be a threat for the rest of our short lives. The realms would burn.

Unfortunately, we fucking needed Finvarra.

So *I* was going to have to be the distraction.

I strolled toward Taraghlan, my new sword in my hand.

Taraghlan spotted me and smiled. "The wolf. Perhaps I'll *keep* you, hmm? As my father did his mother?"

Good fucking luck with that. But the threat in his voice—the thought of being *kept* once more—drew me lunging forward, swinging my own sword. I wanted to shift to wolf, but I'd lose Finvarra's amulet in that form. At the very least, I could distract the king while Finvarra dispatched the guards who'd joined the fight.

Taraghlan waved his hand.

"Kyla!" Finvarra roared, and I ducked, barely avoiding Taraghlan's power.

"Fast." The seelie king smiled. "But you won't be fast enough."

"You like to hear yourself talk, don't you?"

The smile dropped from his face at that, and, with another wave of his hand, gold sparks shot toward me, hot and fiery. I neatly slid beneath them.

The next time he aimed that vicious power at me, I stumbled back several feet. But the power thumped harmlessly off the ward.

Finvarra's little amulet had worked. Taraghlan snarled.

"You're out of your league," he said. "The moment I kill the unseelie bastard, that amulet is done. And I'll chain you to my throne for *centuries*."

Then Finvarra was there, pushing me behind him. "Don't even think about it," he hissed at me. "Stand the fuck down."

I ignored the order but allowed him to stalk toward the seelie king. At least I'd managed to distract the bastard long enough for Finvarra to get close.

Finvarra looked at Taraghlan, and the seelie king finally realized he had no other choice but to face him. Finvarra and his A-Team had taken out most of Taraghlan's most powerful people. From the way the blood was draining from Taraghlan's face, he hadn't been expecting that. With a roar, he launched himself at Finvarra.

One of Finvarra's people shot toward them, but Finvarra held up a hand. "Mine," he said.

I rolled my eyes, but Taraghlan was already grinning. He looked fresh as a fucking daisy, while Finvarra was covered in blood. Most of it wasn't his, but there was a deep slice along the back of his neck between his armor and his helmet.

A hint of movement came from my left. Someone slammed into Finvarra. One of Taraghlan's people. The dirty fucking cheat. As far as I was concerned, that meant I got to jump in too.

But more of Taraghlan's guards had begun pouring in, all of them aimed at the unseelie king. How much longer could he last, even with his most brutal warriors? They were hopelessly outnumbered.

Taraghlan was also at least a century older than Finvarra. He'd had Lutrin spying on him during his training each day.

From the thunderous expression on Taraghlan's face,

Finvarra had been smart enough to hold back. To never let Lutrin see exactly how he fought.

Taraghlan used his power. It hit Finvarra's ward, and I knew him well enough by now—could tell by the tension around his eyes that it hurt. But he merely smiled, sending his dark power back toward the seelie king.

Taraghlan raised his own ward. A standoff.

Did he know just how tired Finvarra was? How much power he'd used so far?

Fear slammed into me. Not for Finvarra. *Definitely* not for Finvarra. But for the realms. For Nathaniel and the pack, Danica and the demons, and the billions of people who would lose their lives if we didn't return that sword to the demigod.

Taraghlan was slowing down, circling now. He lunged, swinging his sword, and Finvarra met it, his expression bored.

I narrowed my eyes as Taraghlan danced back and circled in the opposite direction. That knee bent slightly, and he immediately checked it. Hannah was right. He *did* favor his left leg.

For the first time, I wished I'd allowed Finvarra to teach me how to speak to him in his head.

The fae kings didn't say a word, but I caught Taraghlan's other hand moving at his side, clearly giving some kind of signal. He slashed out, and Finvarra neatly parried, lunging at Taraghlan until he had to backtrack several steps.

A dull flush worked its way up his cheeks.

Right as one of Taraghlan's people appeared out of thin air, burying his knife in Finvarra's back.

I screamed, and for a desperate moment, all I could see was Finvarra's face. All I could feel was the way his lips had caressed mine, the way my heart had tripped each time he'd given me that smile I'd never seen him give anyone else.

I was wolf in my next thought. I heard the amulet clink as it fell to the stone floor. From Finvarra's roar, he knew exactly what had just happened. Too bad.

My wolf had practically been screaming, "It's *my* turn!"

She knew what she was doing. So I allowed her free rein. Her instincts were better than mine, and if I'd been human, I would've grinned as she nipped forward and tripped Taraghlan, snapping at him. He jolted back just in time, cursing at me.

His power came close enough that it singed my fur. I snarled at him.

"You want to play, wolf?"

I ducked, rolled, ducked again. And then I moved faster than I'd ever moved before. Faster than I'd known I could move. Fast enough that it was as if some god were watching over me and guiding me.

My mouth clamped around the seelie king's bad knee, and I dug deep. He screamed, and I darted back just in time to see him limp to the side, to see the gold flash that roared toward me.

I wasn't fast enough to duck this time.

It burned through me, carving through flesh and organs and muscle. I hit the floor.

Finvarra's roar would likely be the last thing I ever heard.

I opened my eyes to slits, just long enough to see

Finvarra swing his sword, taking Taraghlan's head.

Fucking finally.

I choked on my own blood and almost chuckled. Hannah had seen this. She had to have. She'd get the last laugh after all.

Maybe I could hang around and haunt her. It would serve her right.

When I opened my eyes next, it was quiet. But the unseelie king was glowering down at me.

"When will you learn to follow fucking orders?" he snarled.

I flicked my gaze at the ruin of my chest. "Looks like I'm never going to learn that lesson. I'm not all that cut up about it." I attempted a smile. "Well, I guess I am."

"Shut up. Just shut up and focus on not dying."

"I can't believe your face will be the last thing I fucking see," I growled as he roared for healers. "Fate is a nasty bitch."

"Now you believe in fate?"

When I looked at him, all I saw was regret. I closed my eyes.

"Don't you fucking go to sleep."

I kept my eyes closed. "It's not my fault you're boring me."

"I'm wearing fucking armor. What did you think you were doing?"

That was the problem. I hadn't thought. All I'd seen was that knife buried in Finvarra's back, and I'd acted.

For the realms.

And that's what I'd tell myself until the moment I died.

I had a pretty good feeling that moment was coming up.

Finvarra lifted me into his arms, and a choked scream was ripped from me before I could cut it off.

"Sorry. I'm sorry." He pressed his lips to my forehead.

"So you do know that word after all. I'd wondered."

He tensed, but the healers had arrived and were directing him to lay me on something soft.

"Tell Danica… Evie…" My throat thickened. "Nathaniel…"

"Tell them you can't follow a fucking order to *literally* save your life? That's not exactly news to them."

I cracked my eyes open. Finvarra was leaning over me. His face was white, but those gold eyes blazed, brighter than I'd ever seen them.

"Pretty."

One of the healers did something that ripped another scream from me. "Stop," I snapped.

Finvarra caught the hand I'd swung. "They're saving you. And they follow my orders, not yours."

I knew desperation when I saw it. He was trying to piss me off so I wouldn't sleep.

"S'okay," I muttered. "I was always going to die at some point. Selina saw it. Fuck, it hurts."

"You're not dying."

I ignored that. I only had one question. A ridiculous question, considering everything this man had done to me. The healer did something else that made my head spin, and the words were out of my mouth before I realized I'd said them.

"When I'm gone, will you think about me?"

eighteen
Finvarra

"*When I'm gone, will you think about me?*"

This fucking woman. When she was healed, I was going to spank her ass. No one enraged me, bewildered me, and just plain fucking obsessed me like her.

"*When I'm gone, will you think about me?*"

When she woke up, I would make her pay for that alone.

When she woke up.

When. She. Woke. Up.

"Your Majesty?"

I took my eyes off the wolf just long enough to glance at the messenger. "Yes?"

"The seelie king's heir has been arrested. King Aubrey has taken the throne."

"Good. Tell him to get to work cleaning up his court."

"Yes, Your Majesty."

Distantly, I was aware that I was behaving entirely out of character. For *centuries,* I'd planned my revenge. And instead of enjoying it, I was focused on the woman whom I spent the majority of my time either wanting to fuck or wanting to strangle. The woman who'd risked her own life without a second thought.

The woman who was lying in my bed, paler than death.

I couldn't even enjoy my victory, because I was too focused on *her*.

"Why am I not surprised you've ruined even this for me?" I muttered.

Kyla's eyes slit open, the icy blue a startling contrast to her brown skin. "I must be in hell. Because you're still here, bitching as usual."

Relief swept over me, sliding through every cell, making my legs weak, my stomach churn. For a moment, I couldn't speak.

And that relief… I knew what it meant.

I'd never lied to myself until I met this woman. And it was time to acknowledge the dark truth.

When I'd seen her go down, I hadn't cared that she'd stolen from me. That she'd made me *feel* something and had then betrayed me. No, all I'd cared about was that she'd continue breathing. I would have given *everything* to save her.

My entire body tensed, and I watched her as she frowned back at me. Kyla Hill was mine, and she was staying that way.

I had no doubt she would make my life hell when she realized I was keeping her.

A small part of me was looking forward to it.

#

Kyla

Finvarra pinned me with his gaze. For one wild second,

I caught a barrage of conflicting emotions before that expressionless mask slid down over his face.

I closed my eyes, but within a moment, the bed jolted as he sat down.

"Close call, wolf."

I cracked my eyes open again. "I suppose you want thanks or something."

He smirked. "The sound of your sweet voice is all the thanks I need."

Something flickered in his expression, and he got to his feet.

I just swallowed, my mouth achingly dry. "You can take me home now."

"I don't think so."

I attempted to sit up. The bastard watched me flop around uselessly, amusement clear in his eyes.

"You'll need to heal," he said.

"I can heal in my own fucking house." I glanced around and gaped at him. "You put me in your bed?"

"Yes. Now I can keep an eye on you."

"You are deranged."

A satisfied smile curved his mouth. "I know."

"That wasn't a compliment," I ground out as he walked away. A healer was approaching my bed, her hands already glowing.

Finvarra didn't return that night. Or the next.

At least, he didn't return while I was awake. But I knew the creeper was visiting while I was sleeping. My wolf would wake, a whine in my throat and his scent in the air.

The son of a bitch was refusing to let me go, but he

wasn't man enough to face me.

Thankfully, I'd healed enough that I was no longer losing hours at a time to a sleep so deep, even my wolf wouldn't rouse when the unseelie king snuck in.

Tonight, I slid out of bed, taking a long, deep breath as the room spun around me.

Right as Finvarra walked *through* the wall.

The sneaky fae. That explained why I hadn't heard him.

"What do you think you're doing?" he growled. "Get back in bed."

I rolled my eyes. "I was wounded this badly while I was stealing that stupid sword for you, and you know what I did? I womaned up and kept moving."

That wasn't entirely true. I'd never come as close to death as I had just days ago. And Evie's pixie dust had saved my life when we were in the seelie king's castle.

Finvarra didn't look impressed. No, he looked like he was about to have an aneurysm.

"I'm going outside," I announced.

"Oh no, you're not."

I planted my hands on my hips. He stood in front of the wall he'd just fucking *walked through*.

Unfortunately, I wasn't exactly functioning at my best. I didn't like my chances of getting past him and out the bedroom door.

I'd make one last attempt at reasoning with him.

"I'm not going to go for a run. I need some fresh air."

"Fine."

I almost choked. "Fine?"

He stepped forward, and a second later, I was in his

arms again.

I arched my back. "Put me down."

"If you rip open your wound, I'll chain you to my bed with Naud chains until you're healed."

I went still at that. "You brutal asshole."

He just hummed, stalking through the wall once more. Okay, even I could admit that was cool.

"I know you can carry me with your power," I ground out.

"Ah, but then I wouldn't get to feel you in my arms."

I rolled my eyes and fixed my gaze on the ceiling above me.

"I'm not going to rip open my wound," I said, keeping the words slow and clear, so maybe he would understand me. "Did you miss the part where I'm a *werewolf*?"

Finvarra stopped, holding me with one arm while the other caught my chin. "He used death magic on you," he snarled. "You almost *died.* And if you'd put your distaste for me aside, I'd tell you just how many internal organs my healers have had to help you regrow."

I stared back, *hating* that I still enjoyed the feel of his arms around me.

"Distaste? Now there's an understatement."

A muscle ticked in his jaw, and he continued walking. "I had some time to think while you were flirting with death."

He seemed ridiculously put out by the almost-dying thing, and I knew exactly why. Finvarra didn't appreciate anything he couldn't control. If I was going to die, he likely wanted to be the one to make it happen.

"I don't care. I don't care about your thoughts or your

ideas or anything else. I. Don't. Care." My voice cracked, and Finvarra stopped walking once more.

I could feel his gaze on me, but I stared down the hall, attempting to pull myself together.

"Kyla." His tone had softened. I ignored it. He put me on my feet, shifting me back until I could lean against the wall.

"You wouldn't feel this betrayed if you didn't feel something for me. That just means I need to earn your forgiveness."

"You're delusional."

"And you're more harpy than wolf. I love you anyway."

I went still. My gaze met his.

Those eyes burned into mine. His expression was tight, and he looked entirely pissed off. As if he really did love me, and he wasn't at all happy about it.

I laughed, but it came out as a sob. "Enough with the mind games, Finvarra. I'm already fucking wounded."

Both inside and out. Right now, I was nothing but one big open wound, and he was pouring salt on me.

He raised his hand, ignoring the claws I brandished when he caught my chin once more.

"Love doesn't come along often for people like us."

"Speak for yourself," I muttered, and the fucker *grinned*.

"Many men may love you, little wolf, but they can never handle you."

"So, what? It's you or no one? News flash, I *love* being alone."

"You'll love being with me even more."

I stared at Finvarra. Clearly, the seelie king had done

something to impact Finvarra's mental state while I was bleeding out.

Hopefully it was temporary.

He just gave me a faint smile, picked me up once more, and kept walking.

His library. I waited for him to put me down, attempting to accept that he wasn't going to be taking me outside. But he kept walking until we were passing through another wall at the back of the first floor of the library.

My heart thumped, and I scented the air. Finvarra kept walking down the stone corridor and through yet another door.

I went still. We were standing in a large room filled with comfortable furniture. A wave of Finvarra's hand, and the fire began to crackle behind us. But I was too busy staring ahead to pay attention.

Like his private dining room, the wall had been removed, and several chairs waited on the balcony. He strode to the one closest and placed me down. Then he gave me a long look and handed me a blanket. I ignored it. The temperature was perfect. Beneath us, the snow glowed in the starlight, and I itched to go for a long run in my wolf form.

Except I was still so weak and sore, I wasn't even sure I could shift.

Finvarra sat next to me. I glanced at him, but he was staring out at the snow, his brow creased.

"What's with the secret tunnel?"

"This is my place. No one else knows of its existence."

I heard what he wasn't saying. I was the first person he'd brought here. My stomach clenched, and I glanced away.

I didn't believe him. Didn't believe a single lying word he'd said. The thought that he loved me…

"I knew the moment I saw you cut down by his power," Finvarra said casually.

I flicked him a glance, but he was still staring out at the snow as he continued talking. "I saw him hit you, caught the way you stumbled, and knew you were likely dead. And I would have given *anything* to turn back time. I would have handed Taraghlan that sword and allowed him to gut me with it, if it had meant undoing what had just happened."

I remembered his howl of rage. The way he'd roared my name. At the time, I'd thought he was just livid at me for interfering.

When I didn't say anything, he continued. "And then I had to watch you fight death. You were lying so still. In my bed, where you've always belonged. I couldn't celebrate my victory over Taraghlan. Couldn't do anything but sit and *will* you to live."

My throat tightened. "Finvarra."

"But if I'm honest with myself, I knew long before that. I knew I was falling in love with you when we were at the summer palace. By the time I prodded you into going for that sword, you were the only thing I could think about."

"You didn't prod me into anything. I was always going to steal it back."

"I knew you were there. When I was talking to Lutrin."

I closed my eyes. "Of course you did. Tell me one thing. Would you have sent me down to your dungeon if I hadn't tried for the sword?"

"No. Never."

I stayed silent.

After a while, he shifted in his chair. "I know you want to go home. Know you deserve to be with your pack. But I can't let you. Not yet."

"You're just going to make me hate you even more."

"Maybe. But if you already loathe me, I have nothing left to lose. At least this way, I get to see you."

My eyes burned. He caught my hand. For some stupid reason, I allowed it.

"I'm a selfish bastard. And I'm even more selfish than usual when it comes to you. I know you won't believe me, but I'm sorry for everything I've done to you. I wish I could take it back. Could make sure you never ended up in that fucking room. Wish I could make you trust me, instead of forcing you to tell me why you wanted the sword."

I pushed down that spark of hope, refusing to let it ruin me once more.

"What exactly do you think will happen if I stay?"

"I'm hoping you'll find a way to love me back."

I was instantly shaking my head, but Finvarra just tightened his hand on mine. "You came close to loving me once before. I knew what was happening. Knew I was thinking about you more than I should. That's why I pushed you into going for the sword. If you could feel that way about me once, you can feel it again."

"You're wrong. Whatever I felt for you, it's dead."

He just turned, refusing to release my hand as he gazed out at the snow. "We'll see."

nineteen
Finvarra

Days later, Kyla had finally stopped stiffening when I lifted her, cradling her close to my body. The truth was, while she was certainly weakened, she'd healed enough from her wounds that she didn't need me to carry her any longer.

Since it was the only time I was able to touch her, I continued.

Today, she was quiet, allowing me to take her out to the hidden spot we both loved so she could feel the snow on her face.

I placed her in her chair and sat next to her, already mourning the feel of her warmth against me.

"I have a question," she said, her gaze on my kingdom stretched out below us.

"Ask it."

"If I'd…if I'd told you why I needed the sword, would you have given it to me?"

Ah. She wanted to know if all of this could have been avoided. Something I'd thrown in her face when I'd told her she'd betrayed me.

I turned my mind to the man I'd been just weeks ago. The man who'd wanted nothing more than revenge.

"No," I admitted.

Kyla cast me a look from beneath her lashes, and I shook my head at her. "I'm not lying in an attempt to make you feel better. Even if I had somehow believed you, I would never have allowed you to take the sword out of my sight."

She nodded, silent and withdrawn. I stretched out my legs. "If you're searching for someone to blame, that person should be me."

"I could have told you why I was here."

"Your friend Selina said you had to do this alone."

"And look how well that worked out," she said bitterly.

"I still have hope."

"You shouldn't. It's all pointless anyway. You and me."

"And why would that be?" I ground out.

Her icy gaze met mine. "You know what's going to happen, Finvarra. The portals will close. You can help us fight, but you need to get back to your realm—to your people—before the demigod goes back to sleep."

I caught her chin, brushing away the tear that slid down her cheek. "Then we'll make the most of the little time we have."

More tears followed, and I wiped them away. She allowed it.

We sat silently for a long time, until Kyla was almost asleep. I gathered her up, and with a thought, I was in my room once more, laying her on my bed. There was something possessive and dark in me that needed to see her in my room, among my scent, even if I wasn't sleeping here with her.

Something pricked at my senses. Tae was here. I let my power reveal exactly where he was and found him in my library, gazing sightlessly into the fire.

"My father is dead," he said, never taking his gaze off the flames.

I closed my eyes. I hadn't been close to his father. But Tae had.

"I'm sorry."

"He lived a long, full life and wanted to be with my mother. At least, that's what he said last night before he passed."

Tae's eyes met mine, dark with grief.

Despite the wedge between us, I stalked over to him and pulled him into my arms. He stiffened, then buried his head in my shoulder and broke down, as if we were still the young boys who'd only had each other.

Finally, he pulled away, wiping his eyes. "His lands and titles passed to me. I should be at home working…"

But he'd come here. "You need family."

His gaze met mine. "I shouldn't have said what I said to you."

"Yes, you should have." Kings who didn't have anyone to tell them the truth ended up as tyrants.

"How is she?"

"She's sleeping."

His eyes widened. "Here?"

"She almost died."

Tae sat down, and I pulled another chair in front of him, filling him in. "So, you made her come back with you. And you haven't let her go yet. I hope you know what you're doing, Fin."

"I'm in love with her."

His mouth dropped open. When he recovered, he just blew out a breath. "I knew it. But I never thought I'd hear you say the words. It can only end in heartbreak when those portals close."

"I know." But I refused to waste what little time we had left.

"And how does Kyla feel?"

"She loathes me. Wants to leave. At this moment, I don't think she hates me *quite* as much as she did before you left, but that's likely just because she's still weak from healing."

He snorted. "You could have told me you were going after Taraghlan."

"I didn't want you to worry that I'd end up dead and you'd have to rule."

Tae slowly put his drink down on the table. "You're a son of a bitch. Do you really think that's the only reason I'd care if you died, Fin?"

I sighed. "No. But you had enough to worry about with your father."

"Tell me Taraghlan suffered."

"Not enough. He almost took Kyla with him. I've never seen someone come so close to death and live before."

Tae let out a low whistle. "Trust her to spit in death's face. How is she?"

"Stubborn. Mouthy. Beautiful."

I gave a shrug, turning to pour my own drink.

"Things are going that well, then," Tae said.

"I'm not sure how to fix it."

"Maybe you can't."

The words stung, but I embraced the pain. "Perhaps

you're right."

"You made her see the worst moments of her life. Made her relive them. And then you saw those moments. There will always be an imbalance in your relationship."

I frowned at that, considering. "An imbalance."

There was an intimacy to seeing someone's worst moments. Our relationship hadn't been normal. We hadn't had a chance to spill our deepest secrets. To work up to that intimacy. But I'd seen the memories that made her heart crack open.

And she hadn't seen mine.

#

Kyla

I didn't sleep that night.

Or the night after that.

Even though I was still healing. Even though my bones seemed to ache. All I could do was replay Finvarra's words in my mind. All I could see was his expression—the self-loathing in his eyes when he'd talked about what he'd done to me.

His apology wasn't enough.

And yet…I'd certainly betrayed his trust too.

A small part of me wondered where we'd be now if I'd told him about the sword. Would he have surprised me? Would we have worked together?

I'd never know.

Finvarra visited each day. When I woke to find him in my room, he'd take me somewhere—often to his secret room, although he'd shown me a couple of other spots as well. One was a tiny sitting room his mother had loved. Another was an indoor garden.

"You look tired."

I slowly turned my head. Finvarra slid his gaze to the tray of food, noting how much I'd eaten. I glanced away.

"I want to go for a run."

"Have you tried shifting?"

"Yes."

"What did the healer say?"

"She said you're a micromanaging busybody."

"Uh-huh. I have a gift for you," he told me, changing the subject.

"Is it my freedom? 'Cause that would be one hell of a gift."

He ignored that, pulling me to him. Within a second, I was in his arms.

"I'm healed," I snapped. "You don't need to carry me around. Werewolf, remember?"

"Ah, but I so enjoy being this close to your sharp tongue."

I didn't bother struggling. He'd proven just who held the power in this little dance.

I'd expected him to continue walking down the hall. He seemed to enjoy showing me hidden nooks within his castle. But instead, he stepped out into the fresh air.

I sucked it into my lungs, reveling in the cold burn.

"Where are we going?"

"It's a surprise."

He veered toward the stables. Behind the stables, a

trail led into the forest. I hadn't explored it myself, but I'd caught sight of it from my window, my curious wolf half wondering exactly where it led.

Obviously, I was going to find out today.

Except Finvarra continued walking toward the stables themselves. Several horses had been tied to a long post. Waiting.

I went still, and my throat thickened.

For a moment, the betrayal was so deep, I would have gladly taken another slice of the dead seelie king's power rather than stare at those horses.

Clearly, Finvarra had seen my nightmares.

My body shook with rage. Rage and something I didn't want to look too closely at.

Those memories were mine and mine alone. They tormented me, but they weren't for his fucking consumption.

And now Finvarra was mocking my pain. Torturing me by showing me what I could no longer have.

I would never forgive him for this.

Never.

"Kyla." His voice had softened.

Was my lower lip trembling? I took a deep breath and channeled my rage. "You cruel bastard. Put me down before I rip out your throat."

He heaved a sigh. I readied myself to turn wolf. This was it. I'd fight for my freedom right here and now.

"Five minutes," he said to me.

I couldn't breathe.

Cursing, he stopped. With a wave of his hand, a dense fog rolled in, hiding us from anyone who would see or hear us.

"Please don't do this to me." The words came out in a rush, and my voice cracked at the end.

He'd won after all. He'd made me *beg*.

"You stubborn woman." He shook me. "I'm not trying to hurt you. Would you trust me for one fucking moment?"

Tears were rolling down my cheeks as I shook my head. He looked…tortured himself.

"Please. Please, Kyla. Do this for me, and if you still want to leave me, I'll take you back to your pack."

I clung to those words. I could leave. If I just got through the next few minutes, I could go *home*.

My throat was too tight for me to speak, so I just nodded mutely, wiping at the tears on my face.

A muscle jumped in Finvarra's jaw. "I should have known *that* would make you cooperate."

I heard a hint of bitterness in his voice. I ignored him, steeling myself against the pain I was about to experience.

The fog disappeared, and an unseelie man stepped forward, as if it were completely normal for us to disappear behind fog and have a hissed argument.

"This is Opial," Finvarra said, "my personal groom. Opial, this is Kyla."

"Nice to meet you, Kyla."

Greeting him while I was held in Finvarra's arms like an invalid was out of the question.

"Put me down," I ordered the unseelie king, and, surprisingly, he did.

Opial took the hand I offered.

"It's nice to meet you. His Majesty suggested you might

like to be introduced to some of the horses from his private stable."

I took a deep breath. "I'm a werewolf," I said. "If I go near them, they're going to bolt. They may hurt themselves."

Finvarra stiffened behind me, but Opial kept his expression mild. "Ah, but *these* horses are made of sterner stuff than that."

Hope sparked in my chest. I immediately doused it.

I just needed to get through this charade, needed to play one last awful game, and I could go home. I repeated the mantra over and over as Opial strolled over to the horses. I was standing downwind from them, so they hadn't gotten a whiff of my scent yet. But it was only a matter of time.

Opial crooned to the closest horse—a black mare—and unhooked her lead rope. She followed placidly, her head high, eyes glittering with intelligence.

It hurt to breathe.

"Now, why don't you come introduce yourself, Kyla?" Opial invited when the mare was just a few feet away.

I shook my head.

He just smiled. "I guess I should tell you a little about His Majesty's horses. This breed is called *mantuine*," he murmured. "When I say they're made of sterner stuff, I mean it. Mantuines were originally discovered in the middleground—and you know there are all kinds of nasties there. When we're training them, we introduce them to a variety of creatures. Including werewolves, black witches, even His Majesty when he's in one of his moods."

Opial grinned at me. I attempted to process what he was saying. Finvarra leaned forward. "He's saying you don't need to worry about these horses, Kyla. They won't spook or bolt or anything else from your presence alone."

That stupid spark of hope was back, and it was turning into a flame. A flame that seemed impossible to douse. Ignoring Finvarra, I took a couple of steps closer—every one of my spectacular senses paying careful attention to each movement of the horse.

She lowered her head, chomping at some grass.

"Her name is Precious." Opial's dark eyes watched me, and it was the sympathy in them that kicked me into action.

The wind changed. I froze. Precious continued to eat.

I took two steps toward Precious and waited. When she didn't lose her mind, I gently placed my hand on her neck.

Silent tears rolled down my cheeks.

"I need to speak with His Majesty regarding a particular horse," Opial announced, handing me the lead rope. "Why don't you get to know Precious while we have that conversation?"

I sent him a grateful look, and he just smiled.

Precious lifted her head and nuzzled at me. "I don't have any treats," I murmured. "But if I get to see you again, I'll bring you a little something."

A gift. That's what this was. A king's apology.

It didn't make up for what he'd done. But...stroking Precious healed something broken within me. It was still cracked and ugly, but it was no longer in pieces.

I swiped at my face, composing myself while Opial and Finvarra had their discussion. By the time Finvarra strolled over, I'd at least prevented myself from breaking down into full-blown sobs.

"You can come back and ride her when you're a little stronger."

"I'm strong now." I kept my eyes on Precious.

"We'll see what the healer says. But…she's yours, Kyla. Even if you leave here today, I'll have her sent to whatever stables you like in Durham."

I slowly turned. Finvarra was watching me, and for the first time, I noticed just how those brilliant gold eyes had dimmed recently.

"I… I don't know what to say."

"You don't have to say anything." He shrugged like it was inconsequential, but what he'd done for me today was anything but.

We needed to talk.

Finvarra had said I could leave. I'd been convinced I would travel directly to the portal.

But I was confused. Emotionally wrung out. So tired, all I wanted was to sleep. And yet, my wolf was pacing inside me. I needed to shift, needed to run. Needed to think.

Within a moment, I was shaking out my fur, my paws tingling. My clothes were in tatters around me, but I turned my head, watching Precious, who was still completely unconcerned.

Finvarra stepped into my line of sight. "You're leaving."

I hesitated. I didn't know what I was doing. That hesitation seemed to please him, because he let out a breath. In my wolf form, I could see the things I otherwise would have missed. I could see the shadows beneath those gold eyes. The tension in his jaw. The way his hands fisted as if he was struggling not to reach for me.

"If…if you just want to run, my lands are yours," he finally said hoarsely. "Run. Play. Be wild. Just…be careful. There are some creatures in my realm that would consider a werewolf to be a fine pet."

I showed him my teeth—a silent reminder that *he* was one of those creatures.

A faint smile curved his lips, but he nodded to me.

I turned and launched myself into the forest.

twenty
Kyla

The next day, I woke to find Tae in my room, jaw tight, brow furrowed.

Our eyes met, and he forced a smile.

"What are you doing watching me sleep, you creeper?"

He stood, moving in a stiff way that told me he'd been sitting in that chair for hours. Nudging my feet aside, he sat next to me on the bed.

"How are you doing?"

"Better than His Majesty would have you believe."

"Do you want out?"

I blinked, and he just cursed, getting to his feet to pace. "I'll never forgive myself for what I did that day. I almost killed Lutrin when I learned he'd put you in the nightmare room."

"Tae—"

"You saved my life not all that long ago. And I let you be tortured."

"Tae—"

"Say the word, Kyla, and I'll get you out of here right now."

My throat burned, and I pushed myself up. Tae leaned over and shoved a couple of pillows behind me.

"What about Finvarra?"

"He's my cousin. And my best friend. And my king. But he has no right to keep you here, and he knows it."

"Ah, but he doesn't care." I tried out a smile. From the pitying look Tae gave me, it was as pathetic as it felt.

"We're…friends," Tae said. He glanced at my face, and I realized he was waiting for me to agree.

The poor guy was likely just as lonely as Finvarra.

"We are," I said. He angled his head, clearly wondering if I was lying to him. I smirked. "I counted you as a friend the moment you convinced Finvarra to let me go for a run at the summer palace."

"I don't have many friends. Those I do have are aware that I may end up ruling one day, which…changed things over the years. So I don't have a lot of experience with true friendship. But I know I should have defended you that day."

I sighed. I needed to put the poor guy out of his misery or he'd beat himself up for the rest of his life.

"Tae, I watched you trying to convince Finvarra not to use the truth serum that day. He wasn't exactly rational. None of us were. I forgive you."

His eyes glittered, and I threw my legs over the bed, getting to my feet.

I was wearing one of Finvarra's shirts, and I watched as Tae noted that little fact, likely coming to the wrong conclusion.

"Hug it out," I ordered.

He smiled, pulling me close. "I'm serious," he whispered in my ear. "You want out, you say the word."

"I appreciate that. But…" I didn't know how to explain that things had changed.

Tae stepped back, raising his eyebrows. "Well."

"Don't get your hopes up. Besides, if I blow this joint, it's going to be on my own two feet and not because you smuggled me out."

"I'm glad to hear it," Finvarra said, and both Tae and I jumped like startled cats.

Finvarra's gaze swept past me to his cousin. Tae just folded his arms, staring back at the unseelie king. Finvarra… smiled. And that was pride flickering in his eyes.

Men. I'd never understand them.

"If you're finished," he purred, "I have something to show Kyla."

Tae glanced at me. I nodded at him, and he stalked out, giving Finvarra a warning look.

Finvarra watched him leave, contemplation flickering across his face.

"Are you pissed at him for that?"

"No."

I gave him a disbelieving look, and he shrugged. "Tae is a powerful unseelie who would protect you with his last breath. His guilt for what he sees as his inaction that day will haunt him for years. Which means he will never hesitate to act again if he believes I'm at risk of becoming like my father."

A hot ache took up residence in my chest. This man was being torn in two. He'd kept me here against my will, even as everything in him rebelled against the thought of being anything like his father, who'd collected human women and prevented them from leaving.

It was a fine line to walk.

The truth was, I hadn't been here under duress since he'd told me I could leave days ago when he'd given me Precious. Neither of us had spoken about the fact that I'd stayed. The truce between us was a fragile, brittle thing.

And there was another truth. A truth I hadn't faced just yet. In two days, we would both be back in my realm. There was no need to convince Finvarra to let me go any longer.

Because soon, I'd be home, and he would be here, and I'd never see him again.

"Kyla?"

"Hmm?"

"Are you ready?"

"Do I need clothes for this little jaunt?"

His eyes darkened as he took me in, wearing nothing but his shirt. "No. I'm the only one who will see you."

"You know, I have pajamas and sweats in my room." I didn't dare sleep naked. It was a temptation neither of us needed.

Finvarra ignored that, stepping forward to haul me into his arms. I dodged him.

"I'm fine. I'm tired, but I don't need to be carried around."

Surprisingly, today, he finally seemed to agree. I eyed him suspiciously, and his mouth twitched, but he offered his arm. After a long moment, I took it, if only to see the surprise that flashed into his eyes.

"There's something I want to show you," he said.

I never knew what I was going to get with his little

surprises. But I followed him down multiple stairs, until we got to a very familiar corridor.

My heart beat hard enough to rattle my ribs. Surely not. He wouldn't…

My mouth went dry. I knew where he was taking me.

To the nightmare room.

I bared my teeth at Finvarra, pulling on my arm.

Finvarra glowered at me. "Even now, you still don't trust me."

"Trust is earned. And bringing me anywhere near that place erases the little you've built."

"I'm not going to leave you in there. If you like, I'll have the fucking room destroyed."

"Yes, I would like. Do it. Now, let's go."

"Uh-uh. Not so fast."

"Finvarra."

"Just give me five minutes."

The last time he'd asked for five minutes, he'd introduced me to Precious. I hesitated, and he waited me out.

"Fine."

Was I stupid for trusting him? Probably. But something had to change. Clearly, this was important to him.

Finvarra turned and continued walking me down the corridor until we turned left down the next set of stone stairs. The steps were just as steep as I remembered. Only this time, I didn't have armed guards dragging me down.

I shuddered at the memory, and Finvarra stopped, turning and eyeing me. With a low curse, he pulled me close, until all I could hear was the steady thump of his heart. "I will never let anyone hurt you again," he vowed.

I shook my head, and he just held me tighter.

Some of the tension drained from my body, and he turned without a word, continuing to lead me to the nightmare room.

When we finally arrived, he took a gold key from his pocket and handed it to me.

"I'm not going in there."

"You don't have to. All you have to do is hold that key in the room and think of me."

"I don't understand."

"I've seen all your worst memories. All your nightmares. So now, I'm showing you mine."

I was already shaking my head. "I don't want to see them."

"Kyla. Please."

"Why? I don't understand this."

"Because Tae explained to me that after what I'd done, our relationship would always be unbalanced. I would always know the worst parts of your life. The parts that shaped you into who you are. The parts you had to conquer—and continue to conquer, every day. But you wouldn't know mine."

"You can tell me about them."

"This is different. You know it's different. You can stop at any time. But…please."

I studied Finvarra's expression. His brow was creased, his eyes glittering with what looked almost like… desperation. His lips were pressed together, as if he had more things to say but was attempting not to overwhelm me.

"I want you to know who I am. And why," Finvarra said. "I don't understand this need... I don't think I ever will. But it's unfair for me to know your darkest moments while you don't know mine."

"I don't care about fairness when it comes to that."

He took a step closer and cupped my face with both hands. "I do."

"Two days," I choked out. It seemed like such a waste now, all this time. He just gave me a heartbreakingly gentle smile.

"I would take two hours. Two minutes of knowing you're mine. If two days is all we have left, we'll make the most of them."

I swallowed. "I can stop at any time?" My voice was very small.

"You say the word."

"Last time... Last time, I was..."

"You were caught up. Because that's how the room works when you're inside those four walls. That won't happen now. I swear."

I blew out a breath. "Fine."

Taking the key, I held it in my hand, lifting my arm—and just my arm—until it was hanging through the doorway into the room.

It *was* different—watching someone else's nightmares. It was awful, and my heart bled for Finvarra at times. But it was almost like watching a movie. The memories didn't invade me.

And still.

I watched as his mother died, wasting away in her rooms. The poison Taraghlan had arranged had been vicious—something no healer had seen before, with a moss from the underworld that he'd bargained with Lucifer for. It ravaged her body while Finvarra sat at her side, begging her to live.

And even though I was watching his little hands stroking her hair, I could feel his love for her. Could feel his desolation and loneliness as she passed.

Then I was watching his father take a new lover. A human woman he'd stolen through the cracks between realms. A woman who was now trapped in this world, unable to return home without the unseelie king's power shielding her from being ripped apart. Even before the portals had opened, there had been stories in our world about human women being stolen by the fae. Finvarra's father was the reason why.

Finvarra watched as the woman begged those closest to her to take her home, but none would risk disobeying the king. As soon as the lines began to appear on her face—the first sign of her mortality—the unseelie king was done.

But he didn't let her go home.

No, he forced her to stay after he took another mortal woman.

By the time Finvarra had enough power to take another person through the tiny crack between realms, there were sixteen women. Sixteen who had been stolen from their lives.

He'd told me he was planning to keep me. I didn't *think* he was serious, but this was the kind of behavior that had been modeled for him. My stomach twisted at the thought.

But another memory was already sweeping me away.

Finvarra on the day his father had died. Standing at his bedside, watching the old bastard bleed out.

The healers had been called, but it was too late. The knife had been charmed to prevent the wound from healing. And it had been one of his closest advisers who'd stabbed him in the back.

"I only wish your useless mother had given me another son," the unseelie king ground out. *"So I wouldn't have to die with the knowledge that you will ruin this kingdom."*

Finvarra had given him a wicked smile, even as his father's words burrowed deep.

"All those women you stole? The ones who went missing? I was the one who took them back to their realms. They went on to have full lives. Without you."

The king's eyes widened, and Finvarra winked. "Enjoy the other side, Father. Although, something tells me wherever you're going is unlikely to be fun."

The memory faded. But the loneliness and sadness in Finvarra's heart never did. Time lost all meaning as more memories came. Finvarra had lived a long life, and something told me if I were to see *all* of his worst memories, I would be here for days.

Wars. The loss of friends, lovers, family. And throughout it all, time passed, and Finvarra grew cold.

Right up until the most recent nightmares. These were the freshest, and I could feel the underlying emotions Finvarra experienced as he learned I'd gone for the sword.

The betrayal. The justification. The urge to push me

away.

And then the horror when he learned where I was.

I hadn't truly believed him—when he'd told me he'd come for me the moment he'd known where I was. But he had.

Underneath all of it was the need to understand why I'd done what I'd done. He'd justified the truth serum because he was a king who had to protect his people. But beneath that justification was the fact that he was a man who was hoping I had a *reason* to betray him.

Then, when he'd realized why I'd done it...

I gasped at the pain. I'd left, and Finvarra had paced his bedroom, unable to even look at his bed. I'd thought he was unaffected—thought I was the only one dealing with the depression and the betrayal.

But it had hit him too.

He knew what he'd done. Knew he'd lost me forever. And the proud king had fallen to his knees and roared his grief.

While I'd been curled up between Nathaniel and Evie, Finvarra had been alone.

His cousin had left—disgusted by what he'd done. His adviser had betrayed him, and Finvarra could no longer stomach feeding him false information to take to the seelie king. His servants stayed away after he'd bellowed at them.

Finvarra, the unseelie king, was hopelessly, painfully alone.

Finally, he'd come down here to watch my nightmares again. Not so he could taunt me with them, as I'd assumed. But because he wanted to punish himself. And because he missed me so much, he'd take even the worst moments of my life if it meant he could see me again.

But watching my nightmares hadn't helped. They'd only made him truly understand just how he'd betrayed me.

The next memory was even more devastating. He watched as Taraghlan hit me with his power, and I saw it from his point of view, as that magic burned through my body, and…

Those were parts of my insides, strewn on the floor next to me, the blood loss enormous. No wonder he was still treating me like I was made of glass. My stomach swam as he dropped to his knees next to me, sliding in my blood.

He would have given anything to take that moment back. Would have taken the hit from Taraghlan's power a thousand times—without the protection of his ward—if it meant I was okay.

My eyes burned, tears streaming down my cheeks. I'd seen more than enough. I dropped the key, and Finvarra caught it, pulling me away from the room.

His gold gaze searched my face.

"I need some time," I said.

Finvarra's expression shuttered, but he nodded. A few minutes later, I was standing in his bedroom, alone once more.

#

Kyla

I paced in Finvarra's bedroom. It made perfect sense to take some time to think about this. To attempt to come to terms with the way I felt about him.

And yet, with every step I took, we lost another second.

My feet came to a grinding halt, and I almost choked on my own bemused laugh. *This* was the time I'd decided to be logical? To not be impulsive? To think twice?

I could spend a hundred years thinking, and my decision would still be the same.

I opened the door, and my eyes met Finvarra's.

"I know you needed time," he said, more uncomfortable than I'd ever seen him. "I'm just…waiting."

"I wish I'd never met you," I said.

Hurt flickered in his eyes, but he tightened his mouth with a nod.

I stepped closer. "If I'd never met you, I wouldn't feel this way. But you're right, the portals will close, and we'll never see each other again. And I refuse to let that happen without you knowing that I love you."

Pure, unfiltered shock darted across his face. I smiled, and then he was pressing me up against the closest wall.

"You mean it?"

"Unfortunately."

"Kyla…"

"Yes, I mean it. It's excruciatingly inconvenient, and I don't understand *why,* but I'd already fallen in love with you before you caught me in your father's rooms. Even if I didn't want to admit it. It's why I felt so betrayed."

"Even if we weren't down to two days, I'd never hurt you like that again. Never, Kyla."

"I know."

I did know. As much as I hadn't wanted to see his worst

memories, it had let me into his mind. I now knew exactly who he was. And I knew he loved me in a way he'd never loved anyone or anything.

Sliding my hand up to his neck, I urged him closer. He complied, moving his huge body until we were practically glued together.

"You've got me right where you want me," he said.

"Do I?"

His eyes darkened, and then his arms tightened around me as he steered me back into his bedroom.

"Are you sure you're feeling up for this?"

I rolled my eyes, and in a move faster than even the unseelie king could anticipate, I tripped him, pushing him until he was falling back onto his bed.

Surprise and lust mingled on his face. "I'm taking that as a yes."

I stripped off my tank top.

My breasts popped free, and he groaned. "No bra?"

I just sent him a smirk, shoved my yoga pants down my hips, and wiggled until I could step out of them.

"Get naked." I winked.

He gave a lazy wave of his hand, his clothes disappearing.

"You could've done the same for me."

"But then I wouldn't have seen you naked and… wiggling," he murmured.

I took a deep breath. If I did this, there was no going back from it. There was no future for us. No happy ending. But I needed him…

"Hey. Hey."

In the blink of an eye, Finvarra was standing in front of

me, cupping my face in his huge hands. "I won't hurt you."

"It's not that. This won't end well for us. You know that, right?"

His expression tightened, as if he didn't want to be reminded of just what we were going to lose when those portals closed. But he nodded. "I know. But I need you more than I need to breathe right now. At least we'll have this to hold on to."

And then his mouth was caressing mine, achingly tender, infinitely gentle. My eyes filled, and he pulled away to kiss the wetness from my face.

"You're so beautiful. I wish I'd told you that the moment I first saw you. Instead, I wasted too much fucking time."

I wrapped my arms around his neck. "A female wolf. Myth given life. Those were your first words to me."

"I had no idea how fucking right I was. Myth given life, indeed." He let out a strained laugh as I unwrapped my arms, stroking my hands across his chest.

"Don't feel too badly," I crooned, sucking in a breath as his clever mouth found the spot right above my collarbone that drove me wild. "I knew there was something strange between us then too. But I would've rather had my claws pulled out one by one than admit it."

"Obstinate woman."

I laughed, and then I was lying flat on his bed once more, his huge body caging me in. His eyes gleamed at me. "This is where you should've always been."

Where I would've stayed, if the portals weren't about to close.

I pushed that thought away. It probably wouldn't have

worked between us long-term anyway.

"Whatever you just thought, you can go ahead and unthink it," Finvarra purred, nuzzling my shoulder.

He'd gotten a little *too* comfortable with his body sprawled out on top of mine. I freed one leg, and, with my werewolf strength plus a fancy little move Nathaniel had taught me, I managed to take the unseelie king by surprise, rolling us until I was staring down at *him*.

"Dangerous woman."

"And don't you forget it."

Since I had him right where I wanted him, I pressed kisses along his neck, reveling in his scent. My wolf wanted to roll around in it, and for a single moment, she pushed me aside, lifting her head to stare down at him.

Fear rippled through me, but Finvarra could more than handle himself. He just smiled up at me—at *us*—and stroked one hand down my back. "Hello, darling."

My wolf preened, and I took her moment of inattention to shove her aside, my heart pounding at the knowledge that had scraped at the edges of my mind for days now.

I swallowed, my mouth suddenly dry. "You're not afraid of her?"

Finvarra gave me that arrogant, overly patient look that usually made me want to rip out his throat. "Your wolf would never hurt me."

"You're giving her far too much credit."

He just smiled, and I leaned down, nipping at his chin. His smile widened, and his hand caught the back of my head, holding me still as he explored my mouth. Slowly, thoroughly, his lips caressed mine, until I was writhing on him, desperate to feel him inside me.

The bastard simply held me still, smiling against my mouth.

"Something you want?"

"Your dick," I told him.

He nipped my bottom lip, and I laughed.

"I haven't forgotten your comment about getting fae dick anywhere."

"I knew that would piss you off."

He slid his hand to my breast, stroking my nipple with his thumb. "You succeeded."

Finvarra's voice was a dark threat, and it made me shiver. But not in fear. Releasing my neck, he slowly ran that hand down my body, fingertips skimming my most sensitive spots, until he was hovering right above where I wanted him most.

How was it that I was naked, leaning over *him*, and he was still somehow in charge?

Narrowing my eyes, I waited.

"Something you wanted, little wolf?"

"Forget it. I'll do it myself."

"Uh-uh." He caught the hand I'd moved lower, held me in place as I attempted to plant myself on his cock, which was brushing against my ass. I remembered just how good he'd made me feel, and I wanted it again.

Then he flipped us, until I was staring up at him and he was smirking down at me, his cock poised at my entrance.

"Control freak," I muttered.

He slid inside me, achingly slowly, and I lifted my hips.

"My speed," he said, taking his sweet time.

He thrust deeper and deeper. My eyes fluttered closed, and he stopped.

"Look at me," he demanded.

I opened my eyes to slits, and he lowered his head, finding my mouth as he ground against me. I moaned, and he rewarded me by picking up the speed.

Wrapping my legs around his waist, I urged him on. His pelvic bone was hitting my clit with every thrust, and his cock was taking me higher and higher…

I clawed at his back, sucked in a breath, and shattered, my climax shuddering through me. Finvarra groaned against my mouth, continuing his steady thrusts. I went limp, and he buried his head in my neck and emptied himself inside me.

"I guess I can forgive you for your control-freak ways," I panted.

He just laughed, his body shaking on top of mine. I stroked his back, and he rolled off me, pulling me close.

"Love you," he said, closing his eyes.

My throat tightened. "I love you too," I whispered.

twenty-one
Finvarra

Kyla dozed on and off next to me, waking only for more sex. The little wolf was insatiable, and I loved it.

It had been years since I'd taken even a casual lover. There was something infinitely exhausting—and vaguely offensive—about never knowing if the woman beneath you actually gave a fuck about you…or if she was simply attracted to power.

Kyla?

She didn't care about that power. In fact, she seemed to find it vaguely unsettling.

"What are you thinking about?"

I glanced at her. Her voice was hoarse from her throaty moans. *I'd* done that. Smug pride floated through me, followed immediately by bemusement.

Her eyes were all wolf—even lighter than usual—and she grinned up at me, like we were two coconspirators about to embark on our next adventure.

She didn't want me for my crown.

This woman could have any man she wanted, and I'd convinced her to want me.

"Are you going to fuck me, or what?"

My lips twitched. The little brat.

"You have a filthy little mouth."

She just gave me a heated look, and before I knew I'd moved, I'd leaned down and my tongue was tangling with hers. She let out one of those sexy moans—half moan, half growl—and I had to fight the urge to immediately thrust into her.

She tore away my infamous self-control as if it were paper-thin.

I lifted my head, and she reached out, stroking the point of one of my ears. I tensed at the feeling, and my cock hardened further.

"Sensitive?" she purred.

She thought she had the upper hand in our little power play. I smiled.

Her eyes widened, and the shirt she'd worn to bed—*my* shirt—disappeared.

"No fair!"

"You're in my realm."

I took my time nuzzling her neck, enjoying the tiny sounds she made, the way she arched and writhed. My mouth moved lower, caressing one nipple, and it hardened for me, Kyla shuddering as I tongued it, rolling it in my mouth.

I looked up at her. She was staring down at me, eyes wide. I moved to her other nipple, watching her reaction, and those incredible eyes slid to half-mast.

Her brown skin was silky-smooth, heating beneath my touch. I caressed her belly, smiling against her as she rolled her hips.

"Something you want?"

"Fuck you."

"No, little wolf. Fuck *you.*"

I slipped my hand down to the core of her, sliding through the slippery wetness that was just for *me*. Her breath caught, then shuddered out of her as I gently stroked her clit.

"More."

"Demanding little thing."

"Fin…"

I would never let this woman know just how it pleased me for her to shorten my name. As if I were a normal man.

I rewarded her with the flick of my fingers over her clit, and she opened her legs for me, arching her back.

I'd wanted to make this last. If I weren't barely clinging to my control, I might laugh at the thought.

Instead, I moved up her body, meeting that ice-blue gaze. Her wolf looked back at me, and I went still.

Her eyes didn't change, but I knew when I was looking at something *other*.

I adored her wolf. That side of her was one of the reasons she was such a survivor. But I lived in fear that the wolf would win someday. That the woman I knew would be lost. Feral.

That I would start a war, because I would never allow anyone to hunt her down.

Her eyes brightened. My fear pleased the wolf. I gave her a slow smile.

"You're beautiful."

One dark eyebrow arched as if to say *I know*. I laughed.

"But this is not for you."

I was obsessed with both of them equally—the wolf and the woman. But it was the woman I wanted in my bed.

Her eyes changed, and Kyla was staring up at me. Something flickered in that gaze.

"I'm—"

"You better not be planning to apologize."

I slid my hand back down, and she let out a choked gasp. Still ready for me. Good.

With a punch of my hips, I thrust into her, all the way.

She rolled her hips up, demanding more. So I gave it to her. Hard, deep, rough.

I ground into her, and she let out a choked sound that made me pause.

"Don't fucking stop," she ordered, and I nipped at her shoulder.

But I complied, slamming into her, the order freeing me from what little restraint I'd had. Her body tightened, her eyes almost glowing, and I knew she was on the edge.

Slipping my hand down, I rubbed over her clit, still thrusting deep into her.

Her mouth dropped open in a moan that made my body tighten, and I growled. "Come on my cock, little wolf. Now."

She clamped down, shuddering, writhing. "Good girl."

The edges of my vision darkened as I came so hard, all I could do was grit my teeth. I continued pounding into her, my fingers still rubbing her clit, until she was limp beneath me, trembling from the aftershocks.

I was wrung out. I'd never come that hard in my life. I didn't know whether to be embarrassed or amused. Kyla had closed her eyes and was catching her breath. A strange kind of possession took up residence in my gut. I didn't want those beautiful eyes closed while she recovered. While she thought whatever she was thinking. I wanted to *know* each thought.

So I pulled her into my arms, ignoring her grumble as I rolled onto my back. She splayed across my chest, a bundle of warm woman, and when she opened her eyes, they were glassy.

Pride was burning through me now. There was something incredibly satisfying about making the little wolf lose herself in my arms.

She stretched, curling up against me, and my lips curved.

"You're more cat than wolf."

"Watch yourself, fae."

I laughed, pressing a kiss to her nose, and her eyes widened.

My hand automatically stroked her back, soothing her.

Two days. Two days from now, we would be back in Kyla's realm, going to war. And then we would be separated for the rest of our lives.

Bitterness coated my tongue, and I held her tighter.

#

Kyla

Two days later, I leaned into Finvarra and watched the wolves preparing for our meeting.

"Are you ready for this?" Finvarra murmured in my ear.

"No. But it has to be done."

It was strange being back in wolf territory. Most of the wolves were sending me confused looks as they watched me practically glue myself to the unseelie king—who was currently nuzzling my neck. I didn't blame them. It must seem like a quick turnaround from the woman who'd wanted him dead not all that long ago.

Someone had pushed a bunch of tables together, and plates of food were ready to be eaten while we waited for everyone to get here. Meredith waved me over, and I shook my head with a smile.

"Not hungry?" Finvarra murmured.

I shook my head again, and for once, he left it alone. I couldn't even think about eating. My stomach twisted endlessly at the thought of what would happen tomorrow.

When we would send the demigod to sleep, and I'd never see this man again.

Across the clearing, Nathaniel and Evie were deep in discussion with Nathaniel's dominants. Hunter winked at me, and I grinned back at him.

Shadows passed over the clearing. Samael landed, Danica in his arms, as several of his demons fell into formation around him. Bael smirked at me, his eyes flicking to the unseelie king behind me, and I flipped him off.

Danica gave me a wicked grin, wiggling out of Samael's arms to saunter toward me.

"I thought you could fly now," I said.

"I can, but Samael wanted some bonding time. He was feeling insecure."

I choked out a laugh. Across the clearing, Samael

slowly turned his head, raising one eyebrow at his queen. Insecure, indeed.

Danica nodded at Finvarra. "You're lucky she forgave your ass."

"I am."

She angled her head at that, clearly expecting defensiveness. Finvarra just released me to step away and talk to Samael.

"What happened there?" Danica asked, still watching the unseelie king.

"It's a long story."

My eyes met Nathaniel's, and he nodded at me. I nodded back, keeping to my side of the clearing. Okay, so I'd forgiven him for sticking me with Finvarra. That didn't mean I'd forgotten.

"Ooh," Dani said. "Ice-cold."

I gave her a look. She just grinned at me and clapped her hands like a kindergarten teacher. "Let's get this meeting started."

In the end, we were mostly on the same page. Selina still hadn't shown up. I was still pissed at her, but most of my anger had been tempered by worry. The demons and wolves had been questioning anyone who knew the witch, but apparently no one had seen her.

Unsurprisingly, Hannah had agreed to help us. Danica and Evie were working on some of the other witches, who were still fighting among themselves after the death of their coven leader.

"Our biggest issue is going to be the battlefield itself," Evie said. "While the battlefield isn't within the national park, Tikal is close by, and it's a historical site. That means not only does it have archaeological significance, but unless the mages are stupid, they'll have their own witches who can tap into the power of the ruins close by."

Nathaniel frowned. "How much power are we talking?"

Danica shrugged. "It's hard to know. Ancient sites have 'imprints' of the past. Just like everywhere else, Tikal would have seen death, suffering, births, celebrations, and everything else life has to offer. A coven of witches would siphon off as much of it as they could."

"Even if we weren't talking about the potential power they could steal, we can't let them drain the magic from the Guatemalan heritage site," I said.

"So, how do we stop them?" Mere asked, filling a plate with food. Vas pulled out a seat for her. The pregnant tech witch wouldn't be anywhere near the battlefield, but she was helping as much as she could behind the scenes. And she'd be taking down any technology the mages were using to contact one another near the site.

"I believe I can help with that," Finvarra rumbled behind me. "But it will drain me of power. You will need to determine whether you need my power to kill the mages, or if the risk of them channeling the historical ruins is too great."

Samael was watching Finvarra consideringly, and I had a feeling he was attempting to figure out just how much power the unseelie king had. I gave him my most threatening scowl. Shockingly, the underking ignored me.

"How will you do it?" I asked Finvarra.

He stroked my back, and my wolf arched inside me.

The unseelie king smiled at that, but his smile fell as his brow creased in thought. "There is an ancient…spell I can use, which will shift the battlefield to a portal realm. No one will know what is happening until their witches attempt to harness the power of the ruins."

"How do we get out of the portal?"

"You're not truly *inside* the realm. Think of it as an in-between place. It will appear as if we are in Tikal, near the demigod's cave. And yet the grass beneath our feet will belong to the portal realm."

Danica sucked in a breath. "That's impossible."

Samael and Nathaniel watched Finvarra, their expressions carefully blank. Obviously, they were now learning just how powerful he was.

Finvarra only shrugged. "We would cut them off from using the ruins, confuse them, and remove some of their power. But it would mean taking my considerable power from the battle."

"We vote," Nathaniel said. "All in favor of Finvarra using his power for this."

I raised my hand, along with almost everyone else. Vas left his down and shrugged at me when I glanced at him.

"Seems stupid to take one of our biggest weapons off the battlefield."

I didn't like the thought of Finvarra powerless. But I had to believe that we would succeed. That I would return the sword to the demigod and our world would be safe. That the Guatemalans would live to continue to protect Tikal, and the realms wouldn't burn.

In the end, the vote was clear. Finvarra would do it.

"I sent one of my people to examine the cave," Samael said into the silence. "There is a portal hidden behind it."

I scowled at that. "Are you kidding me?" I'd flown in a *baby plane* to get to that cave.

Faint smiles crossed several faces at my tone.

"It's extremely well guarded," Samael said. "But it seems to be a universal portal. Which means anyone who helps you get to that cave can get back to their realm."

"How do you know?" Nathaniel asked.

"The portal is a rainbow of colors."

"In other words, it allows the user to go anywhere they would like." Of course, it made sense that the most powerful portal of all would be hidden behind the demigod's cave.

"Okay," I said. "So anyone who needs to get back to their own realm can use that portal to do it. If they can't get to the one in Flores. Can we use that portal to surprise the mages?"

"Only if we figure out which portals link to it. And that would take too much time," Finvarra said. I glanced at him, and he nodded.

Yes, he could use his secret portal to connect to it, because *that* portal could be used anywhere. But we needed him on the battlefield, keeping the witches from harnessing the ruins.

By the time the meeting was finished, everyone knew their parts. The most dangerous aspect would be when everyone began dispersing to their home realms. The mages wouldn't lose their power until the demigod was asleep once more. And that meant we needed strong magic users on the battlefield until the very last moment.

Then everyone would be hauling ass to Flores. Apparently there was a portal to the middleground close by. They'd arranged for transportation once in the middleground that would take them to their own portals.

My pulse thundered, and Finvarra wrapped his arm around my waist. Across the clearing, Danica jerked her head toward my cabin. I untangled myself from the unseelie king.

"I need some time—"

"To spend with your friends. I understand. I'll be here when you're done."

"Thanks."

A few minutes later, Evie, Danica, Meredith, and I were all on my porch, sitting in glum silence.

"Vas and I are staying here," Meredith announced, surprising no one. "He'll be on the battlefield until the end."

My heart twisted for Danica. Vas was more like her brother than her friend, but she'd bonded with Meredith years ago. Now, she'd lose them as well. Selfishly, I couldn't help but be glad they, at least, were staying. My gaze shifted to Danica, who was smiling at Evie, her eyes glistening.

"I'm staying too."

My mouth fell open. Evie choked on a sob, but Danica just took her hand.

"You can't," Evie got out. "You're a queen, Dani."

Danica gave her a tiny smile. "I left you once before, and it's still the biggest regret of my life. Someone else can rule. Samael and I will figure it out."

"There's no one else." Evie pulled her hand free and got to her feet. "What does Samael say?"

"Samael knows I need my sister."

My own eyes burned as Evie buried her face in her hand. Next to me, Meredith sniffed audibly, tears rolling down her cheeks.

"And I need you too. I thought I wanted to hear you say those words more than anything else, but I know how precarious the situation is in your realm right now. And I can't allow people to suffer because of that need."

"Evie."

"No, Dani." Evie's mouth thinned, her shoulders straightened, and it was clear she wouldn't back down. "It means everything that you want to stay. *Everything*. But you're going home. Where you belong."

twenty-two
Finvarra

I'd fought plenty of wars in my lifetime. So many battles, they blurred together into one long stream of agony and death. I'd come close to that death myself more than a few times in my youth.

But no battle had ever been more important than this.

I glanced at my allies. The underking, the Alpha wolf, and even a few witches Danica had scrounged together.

Kyla and I had spent the night in her small cabin, neither of us sleeping a wink. In between rounds of desperate lovemaking, we'd talked until our voices were hoarse—filling each other in on the small things. The things we would have learned about each other if we'd just had enough time.

It wasn't enough. It would never be enough.

I'd had the protection amulet fitted into a loose collar for Kyla. She'd refused to wear the collar at first, but I'd done something I'd never done before in my long life.

I'd begged.

The thought of her in wolf form, fighting for her life against mages harnessing the demigod's power... I hadn't been able to tolerate it.

She'd agreed—only because the collar was loose enough that she could still shift—more of a necklace than a true collar. And likely because I'd sworn that if she didn't wear it, I'd have her contained until it was safe enough to get her to the demigod's cave.

She'd raged at me, but there were some concessions I refused to make. I may have loved her beyond reason, but that didn't mean I would tolerate her fighting unprotected.

"You're still a possessive, overbearing bastard," Kyla had muttered when she'd finally worn herself out—and realized I wasn't budging.

I'd merely given her a slow smile and used my power to make her clothes disappear.

My little wolf had thrown her head back and laughed.

Now she sidled up to me, still in her human form, the amulet around her neck. Something in my chest relaxed at the sight.

I would be drained of most of my power. Which meant I couldn't protect her the way everything in me yearned to.

I knew what this feeling was. Knew *why* I craved her more than my next breath.

And that knowledge would haunt me for the rest of my excruciatingly long life.

"The mages know we're here," Nathaniel said.

I nodded. Most of us had traveled into Flores and flown here—carried either by demon or…wyvern.

They were gathered now, on the ground, ready to fight.

"The last I heard, those wyverns were wild. Out of control."

Kyla shrugged. "Yeah, well, turns out even the wildest creatures can be tamed, if you know how."

Leaning over, I nuzzled her ear. "Oh, I know how."

She shot me a look, but amusement flickered in her blue eyes. "You think you're so funny." She glanced up. "Holy shit."

I stiffened, hauling her close. Those were—

"Dragons," Kyla breathed. "Some of the demons are bonded to them." She squinted. "The demons have wrapped them in their own wards as a kind of armor. Smart."

Danica strolled up to us. "Nuri's too young to fight, although she begged relentlessly. But her mama's going to be teaming up with Samael to create some chaos."

"Nuri?" I asked.

"Danica bonded with a dragon." Kyla beamed, clearly burning with pride. "Even though she's only half demon, she was still able to do it."

The two women high-fived.

Evie walked over, dressed in armor. My gaze met Nathaniel's, and he shrugged. Clearly, even though his mate was a powerful witch, he was taking no chances.

"I can feel their witches gathering power," Evie said, nodding toward the cave.

This battle would be like none I'd fought before. While we were standing on an empty plain right now, most of the mages would likely remain hidden in the jungle, protecting the cave. That would make it difficult for the demons to spot them.

"Any sign of Gabriel?" Danica asked.

"None so far," Evie said. "He strikes me as a coward."

Around us, everyone went silent. Enough of our army had gathered that it took a few minutes for word to spread into the ranks behind us.

A mage swaggered forward until he was just a hundred feet or so from our front lines.

Kyla craned her head, unable to see.

"Gabriel has sent a messenger," I murmured, my hand automatically drifting to the sword at my side. The sword that would save us all.

The mage opened his mouth, and his words echoed across our ranks, powered by magic.

"You have erred greatly, coming here today," he said. "Leave or die."

Kyla snorted. "That's it? Seriously? Someone needs to teach Gabriel how to write a bad-guy speech."

The messenger slowly turned toward us. Clearly, the power gave him better hearing too. He raised his hand, sending a bolt of green light toward us.

Icy rage swept through every inch of my body. Kyla tensed as I stepped in front of her, raising my own hand.

My flames engulfed his power, and then his body.

Ash rained down on the grass in front of us.

\#

Kyla

It turned out Finvarra was pissed.

I cleared my throat. "If you're done smiting the messenger, you'll need to do your portal work before those witches finish their chanting."

He slowly turned his head, and something ancient and deadly slid through his eyes as he stared back at me.

I just waited him out.

His eyes cleared, and he prowled toward me, sliding his hand behind my head. "My plan to drain my power is strategically sound, and yet..."

"You're worried because you think you can't protect me."

Next to me, Evie snorted. "Because Kyla is a loose cannon. In other news, water is wet."

I shot her a look, and she grinned at me.

Finvarra ignored our little interplay, and I leveled him with a hard stare. "I've got your nifty amulet. Look, Fin, all the reasons for doing what you're doing remain the same."

Evie tensed. "It needs to be now."

Finvarra's mouth found mine in a quick, claiming kiss. "Be careful," he growled.

"I got this."

Samael pulled Danica away for a powwow, likely telling her the same. Meanwhile, Evie had begun doing that creepy glowing thing she did as she gathered her own power.

Butterflies fluttered in my stomach for the first time as my friends found their places.

If one of them didn't walk off this battlefield...

I was pretty sure I wouldn't survive it.

"We cut off the flow of magic, and the mages die," Finvarra reminded me. "The plan remains the same."

While our army was distracting the mages, I would be making my way across the battlefield. Finvarra had insisted on coming with me, even though most of his power would be used to cut off the few witches who'd allied with the mages from accessing the power of the ruins.

Vas had also said he'd join us. Meredith was hidden

in the national park—close enough to ensure her magic continued to stifle their tech, but far enough away that if the shit hit the fan, one of the demons would head directly for her and get her out.

"Unless they're idiots, they know you've got the sword," Vas said when he reached us. "Selina's not the only witch who can use prophecies. I take you through the air, and every mage on that battlefield will aim for us."

"It's okay. The plan was always to go by foot."

Across the plain, the mages had begun banging wooden drums in an attempt to disconcert us. They wore black armor of their own, marching toward our ranks at a steady pace.

I shook my head at that. Samael was in charge of the next part, and he was going to fuck their shit up.

It was the underking's voice that roared over the sound of those drums.

"Attack!"

There was no steady march from our side. Demons, unseelie, werewolves, dragons, and wyverns attacked as one.

The demons launched into the air, many of them astride the dragons, who began blowing fire at the mages' front lines.

The fire burned along their wards, and the mages laughed.

But the wyverns were already attacking next, arrowing into the ranks and creating chaos as they slammed into those wards again and again.

The ward was a green-brown, and I could see exactly where it was weakest. I waved at Evie.

"I see it!" she yelled back. "We need to bring that ward down, or we'll be here for days."

Obviously, the mage council was no longer hoarding the demigod's power among themselves. No, they'd shared that power throughout their people, and every single one of them *burned* with that power.

Stolen power.

Next to me, Finvarra was shuddering as he fought the witches for control. He snarled, and across from us in the tree line, several witches fell to their knees.

"I've got it," he said. "Now we go."

I shifted into my wolf form, joining Danica and Nathaniel, who were hammering at the weak spot in the ward. Samael shielded them with his own dark magic, protecting them from the mages. A few feet away, Evie stood, hair lifting off her face by a wind of her own creation as she aimed her power at the mages' ward. She would be attempting to mimic the ward so she could unlock it, while Danica and Nathaniel weakened it in tandem.

I sprinted for the ward and slammed my body into it, feeling the crack spread. Above me, Vas did the same, followed by a demon I hadn't met who was riding a dragon. The dragon's tail swept through the air, lashing into the ward.

The ward fell.

"Teamwork makes the dream work," Danica crowed.

And then chaos reigned.

I lost track of my friends. Couldn't pay attention to anything except the mages in front of me and the shock in their eyes when their power bounced harmlessly off me, thanks to the amulet Finvarra had insisted I wear.

I could feel him, always within feet of me. He fought with the sword, raging across the battlefield as his power kept the witches at bay, preventing them from harnessing the ancient ruins around us.

"Duck," he roared, and I rolled, instantly launching to my feet as he swung his sword, beheading the mage who'd attempted to gut me. Our eyes met for half a second, and I could see the strain on his face.

Not from using so much magic. But from watching me come so close to death after what had happened with the seelie king.

We were cutting our way through the left flank, but at this rate, there was no way we were going to be able to get to the cave.

Whatever the mages had done to the demigod, it had allowed them to drain a ton of power. We had to shut it down.

Frustration roared through me, and I launched myself at a mage who attempted to strike at Finvarra. Vas had shot toward a group of mages who were targeting Evie.

"This isn't working," Finvarra ground out next to me.

I shifted to human, keeping my wolf claws. The mages hadn't expected to suddenly be fighting a naked woman, and their shock bought me several seconds.

"What do you suggest?" My claws shot out, and I slashed across a throat, ducking as blood sprayed. Most of that blood hit Finvarra in the face, and he glowered at me.

Above us, a demon fell out of the sky. Finvarra did what he could to slow his descent, but the demon was dead before he hit the ground.

I'd seen the blond-haired demon around, joking with Bael. Danica let out a roar, and a chunk of mages surrounding us were suddenly…gone.

Body parts turned to ash, and Danica was instantly there, tears running down her face. Mages turned to run.

We'd broken their left flank. But it had come at the expense of one of Danica's friends.

"They're stupidly powerful. Gabriel prepared for us. We have no shot unless we can cut off that power supply!" Danica yelled at us, her expression still grief-stricken.

We hadn't been able to sandwich their army between ours since that would have meant landing deep in their booby-trapped jungle.

One of Finvarra's people dropped to his knees next to us, and Finvarra hauled him up, shoving him away from the front lines. "Get to a healer," he ordered.

"I'll use Angelica's ring," I said. We'd planned for this. It was our backup.

"You can't," Danica said, slashing out with her power at a mage who dared get too close. "Evie said we took down their main ward, but there was no way to hit their smaller wards. They know we've got that ring, and they've prepared for it."

"A look-away spell…"

"Evie tried. We used everything to take down their ward, and we're using all our collective power to keep it down."

"Kill the witches. Then Finvarra won't need to use his power blocking them." We needed all that power working for us.

"We're trying. We've taken about half of them out, but they're powerful. Hannah is working on the others," Evie said. "My father and uncle are helping her."

Eachann and Lorcan were working with a black witch. Wow.

And then it went quiet. We all turned.

"What's happening?" I demanded.

Vas appeared above us and helpfully pulled me into the air.

My gaze met Selina's.

She was alive. Alive and staring at me over the battlefield, her hand clasped in...Aubrey's.

Behind the newly crowned seelie king, thousands of his people stood in impeccable lines, ready to march with us.

Just a small section of what had been Taraghlan's army just days ago. But it was something.

Selina smiled at me, her teeth flashing white against her dark skin. She and Aubrey raised their clasped hands.

Mages were shoved aside by an invisible power, presenting me with an aisle straight to the cave.

The mages screamed their fury, but it was a ward so thick, it might have been concrete.

It wouldn't last forever, though. We had to go now.

Vas dropped me down. "Gabriel," he hissed.

Danica squeezed my hand. "Get up to the cave. Vas spotted Gabriel, and we're going after him with Hannah."

Vas and Hannah working together. I'd pay to see that.

I looked at Danica, memorizing her face. She gazed back. We wouldn't have time for a proper goodbye. There were no words left to say, and even if there were, we didn't need them. She would kill Gabriel, and then she would go home. To the underworld.

I had so much I wanted to say. I wanted to thank her for taking a chance on a werewolf who loathed authority. For rescuing me from that dungeon. For always having my back. For being the kind of friend I'd always dreamed of having.

Danica just gave me a shaky smile. "I know. I love you too."

The din had quieted as the mages attempted to bring down Selina and Aubrey's ward. Nathaniel and Evie had made their way closer, and Evie…

Evie.

I couldn't be here for her, during the worst moment of her life.

"I know," Finvarra said, his voice tight. And I realized I was shaking with sobs of my own. "I know, Kyla. But it's time to go."

I couldn't. Because the moment I did this hideous thing, he was gone too.

And it was going to fucking destroy me.

"The worlds burn," Selina said from the other side of the plain. But her words were as clear as if she were standing next to me. "If you don't act now, everyone you love will be gone anyway. Go, Kyla."

My heart had cracked open in my chest, but I threw my arms around Danica. "Look after yourself."

"You too."

I didn't hang around. Couldn't bear to see Evie and

Danica saying their final goodbyes. Finvarra took my arm, steadying me, but I shook him off and went wolf.

Shifting helped me push some of my emotions to the side to deal with later. My wolf was all instinct. And she *ran*.

I could feel Finvarra behind me, lightning-fast. Together, we ignored the mages on either side of Selina's ward, all of them snarling and pounding on the ward in an attempt to slow us down.

"You'll never win!" one of them roared. "The demigod is *ours*."

Cute.

Within moments, we were disappearing into the jungle. Finvarra caught me midleap with his magic, only the tension in his jaw showing the strain of using that magic while keeping the witches at bay. He pointed at the trap I hadn't seen.

I'd been expecting something magical. This was an IED.

How *dare* the mages come to this country and leave explosives in the jungle where innocent people could lose limbs and lives.

"Nathaniel will fix it," Finvarra said tightly. "For now, be careful."

Nathaniel would have to be in charge of the cleanup. Because once everyone else went back to their realms, it would only be the witches and werewolves left.

Pushing that thought away, I circled around the next trap. Behind us, shouts sounded. Obviously, the mages were free of Selina's spell. We needed to haul ass.

But Finvarra went still.

I turned, watching as a grin spread over his face.

I knew that grin.

"The witches are dead," he said. And I watched as he pulled his power back into him. He raised his hand, his brow furrowing in concentration. "All of the traps are now dismantled. Run."

We ran. When the shouts got too close, Finvarra did something to make them disappear. By the time the cave came into view through the trees, he looked exhausted once more. He might have access to his power fully back, but that power was obviously drained.

Unsurprisingly, the cave was surrounded by mages.

twenty-three
Kyla

I shifted back to my human form, swaying on my feet, and Finvarra cursed. "How many times can you shift back and forth before you need to rest?"

"I've got a couple more in me. I'm guessing you're almost drained."

"I don't need all of my power to take them—"

We both went quiet as a body hit the ground in front of the cave. The mages pulled their weapons, the strongest among them creating glowing orbs of power in their hands, ready to attack.

Vas hovered in front of them.

"Your leader," he said, gesturing to Gabriel's body. Vas's voice was so cold I shivered. This was torture for him too. Samael was like a brother to him, and most of Vas's other friends would stay in the underworld as well, protecting the fragile peace. "Leave this place, or meet the same end."

Several of the mages attempted to attack. Vas merely used his demon fire in response.

Any remaining mages turned to run.

I darted out into the clearing, and Vas's eyes met mine. "I'll guard the cave entrance," he said.

Finvarra was instantly at my side, nodding at Vas. "Thank you."

Vas nodded back. One of his wings shifted, revealing a tote slung over his shoulder. "Nathaniel thought you might want this."

My extra bag of clothes. I didn't give a shit about the clothes themselves, but I'd tucked something extremely important away in my jeans pocket.

I took the bag. "Thanks, Vas."

He just nodded, glancing between Finvarra and me. "We had people stationed at the portals. They've all called in to say everyone got where they needed to go. Danica has gone." His face tightened, and he swallowed, his eyes hollow. But he took a deep breath and continued speaking. "Samael's gone with her, along with any of the remaining demons who wanted to go home. Aubrey made it back to his realm, along with Selina."

Fresh grief dug a hole in my chest. I'd spent so much time angry at Selina, and now I'd never get to see her again. Her choices had infuriated me at the time, but without them, I wouldn't have fallen in love with Finvarra.

"So, it's up to us now," I said.

Vas nodded. "The wolves and the few demons and seelie who decided to stay…they're keeping the remaining mages at bay. But you need to move now. I'll just be…over here." Vas stalked to the edge of the small clearing, where he could keep an eye on anyone approaching, while also giving us the illusion of privacy.

My eyes met burning gold.

"You have to go," I said.

For a moment, Finvarra looked like he might argue. But we both knew there was no other choice. He had a realm to rule. It was in his blood. And despite every accusation I'd ever leveled at him, I could never accuse him of not caring about his people. Of being an unfit ruler.

Finvarra's problem was that he cared *too* much.

But that was a problem for him to solve. I certainly wouldn't be around to figure it out.

"Go," I said.

Finvarra's eyes flared at my order. He knew exactly what I was doing. The sooner he left and I got this shit over with, the sooner I could work on putting the pieces of my heart back together.

I gestured toward the forest behind the cave and the portal that was waiting for him. "*Go*," I said again, and my voice was so tight, it was exceedingly obvious that I was barely holding on.

"I'm taking you into the cave," he said.

"Fine."

I stalked into the cave, waving at the demigod asleep in front of us. Finvarra studied him, his eyes filled with a dull rage.

Finvarra took a single step closer, and the scent of him, the feel of him so near, I felt as if it might kill me.

"Be careful," he rumbled. "Promise me."

"I promise."

"You're such a fucking liar."

And then his mouth was on mine, and I let out a choked sob against his lips. He stroked my hair, his hand gentle.

I buried my head in his chest. But he was pulling away, just enough that he could take my chin in his hand.

"I love you," he said.

He'd said the words before, and yet this time, they dug into my chest and stayed there.

"I love you too. I wish it could have been different."

"So do I."

A final kiss on my forehead, and he stepped back, his eyes blazing. Then Finvarra handed me the sword. He hesitated for a long moment. Long enough that, for one wild second, I thought he might change his mind. But he whirled, stalking out of the cave.

I knew why he moved so fast.

And I turned away so I wouldn't have to watch him step through that cave entrance.

When I turned back, he was gone.

I fell to my knees. I knew he wasn't dead. Knew he would still be alive and kicking centuries after I was dust. But it felt like he'd died.

My sobs shook my entire body.

Wait. That wasn't just my sobs.

The demigod was creating another earthquake.

Resentment rose, and I launched myself to my feet. "Are you serious right now? This is all *your* fault."

Be careful, wolf.

I held up the sword. "I hold the power here."

For now.

I leaned down and dug through the tote and into my jeans pocket—finding the vial I'd convinced Evie to prepare for me with the witchweed. Perfectly calibrated to remove my memories of the last few weeks.

Sure, it sucked that I wouldn't remember that I was a badass who'd managed to save the realms. But I'd instructed

Evie to tell me all about it…while keeping Finvarra as a footnote. Future Kyla would know we'd managed to work together, but she certainly wouldn't know she'd fallen in love with him.

I'd thought I was strong. Thought I could face anything. But losing Fin…that would be the thing that broke me. And when I broke, I would be all wolf. There was no coming back from that.

I could see my future. Nathaniel would have to kill me himself. He'd never recover. And neither would Evie—or Danica, when she learned what had happened.

No, this was the best way. Some memories had the power to break you over and over again. So I'd protect myself from that.

Vial still clutched in my hand, I took a deep breath and reached for the sword.

But not before I begged. "Please, please don't close the portals."

I will be asleep.

"I know, but surely there's some way…"

You are running out of time.

I couldn't do it. Couldn't be the one. I reached for the vial. I was only removing the last few weeks, which meant I'd still know why I was here. I'd still place the sword in the sheath. And then I'd probably go fucking celebrate.

Unstopping the vial, I studied it.

If…if I removed Finvarra, I removed everything else. I removed the last goodbye I had with Danica. Removed the memory of this battle.

I would erase the fact that I'd loved someone so much it

had *ruined* me. But if I got rid of the pain, I'd also lose some of the best days of my life.

I couldn't do it. Couldn't remove that infuriating unseelie king who had brought something in me back to life.

My wolf would have to handle it. *I* would have to handle it. I'd have to learn to truly lean on the people around me as I grieved the man I loved.

"Don't you *dare*," a low voice snarled behind me.

I went still. A wild, desperate hope fluttered through my chest as Finvarra snatched the vial from my hand and smashed it against the wall.

I could barely look at him standing in front of me, pure male offense written over every inch of his face. "What are you doing here?" I croaked out.

"You think you can just forget me and make it easier on yourself?" His gold eyes blazed down at me.

"I did. But as usual, you messed up all my plans. So, fuck off back to your realm." My voice broke, and I was suddenly in his arms.

"I'm not going back," he growled.

"Yes, you are."

"I've passed the crown to my cousin."

I slammed my palms into his chest, attempting to move back. He ignored that, smiling down at me.

"Are you *nuts?* Tae doesn't want to rule."

"We all have to do things we don't want to do. And he'll make a fine king. I've ensured it."

My head spun. "Don't do this to me."

"Don't do what?" He pressed a kiss to my forehead. The tip of my nose. My lips. "Don't adore you? Treasure you? Love you enough to give up my crown for you?" He laughed. "It was the easiest decision I've ever fucking made."

"You've gone insane," I marveled.

The cave shuddered around us. We both turned to the demigod and snarled.

Finvarra cupped my cheek with his hand, drawing my attention back to him. "I knew the moment I saw you that you'd fuck up my life. I couldn't stay away from you, and I never want to be away from you again. So, here I am. I no longer have a crown to place on your head, but I'm yours."

I burst into tears. Finvarra's expression softened, and he pulled me close, stroking my hair.

"Tell me one thing," he murmured. "If you hadn't needed to be the one in this cave while the portals closed… would you have stayed with me?"

I hadn't let myself think it. But I would have. I would give up everything for this man.

Finvarra caught my chin. He must've read the answer in my eyes, because he smiled. "If you'd removed me from your memories, I'd just have made you fall in love with me again."

He would've. I'd never have been able to hold out against him.

But I had to ask. "Are you sure?"

"I'm more sure than of anything in my life. I was just existing before you swaggered in. All I had was my obsession with revenge and my throne—both of which were making me someone I barely recognized. You woke me up. And I resented the hell out of you for it, until I realized I didn't have to let you go. For once in my life, I could be selfish. And I will be. I'll be the worst, most selfish version of myself if it means I get to keep you. Now let's get this done so I can show you exactly how sure I am."

He chose me.

He didn't care that I was impulsive and snarly, with a tendency to lash out when I was mad. Finvarra wanted me anyway.

I wrapped my arms around him and squeezed. "Okay," I said. "I hope you're sure, because I'm not giving you back to your realm."

He grinned at the possessiveness dripping from my voice. "Good."

The cave shuddered again. "We've got company," Vas called. "Now would be a really good time to magically neuter them."

"Sleep," the demigod demanded in my head.

Since the mages were on their way, I was in agreement with that.

Finvarra released me. Then he began breaking apart the Naud chains. I stared at him.

He just lifted one brow. "They don't work on me."

"We're talking about this later."

Stepping forward, I rounded the demigod's huge feet and shoved the sword into its *true* sheath. It looked like a pocketknife against the demigod's body.

The world exploded.

Finvarra grabbed me, throwing his body over mine. I attempted to roll us, but he ignored that, covering every inch of me with his huge body.

I could feel the rubble hitting him, and I cried out, trying to wiggle free, but he ignored that too, his arms holding tight enough to leave bruises.

Then it was still. And quiet. The dust was so thick in the air, I coughed. Finvarra raised his hand, and the dust gathered into a small cloud, flying toward the entrance of the cave.

"You're handy."

The demigod sat up, the chains falling to the ground. I shivered, fear slithering along my spine. He could smite us with little more than a thought.

"You kept your word," he boomed.

I met his gaze and smelled copper as my eyes began bleeding. Next to me, Finvarra snarled, attempting to push me aside. I tripped him, shoving him off-balance.

"I did," I said, focusing on the demigod's chin. "But please don't let the portals close when you go to sleep. *Please*."

He ignored me, and I took a step closer, ignoring Finvarra's hand on my shoulder as he prepared to haul me back. "I did everything you wanted," I snapped. "And my friends shouldn't have to pay the price."

"You think I care about silly mortal problems?"

"I'll *make* you care," I hissed.

Finvarra shoved me behind him. I just peered around his body, meeting the demigod's eyes, despite the blood that flowed from my own. A smile spread across his face, and my heart stuttered in my chest as he held up his hand, slowly closing it in a fist. With every inch he closed his hand, my heart slowed its beat, until Finvarra whirled, his face ashen as he stared at me.

"This is how you repay those who help you?" I managed to croak. Finvarra summoned his power, aiming it at the demigod.

"The mages stole your power," Finvarra hissed. "Those humans managed to chain you here, and that power allowed them to keep you. But I have much, much more magic than they could ever hope to have."

"You dare threaten me?" the demigod boomed.

Finvarra didn't look impressed. No, he just curled his lip. "If you harm one hair on my *mate's* head, I will make it my life's mission to steal that sword back and make sure you sleep again. And I'm exceptionally motivated. Just ask the last seelie king."

I choked on my next breath. He knew. Finvarra knew. My eyes burned, and he reached back, squeezing my hand.

After. I'd deal with this if we survived the next few moments.

I swallowed, pulling myself together. "Oh, wait. You *can't* ask the seelie king," I said brightly to the demigod, ignoring the dizziness sweeping through me, "because Finvarra killed him."

The demigod released his hand, and my heart raced. I leaned over, recovering, and Finvarra wrapped his arm around me.

"A bargain," the demigod said.

I lifted my head, finding his gaze on my face.

"You'll bargain with *me*," Finvarra said, his voice oozing warning.

The demigod smiled at me, and I kept my gaze on those

pointed teeth.

"What kind of bargain?" I breathed.

"The portals are tied to my magic. If I sleep, the portals close. The only way to keep them open is to lend that power to someone else."

I swallowed, my mouth suddenly bone-dry.

"Me," Finvarra growled. "You'll leave her out of this."

"And give an overpowered fae king enough magic to become a true threat to the gods themselves? I don't think so."

"What are you proposing?" I got out.

"You'll take enough of my power to keep the portals open. Those portals will be tied to your life."

Finvarra had gone still next to me. I could practically feel him searching for an alternative plan. If I weren't careful, he'd go find Vas and demand he step in instead.

"I'm not immortal," I said.

The demigod angled his head. "You will be. Your life will be tied to the unseelie king's, and something tells me he would do *anything* to keep you alive. If I wake in a thousand years, you will serve me."

"Absolutely not," Finvarra hissed.

"This is the only way you'll keep the portals open?" I asked.

"Don't even think about it," Finvarra said.

The demigod waved his hand, and the sound of the battle reached us. Wolves were howling, unseelie warriors roaring as they fought. And died.

"Deal," I blurted.

Finvarra's face drained of color. He opened his mouth,

but it was too late.

The power hit me all at once. I felt my feet leave the ground, but all I could see was a strange light that wasn't light. It glowed, and I screamed as it burrowed deep, burning into my chest until I clawed at my skin.

That was my voice, begging for mercy, and my vision cleared enough to see Finvarra aim his deadly power at the demigod, who simply held up a hand.

And then it stopped.

I fell from the air, landing in Finvarra's arms.

"Hurts," I said.

"I know."

"Now I will sleep," the demigod said. "And when I wake, we will talk about your role."

And *that* didn't sound ominous at all.

I turned my head, and we both watched as the ground parted, swallowing the demigod's huge body until there was no trace that he'd ever been here.

My head spun. The portals wouldn't close. But if the demigod woke again…I would be his bitch.

"I don't fucking like this," Finvarra said, his gaze on the flat expanse of dirt where the demigod had previously been sitting.

"Me neither."

He watched the dirt as if planning a way to dig down beneath it and kill the demigod himself. "He tries to fuck with you, and he's going to see just how much an unseelie king can increase his power in the next thousand years."

Despite the subject, I smirked. Finvarra just turned and narrowed his eyes at me.

"I've made some decisions."

I knew that look. I sighed, waving a hand. "Go on, say the next thing that's guaranteed to piss me off."

He caught my hand and pressed a kiss to my knuckles. I just raised my eyebrow.

"You're hopeless at following orders."

"This again?"

"Because you were never supposed to."

"Well. Someone has finally come around."

He just angled his head, his gold gaze steady on mine. "You were born to give them."

I frowned. He shook his head at me. "I'm not taking the throne back. Not unless you rule by my side."

"A werewolf as the unseelie queen? Are you kidding?"

He slowly shook his head. "I'm not doing it without you. You don't want it, we'll grovel to Tae. You'll have to explain to him about how you were planning to forget him as well."

"Jeez, you're still butthurt about that? I wouldn't really have removed my memories. Probably."

Finvarra smirked at me. "Probably?"

"I'd decided to keep them before you stalked in here and slammed the vial out of my hand. But god, I've never felt pain like that before."

"And you never will again," he promised, with the confidence of a man who was used to controlling everything around him. I just shook my head.

We stared at each other for a long moment. I knew he was standing there in front of me, but some part of me still didn't quite believe it. "Your mate?" I asked, my mouth dry.

He just gave me a long look. "You thought you'd hide it from me?"

"Of course," I muttered. "It wasn't like I was going to see you ever again. When did you know?"

"When I knocked that vial out of your hand. Your wolf looked back at me, and I knew I was yours," he said with a smug, very male smile. But the smile dropped as he narrowed his eyes at me. "More importantly, when did *you* know?"

I took a deep breath. "When I saw that asshole stab you in the back. Right before…"

"Right before Taraghlan hit you with his power," he ground out. "You've known that long?"

I sniffed. "At first, I swore I'd take it to my grave. I loathed what you'd done, and it was the first time I'd actively disagreed with my wolf. And then, once I'd forgiven you… it didn't seem fair."

"It didn't seem fair to tell me I was your mate?"

I planted my hands on my hips. "Are you going to be a whiny baby about this?"

He just gave me a slow smile that told me he wasn't going to let me distract him. "You would've lived your life in this realm. Lived and died while separated from your mate. A piece of yourself missing. All so I could keep my crown."

"Your people needed you. And you needed—"

"You," he said, his voice soft. "I need you. I've always been on the same page as your wolf. It's the woman who managed to perplex me."

I glowered at him, even as I felt my wolf stretch inside

me. Finvarra's eyes brightened. "This is why I always knew when your wolf was nearing the surface."

"Yeah, yeah."

He leaned down and nipped my lower lip. And then he wrapped both arms around me, holding me in place as he lowered his head. I gave back as good as I got, my body tightening as his clever mouth claimed mine.

Something strange burned inside me. I flattened my hands against Finvarra's chest.

Someone cleared their throat. "Uh, guys? The mages are now powerless and fleeing, but the portals are still open. Any idea why?"

I pulled away, ignoring Finvarra's growl as I beamed at Vas.

"Because I'm one bad bitch, that's why."

twenty-four
Kyla

Unsurprisingly, Vas demanded a better explanation, and we filled him in as we made our way back through the forest and toward the battlefield.

A shadow flickered above our heads, and Bael landed in front of us. "I just came through from the portal. Danica sent me, figuring something had gone seriously wrong if the portals hadn't closed."

"Something went right," Vas said. "Kyla did something incredibly dangerous. But she saved all our asses, so we're not allowed to lecture her about it."

Bael just gave me a considering look, a flicker of amusement in his eyes, as I sent him a wide, toothy grin.

"Good luck with *that*," he said. "So, the portals aren't closing?"

"Nope. You're welcome."

He took that in his stride. "I guess I better go tell Danica."

He was gone a moment later. By the time we reached the battlefield, it was strangely quiet. The remaining mages were now humans without any remarkable powers, and they knelt in rows, hands by their sides. Most of them stared blankly ahead, likely coming to terms with exactly what had happened.

Eldan had arranged for a team of healers to join him. They all wore white as they tended to the injuries on the battlefield.

Hunter and Naomi stalked toward me. "What happened?" Hunter demanded.

"Long story. But the portals aren't closing."

His gaze sharpened at that, but I'd returned my attention to the rows of humans.

Naomi turned, gazing out at them with me. "We should make an example of them."

I stiffened. "Are you seriously casually discussing a war crime?"

She just sneered at me. "Human laws." Naomi turned and stalked away. I glanced behind me at Hunter.

"What the hell?"

"She was dating a wolf from one of the other packs Nathaniel convinced to join us. He didn't make it."

"Shit."

One of Finvarra's generals approached. Finvarra released my hand and stepped a few feet away. Not that it would help with all the wolf ears around here.

"Kyla."

A lump formed in my throat. Nathaniel. He was okay. I hadn't doubted it—I would've felt if he'd gone down, even with my currently weakened ties to the pack. But I'd needed to see him for myself.

"What happened?"

I took a deep breath, and it all came out. The portals, the demigod, my new—even longer—life-span. And the fact that if the demigod woke up again, I'd be forced to serve him.

Nathaniel glanced at Finvarra, and satisfaction slid through his eyes as he turned his attention back to me.

I froze. "You *knew*."

One dark eyebrow shot up. "That you were in love with him? Of course I knew. But I wouldn't have allowed you to go with him to kill the seelie king based on that alone. You weren't mated to him then."

The air disappeared from my lungs. Of course Nathaniel had known. He'd probably known I was mated before I did. "Why did you make me go with Finvarra, then?"

"Because I knew the bastard was in love with you too."

I narrowed my eyes at him, and he just smiled. "I want you happy, Kyla. You know that. And you're not happy taking my orders."

I felt my lower lip stick out and sucked it back in. "I *want* to be happy taking orders. Doesn't that count for something?"

Nathaniel laughed, pulling me in for a bear hug. "Sure, it counts for something."

I poked him in the ribs at his lie and felt his chest shake as he laughed again.

Then he heaved a sigh. "Even when you hated the unseelie king, you loved him. I'll never understand it, but I don't have to. And I'll always be your family. *We* always will. The whole pack. You'll come run with us each full moon, and any other time you please. Finvarra does anything to hurt you, and I'll kill him. Even if it means war."

I laughed wetly against his chest. "Thanks."

He patted my back, and I pulled away. "What are you going to do with the prisoners?"

"We're working it out now."

"Naomi suggested—"

"I know what she suggested. I'll keep an eye on her."

Finvarra stalked over and slung his arm over my shoulder. He attempted to make the movement casual, but all of us knew what he was doing.

Nathaniel just grinned and stepped back. "Remember what I said."

He would go to war for me. And just days ago, I'd thought he was kicking me out of the pack because I wasn't enough. Finvarra held his hand out to Nathaniel.

Nathaniel stared him in the eye and shook it.

"Aw, male bonding." Evie sauntered toward us. "Too cute."

There wasn't quite enough attitude in that saunter. She was grieving, even if she was putting on a good show.

Nathaniel pulled her close. "There's something you need to know. Something Kyla has to tell you."

It was good news. And instead of telling Evie himself, he wanted me to be able to.

"You're a better person than I am," I muttered.

He just smiled.

"The portals aren't closing," I told Evie.

"We…failed?"

"No. I made a deal with the demigod. It's a long story, but—"

"Evie."

Evie went still, and then she whirled, the movement

almost wolf-fast.

Danica stood about ten feet away from us. Even from here, it was easy to see how distraught she'd been. Her eyes were red, face blotchy.

Time seemed to stop. Everyone paused, their attention on the sisters.

Evie let out a choked sound, stumbling toward her sister.

Then Danica was there, and they were swaying in each other's arms, talking over each other while everyone in the vicinity smiled.

A few feet away, Lorcan grinned, watching his daughter. He stood next to Eachann, both of them covered in blood and dirt, but alive.

Finvarra squeezed me, and I turned.

Aubrey. And next to him, her braids swinging as she walked toward me, head held high…Selina.

We studied each other. She'd betrayed me. And that betrayal had given me Finvarra. The man I never would have known I needed—and would never have admitted I wanted.

Her betrayal had meant I'd had to stay with him. It had meant I'd seen another side of him. It had meant I'd gotten to see the kingdom he loved, the cousin he treasured.

Selina's insistence that I be the one to return the sword had ensured I'd been caught searching for it that day and that Finvarra had learned why it was so important.

Her deception had cracked my heart wide open in the short-term, but it had led to this. All of us were safe. The portals had remained open, and my life-span was now much, much longer—meaning I wouldn't leave Finvarra alone.

"Do you truly believe I would foresee your death and not search for a way to change it?" She'd said those words to me once.

"That tricky bitch," I marveled, my voice dripping appreciation. Evie glanced at me.

"What do you mean?"

Selina stopped a few feet away. "She means I saw a future for Kyla that was so horrifying, I had to get involved."

I knew what she was saying. Getting involved often came with its own risks. Selina could have made things worse. She could have faced extreme consequences when fate decided it didn't want to be messed with.

And she'd done it anyway.

"I'm sorry for all the names I called you in my head," I said.

She just laughed, holding out her arms, and I stepped into her hug.

"And you?" I asked Aubrey when I was finished hugging it out with Selina. "How much of a part did you play in this?"

He just winked at me, but I caught the heated glance he gave Selina. "I knew it was unusual for her to go missing—especially with everything that was happening. At first… At first, I thought someone had taken her." Aubrey ran a hand over his face, and Selina took his hand, face tightening. I caught the way he stroked the back of her hand with his thumb.

"He came looking for me," Selina said, her eyes narrowing but her body angled toward his, and he wrapped one arm around her waist. "The stubborn man found me somehow."

I gaped at that. "But you…"

"Occasionally get glimpses of the future. Yes. Unfortunately, whichever hand of fate usually steers me… they…"

"Took their hands off the wheel when it came to Aubrey." I grinned, my chest lightening. "He defied fate."

Aubrey sent me a smug look I'd never seen on him before, and I burst out laughing.

"He refused to leave. Until Finvarra contacted him and said he needed to be prepared to take the seelie crown."

I angled my head at the seelie. "You asked me if I'd heard from Selina. That day we took down Taraghlan."

He winced. "I knew you'd expect me to ask."

And he'd seen exactly how furious I was with the witch he loved. It must have killed him not to be able to defend her actions when he knew just how much she was doing behind the scenes.

"You *sneaky* fae," I marveled.

He gave me a mock bow. I surveyed them both. "So, what's next for you guys?"

Aubrey grinned. "I'm attempting to convince this incredible woman to rule with me."

Holy shit.

Selina bit her lower lip and shrugged at me. "We're figuring things out."

twenty-five
Kyla

Precious whinnied, and I smiled, holding out the other half of the apple I'd brought her. "It's right here, greedy girl."

She was a surprisingly delicate eater for a horse, and I petted her soft neck as she ate. It had been two weeks since the battle, and we'd stayed in wolf territory for a large chunk of that time. It was a chance to catch our breaths. A chance for Finvarra to get to know the pack. Danica and Samael stayed at Nathaniel and Evie's for a few days, and they'd convinced Meredith and Vas to do the same.

Selina and Aubrey had needed to get back to the seelie realm, but we were planning to visit them next week.

It would take some time for the human realm to adjust to the imbalance left by HFE and the mages. Danica and Evie were talking about setting up a council with representatives from each faction. I had no doubt they'd succeed.

I felt Finvarra a moment before he appeared behind me, but he encircled me in his arms before I could turn.

Precious continued chomping. She was now used to the unseelie king appearing and disappearing. I spent a significant portion of my time here, and Finvarra liked to "pop in" at various points of the day.

Often, like now, it was because he had a midafternoon craving.

"And just what have you been doing?" I asked as his arms tightened.

"A little of this, a little of that." He pressed a kiss to my temple. "I just received a letter from Tae. You have one too, although he made sure to tell me to tell you he says hi. And thank you again."

I rolled my eyes. Finvarra had set Tae up in the summer palace, and he was currently undoing some of Marnin's mess. Each time he wrote, he made sure to thank me for the fact that his butt wasn't sitting on a freshly vacated unseelie throne.

"Come with me," Finvarra murmured in my ear.

My thighs instantly clenched. I knew what that tone meant. Glancing over my shoulder, I gave him a heated look.

Without any warning, my wolf shoved me aside. Finvarra stiffened. "No," he told her.

She snarled at him. She didn't want to hear no.

Finvarra took my hand and pulled me along the trail leading into the forest. He cupped my cheek in his hand.

"How can I help you?" he asked. And his expression was *tortured.* Unsurprisingly, my wolf—mostly unable to deal with human emotions—decided to bounce.

I chewed on my lower lip. "I don't have a problem controlling her, unless you're around."

He went still. "I make your wolf feral?"

"Yeah. And I think I understand some of it. She wants you to…"

"To what?" He winced. "Please tell me she doesn't want *that*."

"No! God, no. Ew. She wants you to *see* her."

"I have seen her."

This was hideously embarrassing. "Forget it."

"No." He caught my hand, pulling me close. "Explain."

I sighed. Within just weeks, my wolf had gone from wondering if Finvarra was prey, to realizing he most certainly was not, to wanting him to stroke her. She'd known he was her mate before she'd let me in on that little fact, and now…

"Look, I don't understand why, but she desperately wants your approval. She wants you to *like* her."

It was rare that I managed to surprise Finvarra, but this time, his mouth fell open. And then his expression turned so tender I had to swallow around the lump forming in my throat.

"Let her out," he said gently.

My wolf seemed to have been waiting for this moment because, for the first time in a while, my shift was entirely out of my control. Finvarra crouched down and stared at me. At *us*.

"I love you," he told her. "You're my mate. Mine. And I'll protect you always. Both of you."

If my wolf could have purred, she would have as Finvarra stroked my head, unerringly finding the spot right behind my ear. My wolf was proud and would never lower herself to letting anyone else pet her. Would likely bite their hand off if they tried. And yet here she was, guiding Finvarra's hand to her belly.

I shifted back, and Finvarra grinned at me as my wolf receded, and his hand was suddenly in a *very* interesting place.

"I know this is…weird," I said.

He just angled his head. "Your wolf and I have never had a problem."

I felt my lower lip stick out. "You just like her 'cause she lets you tell her what to do." Even when she wanted to rampage, all it had taken was a look of disapproval from him, and she'd fallen in line.

It should've been a rather large clue that he was my mate. Instead, I'd ignored it.

"Something tells me your wolf doesn't act like a golden retriever for everyone," Finvarra said, obviously pleased with himself.

I smirked. "You're the man I happen to be boning. I guess she got tired of you getting pissy every time she came out to play."

"Happen to be boning?"

Now, he really was pissy.

I grinned, and he rolled me onto my back. "You'll pay for that. Say it," he ordered.

I clamped my mouth shut, and he poked one finger into my ribs.

"Fine," I laughed. "You're my mate."

His eyes glittered with satisfaction.

"Now will you come with me?"

"And just where are we going?"

"It's a surprise."

I nodded, letting him lift me to my feet.

The world blurred around us, and a moment later, we were in the throne room. I angled my head as Finvarra released me. At first, I didn't understand.

He just waited me out.

"You…you added another throne."

"You're my queen."

I stared at it. He laughed. "I figured it would take some getting used to. But I have a solution for that too."

My lips had gone numb. We hadn't talked about what the reality of ruling with him would mean. Already, I was helping with the aftereffects of the battle. We were having conversations about what the future of the kingdom would look like. Spoiler alert—I was all for some modernization around this place.

But we hadn't talked about this. About me sitting on a throne next to him and greeting dignitaries.

"You look a little…disconcerted." Finvarra smiled, taking my hand and pulling me over to my throne.

"Go on. Try it out."

I glanced at the doors, but Finvarra was already waving a hand, blocking off the doors and, with a glance at the heavy drapes, the windows.

Hundreds of candles lit at once, casting the room in a warm, welcoming glow. Somehow, the huge, intimidating room was now…private.

This seemed to mean a lot to Finvarra. So, I stalked toward the throne and sat on it.

"Happy?"

He smiled. A moment later, I felt a weight on my head. I yelped, lifting my hands to remove the heavy, jeweled crown.

"Uh-uh," Finvarra purred. Tendrils of his dark magic slid toward me, wrapping around my arms and holding them to the arms of the throne.

"I must admit, this is a private fantasy of mine." His gold eyes practically glowed. I didn't know whether to laugh or curse.

"You've had your kicks. Let me go."

"I may have had *my* kicks, as you put it. But you haven't had *yours*."

I swallowed. "You've been talking to Selina, haven't you?"

"She may have mentioned a little prophecy regarding my queen. My *mate*." He gave me a slow, feral grin.

Finvarra loved that word. Loved that my wolf had claimed him. He'd had a long, lonely life. Thankfully, I was around to shake things up.

"Choose wrongly, and you will be chained to a throne," Finvarra mused. The tendrils of his magic turned to heavy chains and tensed. He stepped closer, his gaze on my face. Watching closely to make sure this was okay. Because he remembered when I'd been chained against my will.

And he wanted to replace that memory. My chest clenched.

"Choose correctly," he purred. "And you'll sit on one."

"I *am* sitting on one," I pointed out. But my voice was breathless, and my nipples had hardened. Finvarra's gaze slid down to my breasts, and he smiled.

"You certainly are."

More chains appeared. Since they were created by the

unseelie king, they were cool, unyielding, and yet they didn't bruise. They did, however, guide my thighs apart until I was spread for him.

"This is perverted, even for you."

He just grinned at me, slowly kneeling in front of me. The sight of the unseelie king kneeling before anyone was enough to make me lose the ability to speak. The fact that his throne was empty while he knelt in front of mine…

"Let this be a reminder," he crooned, slowly sliding his hands up my calves, his fingertips lightly brushing over my skin. "You're more important than anything else. My throne comes second. Always. And if I ever fail to put you first…"

My throat tightened. Finvarra was so, so afraid of becoming his father. And yet, the fact that he was so aware of it meant he didn't have a thing to worry about.

That wasn't what he needed to hear right now. "Don't worry," I assured him. "I'm not the kind of woman who would tolerate being second place."

He grinned. "Truer words have never been spoken."

I narrowed my eyes, but he was already standing, leaning close, nuzzling my neck. I arched, angling my head for his touch. Lifting my hands, I attempted to hold him closer.

The chains tightened, keeping my arms pinned.

I'd thought I would hate it. But instead…

Everything in me clenched, heat pooling in my core. Finvarra chuckled, his mouth finding one nipple, teasing and rolling until all I could do was moan.

He knelt once more, gazing up at me. Those high cheekbones were flushed, his gold eyes blazing. "You've never looked more beautiful," he ground out. "I've dreamed of you like this."

He didn't make me wait any longer. Lowering his head, he kissed his way up my thigh, nuzzling, nipping, until I was lifting my ass as much as I could.

"Do you need more chains?" he rumbled against my skin.

"Tyrant," I gasped out.

He nipped a little harder, and a low moan left my throat.

He gave a dark chuckle, and then one finger was slowly sliding inside me.

"What am I learning about my mate?" he mused.

I closed my mouth as his eyes met mine. He just smiled. "I'm learning that a little bondage makes you *very* wet."

Since he was right—and I was pretty sure I'd never been this turned on before in my life—I kept my mouth shut. His smile widened at my silence.

He slid his finger deeper inside me, following it with a second. He knew just how to angle them to have me shifting restlessly, as much as I could with the chains limiting my movement. His mouth lowered, his thumbs spreading me open as he slid his tongue along me in one long swipe. When he reached my clit, he lingered, unerringly using the perfect amount of pressure.

I was already on the edge, my breath coming out in desperate pants.

My whole body trembled, and Finvarra chose that moment to back off. I let out a garbled string of threats.

He just raised his head, lifting one eyebrow. "I'm in charge here."

That much was obvious. I might be sitting on a throne, wearing a goddamned crown, but Finvarra had managed to show me exactly why I lost my mind when he bossed me around in bed.

"Fin. Please."

That seemed to help. His eyes darkened—either at the nickname or the sound of me begging. Maybe both.

My first climax hit me before I was ready, and I shuddered, unable to even make a sound as my breath caught, the slow roll of pleasure turning my body limp and my mind blank.

"Not bad," Finvarra mused when I opened my eyes. "But I think we can do better."

I opened my mouth, but he was already licking me again, his tongue lighter on my overstimulated clit, but his movements faster, just the way I needed. His fingers thrust inside me, pressing, massaging, finding all my most sensitive spots.

He licked, nipped, *sucked*, and I drew in a desperate breath.

Finvarra let out a pleased growl, and that sound, combined with the vibration…

I heard myself, as if from a distance, while I let out a sound close to a scream. My climax erupted, blazing through my core, along my body, and through every nerve.

When I could focus again, I cracked my eyes open. Finvarra was still watching me, looking exceptionally pleased with himself.

And why shouldn't he be?

I was a sweaty, wrung-out mess.

The chains had disappeared, and I reached up for the crown, removing it so I could take a good look.

It was beautiful, the jewels obsidian. A match to Finvarra's favorite crown, only mine was a slightly smaller, more delicate version.

And in the middle, right above where it would sit on my brow…

A green stone. The exact same green as the amulet I'd worn into battle.

I swallowed, my mouth still dry. "How?"

"I bargained for another amulet and had it set into your crown."

"I…I have power now."

"I'm taking no chances." He held out his hand. "If you're not planning to wear it…naked for the rest of the day…"

I laughed, handing it to him, and he did something to make it wink out of existence.

The two orgasms he'd given me hadn't even been enough to take the edge off. Not with him standing in front of me looking so ridiculously sexy.

"Not here," he said, taking my hand and hauling me up. I swayed, and he pulled me close. "I need much more room for all the things I'm about to do to you," he said, and my skin tightened in anticipation. "But first…I have something else to show you."

"As much as I'm down to wander around this place naked, I might need some clothes."

"We won't be long," he said, but a robe appeared out of thin air, and he wrapped me in it.

"Where are we going?"

He just pulled me close, and I went still as our surroundings went blurry.

When those surroundings turned sharp once more, I frowned.

The portrait hall. I'd walked down it once before, when I'd first arrived, silently mocking Finvarra's stoic ancestors.

"It's tradition for the unseelie queen to have her portrait painted before her coronation," he said.

"Are we going to have issues with the fact that I'm not unseelie?"

"No."

"Fin."

He shrugged. "There will be rumbles. But according to my spies, the unseelie have already taken to their loudmouthed, sticky-fingered werewolf queen. They like that you're different—and they figure you'll shake things up a bit. Which is why I've already had your coronation painting commissioned."

Finvarra turned me in his arms, until we were both facing the wall.

I burst out laughing. This was no solemn, regal portrait. Not for me. There I was, on Virtus's back, Finvarra's sword slung over my shoulder, my middle finger stabbing into the sky.

"You think you're so funny, don't you?"

Finvarra nuzzled my hair. "This is the moment I realized what I'd done. I knew you'd never forgive me, and I also knew I'd *crawl* for that forgiveness. But I had to strategize, because you were tricky."

"*I* was tricky?"

"Mmm-hmm." More nuzzling that made my toes curl. "My tricky, sneaky, cunning wolf."

We were both silent for a long moment, and I studied the portrait. I had been so fucking mad at Finvarra in that moment. But beneath that anger had been pure devastation. I should've known I was in love with him then. No one could make you more furious than the people you loved.

"What will your advisers say?" I asked, gesturing to the portraits on either side. Finvarra's ancestors were covered in jewels, their expressions placid, eyes serious.

"I don't care," Finvarra murmured. "It was either this one or…"

My breath caught at the dark promise in his voice, and I wiggled until I could turn in his arms.

"Or?"

"Or a portrait of you the way you were just minutes ago…chained to my throne, back arched, looking so fucking sexy I couldn't breathe as you lost yourself in your pleasure."

My mouth dropped open. He just smiled down at me. "Don't worry. That portrait will go in our bedroom."

My cheeks blazed, and his laughter echoed through the hall. Despite my embarrassment, I grinned up at him. He laughed so infrequently, the sound burrowed into my heart every time.

"As if you would trust someone to paint that portrait of me."

"Oh, I don't need to." The smile slid from his face, and his eyes sparked at the suggestion. "Since it's just for us, I'll use magic."

"You're kidding, right?"

He was already taking my hand and leading me to our bedroom.

"Fin. Please tell me you're kidding."

He just threw back his head and laughed, picking up the pace.

* * *

Printed in Great Britain
by Amazon